Flying Off the Candle

~A Glenmyre Whim Mystery~
Sarah E. Burr

This book is a work of fiction. Any similarity between the characters and situations within its pages and places or persons, living or dead, is unintentional and coincidental.

Copyright © 2024 by Sarah Burr

All rights reserved. This book or any portion thereof
may not be reproduced or used in any manner whatsoever
without the express written permission of the publisher,
except for the use of brief quotations in a book review.

First Printing, 2024

www.saraheburr.com

Other books by Sarah E. Burr

Glenmyre Whim Mysteries

You Can't Candle the Truth
Too Much to Candle
Flying Off the Candle

Book Blogger Mysteries

Over My Dead Blog
Dearly Deleted

Trending Topic Mysteries

#FollowMe for Murder
#TagMe for Murder
DM Me for Murder

Court of Mystery

The Ducal Detective
A Feast Most Foul
A Voyage of Vengeance
A Summit in Shadow
Throne of Threats
Paradise Plagued
Burdened Bloodline
Sovereign Sieged
Crown of Chaos
Harrowed Heir
Ravaged Reign
Innocence Imprisoned
Ardent Ascension
Eternal Empire

www.saraheburr.com

Praise for the Glenmyre Whim Mysteries

"With the setting, characters, and mystery storyline all on point, *You Can't Candle the Truth* is pure delight." —**Carol E. Ayer, author of The HSP Mysteries**

"*You Can't Candle the Truth*, like its heroine, Hazel Wickbury, is absolutely enchanting…the magic is threaded with persuasive charm into the fabric of the story." —**Lori Robbins, award-winning author of** *Murder in First Position*, **an On Pointe Mystery**

"*You Can't Candle the Truth* is a unique, charming, feel-good story that fans across the entire mystery spectrum will enjoy. Treat yourself to a trip to Crucible…You'll be glad you did." —**J. C. Kenney, author of the bestselling Allie Cobb Mysteries**

"What a great beginning for a new series! Burr has crafted an entertaining and unusual mystery in *You Can't Candle the Truth*. The world she creates is immersive and engaging, with some interesting, light paranormal touches (think *Bewitched* meets the Hamptons)" —**B. J. Bowen, author of** *Music is Murder*

"There are twists and turns in this cleverly woven mystery with enough intriguing characters, red herrings, and genuine clues that challenged me to decide who killed the victim. Admittedly, I was surprised but totally satisfied with the ending, and I can't wait to read more in this exciting new series." —**Bailee Abbott, author of the Paint by Murder Mysteries**

Dedication

To Melissa, an incredible publishing partner

Acknowledgments

I am continually awestruck that I get to murder people—fictionally—for a living. The only way I know how to thank my wonderful readers is by writing more stories for you to enjoy. With *Flying Off the Candle* now in your hands, I must take a moment to thank the individuals who helped shape this book.

Thank you to my editor, Sarah Wu, for her continued partnership and dedication to this series. Many thanks to Carol Ayer for her thoughtful suggestions and for seeing the big picture when I couldn't. I'm so grateful to Melissa Green, the voice actor for the Glenmyre Whim Mysteries audiobooks. Hearing my characters come to life through her is a magical thing.

Chapter 1

"Holy hexes!" Poppy Glenmyre gripped the steering wheel, her blue eyes wide. "This doesn't look good."

I shifted in the passenger's seat of her Subaru, trying to get a better vantage point of the scene playing out in front of the Sherwin Memorial Library. "Whoa, is that Marjorie? What is she still doing in town?" I glanced at my thirty-three-year-old best friend and aunt. "I thought Constance tossed her out."

"She did." Poppy's right eye twitched as she slowed her SUV to a halt. "And I think that's part of the problem."

I swallowed back a barrage of questions. There would be time later to ask what Poppy had seen in the auras of the two women currently raging at each other in the shadow of the stately library. It didn't take a supernatural ability to see there was something dreadfully amiss.

I unbuckled and tossed an apologetic look over my shoulder at the backseat. "Sorry, girl. You stay here for a few minutes. We'll be right back."

Magnolia, my border collie-corgi rescue, or "bordgie" as Poppy called her, sat secure in her safety harness, a goofy grin on her face.

She was just happy to be along for the ride.

With the windows cracked to allow Noli plenty of fresh springtime air, Poppy and I hopped out of the SUV and hurried toward the tense scene that we could hear clear across the parking lot.

"What part of 'get out of my life' did you not understand?"

Our good friend Constance Crane ran an aggravated hand through her honey-colored hair. Normally a cheerful ray of sunshine, Constance looked like she'd just gotten back developmental edits from her editor and hated what she saw.

Standing opposite her was sharp, sophisticated Marjorie Zeller. Constance had introduced us a few weeks ago during trivia night at Cold Cauldron Brewing. Marjorie was a college friend of Constance's, visiting while the two did "writing sprints" together. At the time, Poppy and I just nodded along, as neither of us had any idea what writing sprints were.

"Look, Con, you can throw me out of your house, you can ice me out, but you can't run me out of town. You don't own this place." Marjorie folded her arms across her chest. "Besides, I'm not even bothering you by being here. *You're* the one who got up all in my face."

Constance scoffed. "Not bothering me? Just looking at you makes me sick. I can't believe you. I can't believe what you did!" She stomped her feet on the pavement, her hands balled into fists. "I swear, if I ever see you again—"

"Constance!" Poppy interrupted the heated argument, her tone uncharacteristically cool. "Maybe we should take this conversation elsewhere," she suggested through gritted teeth.

Constance stepped back, clearly startled by our sudden appearance. "What? Why..." Her voice trailed off as she answered her own question. Curious faces were glued to the windows of the library, staring eagerly at the stormy spectacle. Several of the library's patrons had come outside to blatantly watch the confrontation unfold. Luckily, it didn't look like anyone had pulled out their phones to livestream an argument featuring one of America's most famous mystery authors. Yet.

Constance tugged nervously at the neck of her cable-knit sweater as if trying to hide her beet-red face.

I hurried to her side and threaded my arm through hers. "Let's get some food in you, C." To a wary Marjorie, I joked, "I'm sure you know how hangry she can get."

Poppy and I didn't wait for a peeved Marjorie to respond. Together, we escorted Constance to my aunt's SUV before she could make an even bigger scene.

"What in broomsticks was that about?" Poppy asked as soon as the doors were closed and the windows were rolled up.

Constance scratched Noli's left—and only—ear before muttering, "I don't want to talk about it."

"What is Marjorie still doing in Crucible?" I prodded her for more details as Poppy started the engine and drove toward Lakeside Mulligan's, our intended dining spot. "I thought she left a couple of weeks ago."

Constance folded her arms as she sank into the backseat. "That's what I was trying to figure out. Ugh, I can't *believe* her!"

At the fifty-eight syllables Constance added to the word 'believe,' Poppy and I shared cautious glances. "Hey, we're here for you. You know that, right?" Poppy hedged, her gaze flicking to the rearview mirror. "But going off on Marjorie like that in public isn't a good look. Not when everyone has a camera at the ready, waiting to take down a high-profile figure online."

Constance rolled her eyes with a huff, and for a moment, she reminded me of an angsty teen rather than an accomplished author in her thirties. "She deserved it after what she did."

I chewed on my lower lip as I turned around and settled into the front passenger's seat. Neither Poppy nor I knew what Marjorie had "done" to cause Constance to throw her out of her waterfront colonial home. Over the past two weeks, whenever we tried to get Constance to open up about the vexing situation, she'd change the subject. Eventually, we took the hint and stopped asking.

Silence settled over the car, save for Noli's dog tags clinking together whenever the Subaru drove over a bump.

"Oh, shoot," Constance grumbled a minute later. "Hey, sorry, guys. Can you turn around? I left my notebook at the library. It's got an outline in it that I can't have people snooping through."

Poppy paused a moment, her right eye twitching as she assessed Constance through the mirror. My aunt was undoubtedly using her whim to see if Constance truly had a handle on her emotions. "Sure," she agreed after a beat.

Within five minutes, we were back at the library. As soon as Poppy hit the brakes, Constance hopped out of the car. She scanned the parking lot before knocking on my window.

I hit the switch to roll it down.

"Why don't I meet you guys at Lakeside Mulligan's?" Constance tucked a strand of hair behind her ear. "I appreciate the offer to chauffeur me, but I think I'll just head home after we eat instead of coming back here to work." She had been holed up at the library all week, going through copyedits for her upcoming Misthollow Mystery release.

I raised an eyebrow. "You sure?"

"It's no trouble to bring you back," Poppy said as she leaned across the front seat to insert herself into the conversation.

"Yeah, I'm fine." Constance motioned to the parking lot. "I don't see Marjorie's car here, so she must have left." She plastered on a reassuring smile. "And besides, I need to grow up and move on."

Internally, I was bubbling over with curiosity about *what* Constance needed to move on from, but I didn't feel it my place to pry when clearly, our writer friend wasn't ready to talk about it.

"All right, we'll grab a table then." An effortless smile eclipsed Poppy's pretty face. "See you there!"

As Constance retreated up the path toward the library doors, Poppy put the car in gear, her expression shifting as well. "Curses, what is going on between those two? One minute, they're giggling like sisters, the next, the mere mention of Marjorie sends Constance's aura into a storm of anger and betrayal. Yeesh, I was in full-blown panic mode when we came upon them earlier. My whim had me worried that Constance was about to slug Marjorie."

"I don't think you'd need a whim to see that," I pointed out tactfully before rolling up the window to ward off the chill in the upstate New York air. "I mean, if looks could kill...I do wish Constance would confide in us about what's going on. You'd think she'd know by now that she can trust us."

Constance was an international best-selling author and a very popular public figure. In the six-plus months we'd known her, we'd yet to spill any of the secrets she'd shared as our friendship had grown. We hadn't told the world that she loathed the male lead in the Misthollow Mysteries. We hadn't spread the news online about the real people she'd modeled some of her less-than-flattering characters after. And we certainly hadn't spilled the beans that she was crushing hard on our cousin, Crucible's new chief of police, Holden Whitfield.

Poppy gave me a sad smile. "Yeah, but I get why. In her position, it's hard to ever know who's a friend and who's just using you as a stepping stone." Her smile grew a bit more devious. "And it's not like we don't have secrets of our own."

I laughed. "Touché, Auntie Dearest."

She stuck out her tongue at the teasing nickname.

Poppy, Holden, and I were the last remaining descendants of the Glenmyre clan, one of Crucible, New York's five founding families. But being one of the town founders wasn't what made us special. Our powers, what we Glenmyres called "whims," did. For reasons I'd yet to understand, our family had been gifted with supernatural abilities, and for over three centuries, the Glenmyres had used these whims to help the people of Crucible. *With our whims, do good* had long been the family mantra.

Poppy was the living embodiment of the Glenmyre motto; she used her aura-reading skills whenever she could, gauging a person's mood or feelings to determine if they needed help. Her gift had also come in handy big time during our forays into solving mysteries.

My whim…not so much.

"Maybe once we get some of Nora's mashed potato casserole in her, Constance will spill the tea," Poppy suggested as we continued our drive around Lake Glenmyre.

I absently bobbed my chin in agreement, my gaze taking in the less-than-inviting frozen waters. Lake Glenmyre, named after a town founder and our ancestor, Jedidiah, was a sparkling blue, pristine paradise during summer and fall. However, for the past four months, it had been a chunk of ice.

That ice wouldn't last much longer, though. With springtime

temperatures beginning to inch slowly upward, parts of the lake had started to thaw. Despite the rising temps, I still spotted a few ice fishing shacks peppered across the slick top. "Dom and Lamonte better get a move on, or those are going to end up at the bottom of the lake." I pointed with an ironic smirk to several red-topped shacks boasting the It Floats logo. Dominic Gains and Lamonte Daniels owned the local aquatic sports rental shop, which, in the winter, rented ice fishing equipment to tourists and residents alike.

Ten minutes later, my phone chirped with a notification as Poppy turned into Lakeside Mulligan's parking area.

"Constance texted our group chat," I said before reading her message with a growing frown.

Sorry to bail, guys. Not feeling up for an evening out. Just gonna head home & Netflix. I'll text you later.

Once Poppy had parked the SUV, she read the message for herself. "Hexes. I was hoping we could cheer her up."

"I know." I patted my aunt on the arm. With her whim, it was hard for Poppy to see people suffer and not take immediate action. "At least that reality show she loves just dropped some new episodes. Hopefully a cozy night in will do her some good."

Hindsight being what it was, I wished Poppy and I had tried a little harder to convince Constance to join us for dinner. At least then, our friend would have had an alibi.

Chapter 2

"Come on, Noli." I gently tugged my sweet girl's leash toward the newest eatery in Crucible. The owners of Lakeside Mulligan's had made great use of their rustic, wraparound deck by installing large kerosene heaters. Patrons could eat outside in colder temperatures, all while enjoying the picturesque scenery. The establishment was also dog-friendly to folks sitting outdoors, so Noli could hang with us while we ate.

Poppy surveyed the crowded deck. "Yikes. Why is this place so busy?"

I glanced at my watch. "It's already five." We'd been hoping to beat the Friday dinner rush by getting here earlier, but the drama with Constance and Marjorie had delayed us.

"I think I spy a table in the corner." Poppy jogged toward the porch steps and flagged down the host.

Remy Potsdam smiled as we approached. Dressed in a vibrant floral dress shirt befitting of spring, the co-owner of Lakeside Mulligan's gave Poppy a hug. "Hello, darling. Radiant as always." He gave her a playful wink.

As Poppy giggled, Remy greeted me with a kiss on each cheek.

"So happy to see you, gorgeous. It's been a while. That hunky man of yours keeping you busy?" He wiggled his salt-and-pepper eyebrows, a mischievous gleam in his periwinkle eyes.

My introverted instincts kicked in, eager to keep my relationship with my boyfriend, Ezra Walters, private. I gave a light laugh and batted the question away. "Tonight is ladies' night."

Remy rubbed his hands together. "Then I've got some honeydew margaritas with your names on them." He ushered us toward the open table Poppy had spotted, conveniently located next to one of the glowing outdoor heaters. "Anything I can get for Miss Noli?"

I stroked Noli's head after claiming my seat. "She's all set. Thanks, Remy." Poor Noli had a medical issue that required a prescription diet, so she always had to pass on the "Puppers Menu" Lakeside Mulligan's offered.

Remy handed us the human menu and excused himself to collect our drinks.

Poppy's eyes widened as she read the specials. "I thought I was going to do the mashed potato casserole, but this duck confit fried chicken is calling my name."

I licked my lips in anticipation as I skimmed the featured entrees. Remy Potsdam and Nora Malone were longtime business partners, having opened several restaurants in the New York City Midtown area. Unfortunately, the cutthroat nature of the urban dining world had also seen them close those same restaurants. Hoping to find lasting success in a more intimate setting, Remy and Nora had opened Lakeside Mulligan's this past December. In the months since, the sophisticated gastropub had quickly become a hotspot in our quiet, upstate hometown.

"I'd try the crispy sweet potato fritters if I were you," a familiar voice murmured from over my left shoulder, "I had them a few nights ago, and they were to *die* for."

I turned around to greet the tall, athletic figure hovering behind me. "Hi, Tula. Long time, no see."

Poppy glanced up from her menu. "Hey, lady! I didn't realize you were back in town."

Tula Sardolous tossed back her mane of sleek, black hair. "Yes. I've been keeping busy, what with the family returning home last week."

She was referring to the Finchmores, of course. Tula served as the estate manager for billionaire Grant Finchmore and his influential clan. Grant was the CEO of Finchmore Power Technologies, a world leader in innovative energy solutions. Its campus was located on the outskirts of Crucible and employed thousands of people in the area. As one of Crucible's founding families, the Finchmores were more like royalty in this neck of the woods. Their home base was Finchaven, a sprawling, eco-friendly manor in northern Crucible, and Tula managed its operations with the dedication of a naval captain.

"Ah, yes," Poppy nodded with faux sincerity, "how could we forget their annual sojourn? The Finchmores aren't ones to weather the winter alongside us mere peasants, even if it means hopping on a private jet that destroys the environment they claim to care so much about."

Tula glared at my aunt, clearly not appreciating Poppy's attempts to throw shade at her globetrotting employers.

I, too, sent Poppy a reprimanding stare. She didn't usually badmouth anyone—let alone the Finchmores—to their employees' faces. "Did you go on vacation with them this time?" I jumped in to redirect the conversation.

"No. I opted to go to Mykonos." Tula rolled up the sleeves of her cashmere sweater to reveal her tanned arms. "Why my grandfather ever left there, I don't know." Both her and her late husband's families had immigrated to the U.S. in the fifties.

"I hope the adjustment back to reality hasn't been too harsh." Poppy offered a sympathetic smile, her snarkiness now gone.

Tula waved away her concern. "I can't complain. Finchaven is beautiful in the budding spring." She cast a quick glance at her watch. "But I am looking forward to having dinner with my son tonight. He joined the family in Turks and Caicos, and since they all got back, Grant's been keeping him busy with fundraiser stuff." She folded her arms as she surveyed the deck. "Speaking of Tobias, he should be here soon, so I'm off to secure a table. Always nice to see the Glenmyre Girls." She gave Noli a pat on the head before going inside.

Poppy stared after the estate manager. "Man, I wish I had a boss who let me tag along on trips to the Caribbean." Tobias Sardolous, Tula's pride and joy, also worked for the Finchmores as Grant's personal assistant.

I chuckled. "You *are* your own boss. Why not just take a vacay?"

Before she could respond, Remy returned with two very large salt-rimmed glasses. "Drink up, ladies!" he announced with a sassy shimmy. "Can I get some apps going?"

We gave Remy our gluttonous order of crispy sweet potato fritters and smoked gouda spinach dip. I mentally promised myself I would take Noli for an extra-long walk later tonight to help counteract all the cholesterol.

Poppy answered my lingering question once Remy had floated over to another table. "I'm too swamped with the greenhouse right now, and soon, wedding season will be in full swing. I already have centerpiece orders up the wazoo." She began to massage her temples as if the thought gave her a headache.

"What about a weekend getaway?" I sipped my honeydew marg and relaxed as the sweet melon tequila tickled my tastebuds. "You know, spend some quality time with Fitz?"

When Poppy didn't immediately answer, a surge of worry spiked through me. "Is everything okay between you two?"

My aunt had been dating the Massachusetts-born proprietor of Cold Cauldron Brewing for several months now. Fitzgerald Ames had harbored a huge crush on Poppy for years, and I'd always suspected the same of Poppy. It had just taken them some time to get together, much like Ezra and me.

"Oh, *pft*, Fitz and I are great." Poppy rolled her eyes, and I got the sense she was annoyed.

"Then what's the matter?"

Poppy dropped her gaze as she stirred the crushed ice in her drink. "I don't know, Hazel. It's hard to describe it."

"Try." It was moments like this that I wished I had a whim as useful as Poppy's rather than my own morbid ability. All I could tell from Poppy's appearance was that she seemed a bit tired.

My bestie sighed and gazed out across the frozen lake. "I guess with everything finally feeling back to normal, I'm worried about what will happen to the town if I take my eye off things."

I chewed on my lower lip as I considered her confession. "Pops, Grandmaster Jedidiah's shield is gone. We've got to accept that."

After Crucible's founding, Jedidiah Glenmyre and his kin, people able to harness awe-inspiring supernatural power, had cast a protection spell over the area to keep Crucible safe from the evils of the world, both natural and manmade. However, due to the lack of Glenmyres left, the shield's strength had deteriorated. Without the enchantment's mystical protection, Crucible was no longer the haven it had once been, and a recent string of terrible murders had afflicted the town. As the current matriarch of our clan, Poppy clearly felt responsible for the enchantment's demise.

"We've got to learn to live without the shield's protection," I continued in a low murmur. "Yes, we should use our whims to help when we can, but we also can't spend our lives hovering over Crucible like helicopter parents."

Poppy shuddered at the unflattering term. "I know you're right. It's just hard not to feel like this is all my fault."

"Hey," I said, reaching across the table to squeeze her hand. "We're in this together. You, me, and Holden."

Poppy chuckled softly. "I guess the town's safety should rest more on our police chief's shoulders than mine."

Happy to see her sense of humor returning, I sat back and took another refreshing sip of margarita. "Based on how little we've seen him lately, Cousin Holden understands that, too."

"We should invite him and Constance out the next time we double up with Fitz and Ezra." Poppy rubbed her hands together in eager anticipation. We'd been trying to set Holden and Constance up for what felt like forever, but our matchmaking efforts had yet to yield any positive results. Without fail, either Holden was called away to assist with police matters, or Constance's numerous professional commitments got in the way.

I reached down to scratch Noli behind her ear. She sat at my feet, happy to be at my side. "Now that Constance is almost done with her latest Misthollow book, she won't have an excuse to say no."

We set about making plans for a fun group date and thanked Remy when he delivered our drool-inducing appetizers. Somewhat mindful of our arteries, we placed orders for grilled chicken Cobb salads and another round of margaritas.

Dining out in Crucible wouldn't be complete without several familiar faces stopping by our table. By the time Poppy and I paid the bill and left Lakeside Mulligan's, it was going on eight.

"I'm so happy for Ione," Poppy gushed as we strapped ourselves into her car. "Kingston's a great guy, and after everything she went through with Dumb Darren, she deserves the world."

I giggled at Poppy's nickname for Ione's ex. I had a more unflattering choice of words for the man who had cheated on our dear friend, Ione Martin. But having spotted Ione and Kingston Hughes, the Crucible Historical Society curator, enjoying a cozy date at Lakeside Mulligan's, I couldn't agree more with Poppy's assessment.

I turned around in my seat to smile at Noli. "Ready to go home and see Berg?" Bergamot was my three-year-old gray short-haired cat and Magnolia's brother from another mother.

"Didn't you need me to swing by the store?" Poppy asked as she maneuvered her Subaru through the bustling parking lot.

I shook my head. "Iggy texted and said he dropped the new labels off on my front porch on his way home."

"These are the ones Cora designed, right? I can't wait to see them."

I beamed. "Me neither. She sent me mockups, and they were breathtaking."

Four and a half years ago, I turned my love of candle making into a small business and opened my shop, A Wick in Time. One of the best parts of my job was experimenting with new fragrances and scent pairings, and my most recent candle collection had been inspired by both Poppy and our friend, Cora Donahue. Cora was the art teacher at Crucible Grammar School, and in her free time, she sold watercolor paintings on Etsy. Back in January, she'd been commissioned to paint orchids for a client's Valentine's Day gift and had asked Poppy if she could use her flowers as still-life models.

I was visiting Poppy at the time, and while Cora was out sketching in the greenhouse, I'd had a flash of candle-making brilliance; I'd reimagine my own take on an English garden. "Poppy's Patch" candles would showcase the beautiful flora from the gardens, greenhouse, and conservatory cultivated by my spirited aunt. Enthused by the idea, I asked Cora if I could employ her talents to design the product labels, each bearing a watercolor graphic of the flowers represented, and was thrilled when she said yes.

"I still can't believe you're naming a candle collection after me." Even in the nighttime darkness, I could see Poppy's cheeks glow red with delight.

I shook my head. "I can't believe I didn't think of it sooner."

We drove around Lake Glenmyre in companionable silence, our stomachs and hearts full from a good meal. Sleep tugged at my eyelids just as we rounded the last bend before my driveway. I couldn't wait to cuddle up on the couch with my fur babies when I got home.

The sudden pulsing of red and blue lights doused my drowsiness like a bucket of cold water had been tossed over me.

"Holy hexes! What do you think happened?" Poppy shot me a concerned look before pressing the gas pedal and speeding past my driveway.

I opened my mouth to protest and plead for Poppy to just drop me off at home, but the sight of several police cars and black SUVs silenced me. Curiosity overtook the rest of my senses.

We pulled onto the side of the road behind a familiar Ford Explorer. The words "Crucible Chief of Police," painted on the back, were easy to read in Poppy's headlights. Holden's new set of government-issued wheels.

After giving Noli murmured reassurances that we would return soon, Poppy and I darted out of the Subaru and jogged toward the unnerving activity ahead. An ambulance's lights flashed, but the vehicle remained stationary, parked on the opposite shoulder. Yellow police tape was everywhere, and one of Holden's new part-time officers, Theresa Jacobs, stood at the ready to redirect traffic.

"They've completely closed down the road." Poppy frowned as she scanned the chaotic nighttime scene. She'd have to backtrack into town to make it home now.

I stood on my tiptoes, trying to catch sight of what was going on. A trio of emergency vehicles blocked my view. The lettering on one van caught my eye. "Why would the Bureau of Criminal

Investigation be helping at a car accident?" Holden had been a homicide detective with BCI before becoming Crucible's police chief. Their presence here didn't make much sense.

Poppy wrung her hands, her right eye twitching every time she caught sight of a first responder darting in between vehicles. "I don't think they're dealing with an accident, Hazel."

My stomach flipped, and I immediately regretted my heavy dinner of fried food. "What do you mean—"

Two BCI officers suddenly appeared and climbed into the SUV nearest to us. A heartbeat later, they drove away, the ambulance following after them at a slow, dispiriting pace. The gap left by their departure allowed us a better view of the scene, still painted red and blue from the pulsing lights. An orange BMW with New Jersey plates sat parked on the side of the road, about twenty feet from where Poppy and I stood. The car door was ajar with numbered yellow markers peppered all around it. It looked like a scene straight out of *Criminal Minds*.

"Excuse me, I'm going to have to ask you—oh, it's you two."

I tore my horrified gaze from the car and settled on the pinched expression of Detective Declan Shroud. When Declan Shroud first came to town, he and I had not gotten off on the best foot, what with his initial belief that my friend Iggy Alewell was a cold-blooded killer. However, the young detective had eventually owned up to his mistake and apologized to Iggy, for which I had to give him credit.

"Hey, Declan." Poppy hugged herself. "What happened?"

Declan straightened his shoulders. "I'm not at liberty to say, Ms. Glenmyre. I do have to ask you both to leave."

Confused by the formality of his words, Poppy and I shared an agitated look. "Who's been hurt?" I asked.

Before Declan could respond, another familiar voice reached my ears. "I should have guessed our nosy looky-loos would be you two."

Holden Whitfield emerged from the shadows, the red and blue flashing lights dancing across his bronze skin. He wore his crisp new uniform, looking very much like the man in charge.

He tipped his hat at Declan. "I've got this, pal. The medical examiner wants you."

With a curt nod toward Poppy and me, Declan wove through the sea of parked vehicles and disappeared.

"Medical examiner?" I repeated, feeling nauseous. Someone wasn't hurt. They were dead.

Poppy sagged against me. "Someone's been killed?" Her voice trembled at the question.

Holden stared at us, his dark gaze full of sorrow. "I'm afraid so."

"Who?" Poppy and I burst out in unison.

Our cousin sighed. "I can't tell you that. Not yet, at least." He motioned with his elbow in the direction Declan had gone. "I may be Crucible's chief of police, but BCI still has jurisdiction in a case like this."

The fried food in my stomach hardened into a massive rock. "In a *murder* investigation, you mean."

Holden shifted on the balls of his feet, clearly uncomfortable. "A statement will be shared with the public soon."

My stunned gaze flicked over his broad shoulder, back toward the orange BMW.

A fluttering movement caught my eye near the open driver-side door. Something hanging off the side of the front seat twitched in the cool breeze.

I narrowed my gaze as a crime scene tech's flashlight illuminated the scene. It was a silk scarf dangling from the seat belt. From here, it looked to be coral with a bow-tie pattern.

I grabbed Poppy's arm so hard she yelped in surprise. I remembered the last time I'd seen that design. It'd been two weeks ago at Cold Cauldron Brewing, around the neck of a dear friend.

"Oh my gosh." Tears sprang to my eyes. "Pops, isn't that scarf *Constance's*?"

Chapter 3

"Constance?" Holden's jaw went slack. He looked as though he had been punched in the gut. "Are you sure, Hazel?"

Poppy's hand covered her mouth. "Omigosh. You're right. She was wearing it the last time we did trivia together. That's—I-I can't believe it."

"Constance?" Declan's voice startled us all. He popped up beside Holden. His chat with the medical examiner must have been quick. "You mean Constance Crane, the famous mystery author who moved to the area last year?" In his hands, Declan had a notepad and pen at the ready.

Poppy ignored him, her right eye twitching as she studied our cousin. Her horrified expression turned to one of growing confusion. Ugh, if only I could see what Holden's aura was revealing about the situation.

Instead, I was left to ferret out information the non-whim way. "Holden, please, tell us Constance isn't—"

"Constance is *fine*," he cut me off in clipped reassurance. "That we know of." He shot a wary glance toward Declan.

As soon as Holden's attention was diverted, I felt a sharp nudge in my side. I turned to chide Poppy and her careless elbows but swallowed my words when I met her panicked gaze. Her eyes were wide, and her lips were pressed tightly together. I didn't need a mind-reading whim to know what she was trying to wordlessly convey.

Don't say anything else. Keep your mouth shut.

I nodded my understanding a second before Holden's attention settled back on the two of us. "You ladies are certain that scarf belongs to Constance?"

My tongue went dry. I couldn't lie to my cousin, let alone to an officer of the law.

"I mean, we can't be *certain*, Holdie." Poppy, however, seemed to have no such reservations.

"But Ms. Crane must own a similar scarf if you thought it belonged to her?" Declan's left eyebrow arched as he probed further, his pen poised to note a response.

Static and beeping erupted from the radio clipped to his belt. "Shroud? We've got something."

The detective cursed under his breath as he shoved his pen into his jacket pocket and grabbed the device. "Roger that." Once he secured the radio to his waist, he clasped Holden's shoulder with his hand. "Deal with these two, will you?"

Holden obediently bobbed his head, and I frowned at the new power dynamic between them. When Holden had been with BCI, he'd been Declan's supervisor.

Once we were alone, Holden heaved a sigh. "This is not good," he muttered, more to himself than to us.

Poppy checked her watch on her left wrist. "Oh, curses. Look at the time. We should get going." With her right hand, my bestie grabbed my arm and dragged me away from the barricade.

"Hey, wait!" Holden ducked under the yellow tape and hurriedly followed, catching up to us just as we reached Poppy's car. "We need to talk." He put his hands on his hips. "Glenmyre-style." Anxiety swam in his dark eyes.

"Seems so. We'll be hanging at Hazel's." Poppy opened her door and hopped into the driver's seat.

I gave Holden a sympathetic smile, although I was beyond

confused by Poppy's cryptic behavior. "I guess we'll be at my place."

He nodded. "Okay, sit tight. We're wrapping up here. I'll be over once I'm done."

As soon as I said hello to Noli and buckled myself in, I turned my wary focus to my aunt. "What in the hexes did you see in their auras, Pops?"

She put the Subaru into drive and executed a perfect three-point turn. "Oh, man. I think we messed up big time, little niece." Poppy gnawed on her lower lip as she sped toward my driveway.

"What do you mean?"

"The scarf." My bestie winced. "We shouldn't have said anything."

"Why? Holden was the one being cagey." I bristled in my own defense. "Goodness, I thought Constance had been killed!"

"I know, I know." Poppy tenderly shushed me as she parked her car next to mine. "It's just—we've complicated things."

Why was Auntie Dearest being so guarded with her words? Now that we'd arrived at my secluded lakeside cottage, it wasn't like anyone could hear us.

I helped Noli out of the car and watched as she bounded enthusiastically toward the front porch. Her nubby tail wiggled as I followed after her. "I'm sorry, girl. I know it's past your dinnertime."

I unlocked the front door and let the pup inside, checking behind me to see what Poppy was doing. Oddly enough, she stood off to the side of my house, her gaze intent and focused on the dark frozen waters of the lake. "Hey, you coming in?"

She jumped as if she'd been in a trance. "Yep. I just need a minute to clear my head."

Impatience bubbled within me over her strange behavior. Poppy had never been hesitant to share an aura reading with me before. She didn't have the kind of hang-ups I did about my own whim. But really, who wanted to know when everyone around them was destined to die?

I took a deep breath. I wasn't being fair. Maybe Poppy had seen something in Holden's or Declan's auras that had left her reeling. Broomsticks, there had been plenty of times when I'd accidentally seen that dreaded, glowing countdown hovering over a person's head and felt like I'd been walloped in the stomach.

Subconsciously, I touched the bridge of my glasses, glad to find them securely in place. It was a nervous habit I did a hundred times a day to reassure myself they were still there. I didn't need my purple-and-gold frames to see clearly. I wore them to hide the creepy lifeclock that floated above the heads of everyone around me. An enchanted gift from my beloved Great-Aunt Ruthie, who'd had the same macabre whim as me.

A flash of smoky gray darted out from under the couch and into the kitchen. A scuffling of nails on the polished wood floor ensued. I sighed. I'd give Poppy a moment to collect her thoughts while I tended to the pressing matter of feeding my fur babies.

I found Bergamot perched on the kitchen windowsill next to his feeding tray, his tail swishing with impatience. Noli danced on the floor below him, bouncing back and forth from saying hello to him to examining her empty food bowl.

"Greetings, good sir." I scratched the short hair under his whiskered chin. When I first brought Berg home, I thought having three legs might limit his ability to climb all over my house, but I'd been proven wrong almost immediately. He was as graceful as any cat I'd ever met, hopping from my kitchen countertops onto the top of the fridge and then onto the bay window ledge. He treated my entire cottage as a jungle gym, and I was happy to let him.

Once I filled Berg's bowl with his cat food and Noli's with her prescription kibble, I heard the front door open. I hoped this meant that Poppy was finally ready to talk. I grabbed two seltzers from the fridge and headed into the living room.

My subdued aunt sat on my jersey-blue couch with her feet curled up under her.

"You okay?" I handed her a can, which she gratefully accepted.

"Yeah, I'm sorry I'm being so weird." Poppy cracked open the seltzer and took a long drink. "I thought we were done with all this. I thought whatever evils were plaguing Crucible had finally blown over." She rubbed her eyes, and I realized she'd been crying.

"Pops, this isn't your fault." I sat down on the couch next to her, draping a comforting arm around her shoulder.

"I know. But another *murder*?" Poppy sniffed. "Is this what our lives will be like going forward? Is this karma for our town having peace and prosperity for so long?"

I didn't have an immediate answer. Grandmaster Jedidiah's protection shield had ensured Crucible's safety for over three centuries. With its deterioration, was murder and mayhem going to be our new norm?

"Whatever's going on, we'll face it together," I pledged with as much confidence as I could muster.

My aunt squeezed my hand. "You're sweet to try and make me feel better." She chuckled lightly. "You're nearly bursting at the seams to know what I saw in the boys' auras, aren't you?"

I rolled my eyes. While our Glenmyre whims didn't normally work on members of our own family, for some reason, Poppy could see my aura, as well as Holden's. It made it really hard to keep my emotions and internal reactions private. Although, I was very thankful that it wasn't the other way around. I had no desire to know when I would eventually lose my best friend in the world if my glasses accidentally came askew in Poppy's presence.

"What's the big issue with the scarf?" I propped an elbow on the cushions and stared at her. "How have we complicated things?"

Poppy didn't meet my gaze. "When we mentioned Constance's name, Holden's aura went on high alert. Not sorrowful, mind you, but like he was scared and unnerved." She took a deep breath. "Declan, on the other hand, grew super suspicious and excited all at once."

"Excited?" I wrinkled my nose. "That's a weird emotion for a crime scene."

Poppy's blue eyes widened. "Haz, I think they believe Constance had something to do with the murder they're investigating. Both Declan *and* Holden."

"What?" I sat back as a nervous cackle sputtered across my lips. "You can't be serious."

Poppy tilted her head. "Why else would they be so curious about whether that scarf belonged to Constance?" Her incredulous expression made me feel like I was missing some blatant point.

"Well, uh, I don't know." My phone buzzed from my sweater pocket, saving me from having to answer Poppy further. I had somehow missed a call and a text from the same person.

Hey, luv. I heard there's an accident by your house. You ok?

Ezra's message brought a small smile to my lips, and the growing tension in my shoulders loosened just a bit. **I'm fine. Not sure what's going on, tho. Will let you know what I find out.**

His response was almost immediate. **Figured you'd be on the case. Be careful, pls.**

Will do.

"Ezzie, I presume?" Poppy squirmed in her seat and extracted her own buzzing phone from her pocket. "Word must be getting out. This is Fitz."

She tapped the Accept button and then the speakerphone icon. "Hey, babe. I'm here with Hazel. You're on speaker."

"Good to know." Fitzgerald Ames's earnest, deep voice filled my cozy living room. "Hey, Hazel."

"Hi, Fitz." I waved for emphasis, even though he couldn't see me.

"Just calling to check in," he admitted. "Heard about a nasty accident on the southeast side of the lake. Relieved to learn you two weren't involved."

Poppy grimaced. "Depends on your definition of involved."

"What do you mean?"

I knocked her in her side and mouthed, *Don't you dare say anything before we talk to Holden.*

Duh, Poppy wordlessly answered back. "Well, the whole thing happened practically on Hazel's doorstep. Not that the police are telling us much." She gave me a thumbs-up sign.

I nodded my satisfaction. Fitz, God love him, was a notorious gossip. It was one of the many reasons he was such a popular brewer and bartender. And while we normally tried to stay away from the Crucible rumor mill, tonight, Poppy and I could use Fitz's chattiness to our advantage. No doubt, he would make sure everyone in town knew that the Glenmyre Girls had no more information than they all did. We'd bought ourselves some time from having to field a slew of prying questions.

I tuned out the rest of Poppy and Fitz's animated conversation, scanning my phone for updates about the incident from the local news station. Nothing.

Noli, having finished her dinner, jumped onto the couch and curled up into a ball next to me. I stroked her soft fur as I surfed the web for intel. It wasn't until car lights flashed through the living room window that my trance was broken.

"I'll swing by tomorrow. Night, babe." Poppy quickly signed off her call and beat me to the door to greet our visitor.

"Start talking," she instructed Holden as soon as he stepped over the threshold.

I shot her a scolding glance. "Give him a chance to breathe, will you? Can I get you anything, Chief?" I asked our weary cousin. "Food? Drink?"

Holden removed his cap and ran a hand over his dark, close-shaven hair. "Nah, I'm good. I don't feel much like eating right now." He knelt to say hello to Noli as he removed his work boots. "What a night."

"Hazel and I have been dying for deets over here." Poppy winced as soon as she heard herself. "Sorry. Poor choice of words."

Holden gave her a pointed look. "Not the first time you've put your foot in your mouth this evening." He rubbed his temples before sighing. "What I'm about to tell you stays between us, all right? No Ezra. No Fitz. No *anyone*."

Poppy and I bowed our heads in solemn promise. "Cross our hearts." Poppy even drew an X on her chest to seal the deal.

We all settled into our usual spots in the living room, although Poppy and I sat more on the edge of our seats, eagerly anticipating Holden's news.

"What's going on, Holden?" My aunt broke the tense silence. "*Who* was killed tonight?"

Holden clasped his hands together, his expression grave. "According to the name on the driver's license, a New Jersey resident called Marjorie Zeller."

"Marjorie?" I choked out.

Poppy gasped as we shared a horrified look. The victim was Constance's writing friend?

Holden cocked an eyebrow. "You guys know her?"

Poppy held my gaze before giving me an encouraging nod to keep talking. "Kinda." I swallowed. "Through Constance."

At the mention of the renowned author's name, Holden flinched. "I was worried you'd say that."

"Constance didn't kill Marjorie." Poppy's tone was measured and confident. "So get that outrageous idea out of your head."

"I would, if I could." Holden wrung his hands. "But now that Declan knows about the scarf—"

"That scarf *could* belong to anyone," Poppy cut in. "Who knows how many like it exist in the world?"

Holden's gaze narrowed. "'That scarf,'" he replied sharply, using air quotes, "is our murder weapon."

I involuntarily gathered Noli in my arms and hugged her to my chest.

"What?" Poppy whispered through her fingertips. "How?"

"The poor woman was strangled." Holden momentarily glanced down at the floor before lifting his head to meet our stunned gazes. "We'll know more once the ME does an autopsy. But until then, the optics don't look great for Constance—especially since she was friends with the victim. No doubt, Shroud will be knocking on her door and soon."

"Oh my gosh." My chin quivered as regret pricked at my eyes. When would I ever learn? Me and my big mouth were now responsible for setting the police on a dear friend. Again. "But Constance had nothing to do with this. She couldn't."

"Unfortunately, cuz, your reassurances won't hold up in court." Holden's expression was all business. "Tell me what you guys know about her relationship with Marjorie Zeller."

I nervously twisted a long strand of my dark brown hair around my finger. "I mean, we don't know all that much. Marjorie was a college friend from Constance's writing circle who came to Crucible for an extended visit. Constance said they were doing a self-imposed writing retreat at her place. Until two weeks ago, that is."

Holden frowned. "What happened two weeks ago?"

I gnawed on my lower lip, dreading the ramifications of what I was about to reveal. "Well, Constance and Marjorie had a little disagreement that resulted in Constance asking Marjorie to leave."

"Little disagreement, huh? Great, this keeps getting better and better." Holden snorted with heavy sarcasm. "Do you know what their dispute was about?"

Poppy shook her head, relieving me of storytelling duty. "No. And for all we knew, Marjorie had left town. Until we saw her at the library earlier today."

"Today?" Holden straightened in his seat.

"Yeah. We had dinner plans with Constance, so Hazel and I offered to pick her up at the library." Poppy then explained to Holden the heated scene we'd found when we arrived. "Since the whole ordeal had put her in a bad mood, Constance ended up going home instead of coming to dinner with us," she concluded.

I tried to get a read on Holden's face, but he was giving me nothing. Poppy's right eye, however, was twitching a mile a minute.

"So," Holden began with a labored sigh, "you two can't account for Constance's whereabouts at five twenty-six this evening, can you?"

I held up a hand. "Five twenty-six? That sounds oddly specific."

"Yeah," Poppy said in sly agreement. "How could the medical examiner give such a precise—oh, holy hexes, of course!" She leveled a finger at Holden. "Your *whim!*"

The corner of Holden's lip twitched at Poppy's dramatics. "I'm surprised that wasn't the first thing you asked me about."

Much like my ability to see when someone would die, Holden had a very morbid power of his own. He could hear a person's final thoughts before their demise.

"You were able to get a reading on Marjorie?" Sympathy bloomed in my chest when he nodded. That couldn't have been pleasant for him.

Poppy scoffed. "Then you must know Constance had nothing to do with Marjorie's death."

When Holden didn't immediately respond, I gulped. "Constance had nothing to do with Marjorie's death, right?"

"As of now, I don't know what to believe." Holden flopped back in his seat, throwing his arms up in defeat. "And I certainly don't have anything that I can share with the DA's office."

"What did Marjorie's memories tell you?" I pressed. Now I knew why Holden wanted to talk with Poppy and me after finishing up at the crime scene. He couldn't share the burden of his whim with anyone else. Not only were our whims a long-kept family secret, but who would believe that he'd heard a recap of Marjorie's last moments?

A haunted look loomed in Holden's brown eyes. "It was awful. A real struggle. Marjorie didn't reveal a face or name. Whoever attacked her must have taken her by total surprise while she was sitting at the side of the road in her car, staring at the clock on the dash."

"Five twenty-six." Poppy's skin grew pale. "That's why it came through so clear in your reading."

Holden's gaze dropped to his fidgeting hands. "Her memories were a panicked jumble, a complete mess, but I was able to make out a few coherent sentences." He took a steeling breath. "She thought, *'Please, no. I swear, I'm not here to cause trouble. I'm just so close. Stop. Please, someone help me. I need to find—'* and then everything went quiet."

Silence settled over us as the horrifying magnitude of Marjorie's final words sunk in. Holden wiped a stray tear off his cheek, and my heart ached for him.

Poppy reached for his forearm and squeezed.

Our cousin cleared his throat. "She didn't provide me with a name or face, but given the circumstances, a pretty bad picture is beginning to take shape."

I tilted my head. "Circumstances being?"

"Shroud will have to follow the evidence, and so far," Holden replied, holding up his fingers as he presented his material, "we have a friend of Constance Crane found dead in her car, killed with a scarf potentially belonging to Constance, two weeks after they had a falling out and barely an hour after they had a fiery confrontation in front of the public library."

Poppy folded her arms. "But you know Constance didn't do this, Holden."

"I want to believe she's innocent. Believe me, I do…" He hung his head.

"But because Marjorie was likely attacked from behind, her final memories don't prove one thing or another," I finished his train of thought. "And as of right now, the evidence will lead Shroud straight to Constance." I put my face in my shaking hands. "Ugh, if only I hadn't said anything about that scarf."

Poppy patted me gently on the back.

"Don't beat yourself up about this, Hazel," Holden offered. "For all his faults, Shroud's a good detective. He would have uncovered Marjorie's connection to Constance one way or another."

His reassurances didn't make me feel any better. "We have to help her. We have to find out who really did this."

"Obviously." Poppy rolled her eyes. "That's why we're all here, isn't it?" She shifted in her seat and raised her brow expectantly at Holden.

"As chief of police, *I* will be assisting BCI when and where I can." Holden glared at her. "*You two* will have to be more discreet."

Poppy and I grinned.

"I'm breaking every rule in the book by sanctioning this, but the book doesn't account for the power of our whims. Besides," Holden paused as his gaze trailed out my front window, "I don't want Constance to get dragged into this mess any more than you do. She's a good person. She doesn't deserve this."

I pressed my lips together, suppressing the little *aww* bubbling inside me. He clearly cared about her, even if our efforts to play matchmaker hadn't yielded any fruitful results.

"All right, now that we're done dancing around the fact that we're inserting ourselves into yet another police investigation…" Poppy dusted her hands off like a job well done. "Where do we start?"

"I start by leaving." Holden rose from his cushion and headed for the door. "I need a little plausible deniability about this whole thing." He gave us a crooked smile, and we chuckled. "And I won't be sharing anything about the official investigation from this point on. You got that?"

Poppy saluted her understanding. "Yes, sir."

"Be careful, Chief," I reminded him as we bid Holden goodbye.

With our cousin gone, Poppy began nervously tapping her foot on the polished wood floor. "We've always had Constance to help us kick off our crime-solving antics. Where do we begin this time?"

"I've got an idea." I motioned for Poppy to follow me into the kitchen. We stopped in front of the whiteboard hanging by my stove. It once served as a place for me to brainstorm candle scents, but tonight, it would play a different role.

I grabbed a red marker and wrote the question burning inside me.

Who killed Marjorie Zeller?

Chapter 4

"Who *is* Marjorie Zeller might be the more pertinent place to start," Poppy suggested as she studied the whiteboard with a frown. "I mean, she was just visiting Crucible. Why would anyone here have reason to kill her?"

I recoiled. "That's another strike toward Constance, then." I wrote our friend's name underneath the victim's. "She was Marjorie's only connection to the area."

"At least, that's what we think," Poppy countered. "What the heck was Marjorie still doing in town? Where was she staying? Constance kicked her out of her house two weeks ago. A Thursday, wasn't it?" Her hands went to her hips as her nose wrinkled. "Could Marjorie really have made another enemy that quickly?"

My stomach lurched as I considered the notion. "Yeesh, that's disheartening to think about."

"Right? If Grandmaster Jedidiah could see Crucible now." Poppy hugged herself, her expression forlorn. "We should talk to Constance in the morning. Before Declan and BCI do, if possible."

"Let's hope he hasn't already gotten to her." I glanced at the half-moon clock hanging from my kitchen wall. It was close to ten, and I still needed to take Noli for her nighttime walk. "Iggy's opening the shop for me tomorrow. Shall we meet at her place at eight?"

"Sounds like a plan." Poppy's phone buzzed a second later. She reached for it, and as she read the screen, her face lost all color.

"What is it?" I leaned forward, eager to see what had caused such a reaction.

Poppy dropped the device into my palm. "My friend Reagan just sent it to me. Looks like someone *did* whip out their phone during Constance and Marjorie's heated spat."

My stomach hardened like a curing candle as I watched the TikTok video Poppy's pal had shared. With a demeaning caption that read *Girl has lost the plot*, the short clip showed Constance yelling at Marjorie in front of our library. Well, *I* knew it was Marjorie, but the video only captured her from behind.

"Oh, no."

Poppy massaged her temples. "Check the timestamp. It was posted even before we got there to intervene."

"Which means most of Crucible already knows about their blow-out." I cringed. I already assumed the town rumor mill would have spread the news, but I thought we'd escaped the Internet's scrutiny. But with eleven thousand views and climbing, those hopes were horribly dashed.

Poppy gritted her teeth. "Within seconds of that video being uploaded, too. This, paired with Marjorie's murder? I can only imagine what people will say about Constance."

Out of curiosity, I reviewed the user profile that posted the argument. "Curses. Looks like some high schooler." While the kid was probably hoping to stir the pot with his video, I doubted he'd meant anything overtly malicious by it. But now, the clip would likely be added to the growing pile of circumstantial evidence against our friend.

Summoning what little humor I could, I batted my eyelashes innocently at Poppy. "What are the chances Declan won't see this?"

She folded her arms. "We can only hope." Her confidence sounded non-existent.

~∞~

When I pulled into the driveway of Constance's stately lakeside colonial home Saturday morning, I found my aunt leaning against her Subaru with a wicker basket nestled in the nook of her arm.

"Lemon poppyseed muffins," Poppy announced in greeting.

"Stress baking?" I guessed as I stuffed my hands deep into the pockets of my peacoat. Much to my dismay, there'd been a layer of frost on the ground when I'd awoke. Warmer temperatures could not get here soon enough.

Poppy chuckled. "You know it. I was up all night trying to find intel on Marjorie. Other than BookTok hype for her upcoming release, I couldn't unearth much."

"Me neither." I'd tried playing cyber sleuth after crawling into bed with Noli and Berg, but it hadn't amounted to anything useful. Marjorie maintained several professional social media accounts, but none revealed much about her life other than her love of writing. "Let's hope Constance will pull back the curtain for us."

Poppy straightened her shoulders with determination. "We also need her to tell us what they fought about." Despite her resolute posture, she looked tired. "The Internet sure has its theories after that video making the rounds."

We ambled along the pathway to the front porch, still cloaked in early morning shadows. Swallowing the sudden burst of nerves threatening to clamp up my throat, I grabbed the brass knocker and rapped it against the red-painted door.

Poppy peered through the panel of distorted glass running alongside the entryway. "She's usually up by now." Constance always touted the perks of being an early riser and how it helped her manage her busy writing schedule.

I knocked again. "Constance?" I called out. "Are you in there? It's us."

Poppy jumped back from the window and hurried to my side. "Incoming."

The front door inched open a crack, and I heard a whimper on the other side. "Thank goodness it's you girls." The door swung inward, revealing our disheveled friend. The award-winning author's blonde hair was in a messy topknot, and her forest-green eyes were red and watery.

Wordlessly, Poppy held out her arms, her face exuding concern, but I noted the sincere relief that mingled with her sympathetic expression. Whatever Poppy had seen in Constance's aura, it was not that of a killer.

"I-I can't believe this is happening." Constance sniffled as Poppy gathered her in a tight embrace. "I can't believe—Poor Margie."

Once Poppy released her, I gave Constance a hug of my own. "How'd you find out?" Had Shroud already paid Constance a visit? The police hadn't yet issued a statement about Marjorie's death, so it wasn't like the details were common knowledge.

Constance wiped her eyes as she beckoned us inside her home. "My agent called me. Around midnight. She wanted to break the news before I read about it online."

Poppy's brow furrowed. "How'd your agent find out so quickly?"

"Word travels fast in publishing circles." Constance shrugged off the remark as we grabbed seats at her kitchen counter. "Our agents are friends. The police called Lauren Johnson, Margie's agent, to inform her about Margie's passing. I guess Lauren was listed as her emergency contact."

Passing? I shot an inquiring look at Poppy. Did Constance not know the tragic way in which her friend had lost her life?

Constance dabbed at her wet cheeks once more. "Margie was young. Healthy. Our age. How could she just *die*?"

Guess I had my answer. "Um," I hesitated, trying to find the right words, "did your agent tell you anything else about Marjorie's death?"

"No." Constance rubbed her pert nose with the back of her hand. "She just told me it happened suddenly last night, and that Margie's death would probably bring a little uncomfortable media attention since she was visiting me at the time."

I cringed at Constance's rather cold tone. She was normally a warm, caring person, so this had to be the shock talking.

"I think there'll be more than a *little* media interest in this case." Poppy took a fortifying breath. "We have some unsettling news to share. Marjorie was murdered."

"What?" Constance let loose a nervous chuckle, her expression growing alarmed as we remained sincere and stone-faced. "*What?* Is this some sick joke? Please tell me—"

"We're so sorry." I reached for her left forearm. "But it's true."

She dropped her head into her palms, and for the first time, I noticed she had a large bandage wrapped around her right hand. *Ouch.*

"*Murdered?*" Constance finally whispered through her fingers. "This can't be happening. Who would want to kill Margie?"

"Have you eaten anything? You look a bit peaked." Switching to mother-hen mode, Poppy jumped down from her barstool, grabbed some plates from the white cabinets, and began dishing out her freshly made lemon poppyseed muffins.

I joined in by making some coffee. We'd eaten at Constance's home enough times to be comfortable navigating our way around her enviably large kitchen.

"Thanks." Constance picked at the muffin, tearing it into pieces, but never put a bite in her mouth. The coffee, however, she gratefully accepted and drank.

"Murder," she murmured a few moments later, sounding more composed. "Gosh, this reads like one of my books. I hope the police figure out who did this. Margie and I may have had our differences of late, but she—she didn't deserve this." Her chin began to quiver.

I cleared my throat. "I'm afraid we've got more bad news. Poppy and I got a look at the crime scene last night. Someone attacked Marjorie in her car. Holden was there, helping the BCI team."

Constance shuddered.

"At the scene, the police found a scarf. A coral scarf in Marjorie's car..." I trailed off, letting my words sink in. "A scarf that looked like one you own."

"The pretty bow-tie pattern one," Poppy added. "I told you how much I liked it when we saw you at trivia night a few weeks ago."

Constance tilted her head in confusion. "You mean this one?" She got up and hurried toward the first-floor primary suite. When she didn't immediately return, we trailed after her. We found Constance pawing through an accessory tree hanging in her walk-in closet, her expression growing increasingly more panicked. "Where is it? You guys, it should be here!"

Poppy and I shared worried glances.

Constance blew a loose strand of hair out of her face. "I know I put it back once Margie and I returned home from Cold Cauldron. I even remember Margie saying—" She cut herself off, her eyes widening.

"Saying what?" Poppy and I asked in unison.

Constance's gaze grew stormy. "Saying how I always knew how to spot a good find. She kept fawning over the scarf and how it would look *sooooo* good with her skin tone." Her grip tightened on a huge orange belt dangling from the hangers. "She couldn't. Margie—hold up." She suddenly whirled on us.

"Omigosh. Why didn't I suspect something sooner? There's a death in Crucible, and the Glenmyre Girls show up on my doorstep first thing the next morning?" Her voice inched upward with every word. "Are you here as my friends or to question me as a suspect?"

Poppy held up her hands in defense. "Of course we're here as your friends!"

"We're here to help you," I hurriedly reassured Constance. "We know you had nothing to do with Marjorie's death. But—" I bit my lower lip "—the police will probably think otherwise. And it's all my fault." The words tumbled from my lips, a wave of guilt threatening to drown me. "I saw the scarf dangling from Marjorie's car, and I recognized it as looking like one you owned, and I thought *you* were hurt, and I stupidly asked if you were all right."

Much to my surprise, Constance had her arms around me when I finished my rambling confession. "You guys." She stretched out the words into ten syllables. "Thank you. It means so much that you're here."

I stared at her, worried that I'd misheard her. "But it's *my* fault that the police will be looking at you." Neither Poppy nor I could mention Holden's troubling reading of Marjorie's final thoughts.

Constance batted the idea away. "Oh, please. After the scene I made at the library yesterday, the police will learn sooner or later that Marjorie and I were going through a rough patch. Yeah, yeah, I saw the TikTok video." She rubbed her hands together, her eyes glowing with intrigue. "At least now we know what I'm up against. I mean, if it was found at the crime scene, obviously, Margie stole my scarf from me."

Her sudden change in mood left me unsettled. How had Constance jumped to the conclusion that her scarf had been stolen? If Marjorie had been so taken with it, couldn't she just have bought one for herself?

"Hey, girlie, slow down." Poppy placed a comforting hand on our friend's shoulder. "You've had a terrible shock. I think it would be best for you to give yourself some time to heal and process what's happened."

Constance's gaze darted between Poppy and me. "But the police will likely be here soon. We need to get to the bottom of this."

I draped my arm over her shoulders. "*You* need to focus on taking care of yourself. Leave the sleuthing to us."

Poppy nodded. "Remember how much the Misthollow police hate it when Jinx gets involved in a crime when she's a suspect?" she asked, perfectly referencing the main character in Constance's mega-popular book series. "You need to stay on BCI's good side."

My aunt's gaze dropped to our friend's right hand. "And speaking of healing, what the heck happened there?" She pointed to the thick, gauzy bandage.

Constance grimaced as she led us out of the closet and back to our abandoned muffins in the kitchen. "Like a total idiot, I grabbed the hot end of my hair straightener this morning. As you can guess, my mind has been elsewhere." Her grief-stricken demeanor returned. "Are you sure I can't help? I feel like I owe it to Margie. I'm the reason she was even in Crucible in the first place." Tears spilled down her cheeks once more.

"Tell us about her," I suggested softly. "How did you two meet?"

"Gosh, it was years ago." Constance grabbed a tissue and blotted her eyes. "My sophomore year of college. We were in the same creative writing course elective. Margie was an accounting major in her final semester and felt so out of her depth. We teamed up for a project and became great friends. Margie totally got the writing bug." A smile spread across Constance's face as she recounted the memory. "Even though she graduated and moved to NYC, we kept in touch through the years. I moved to the city after college, and we joined a Brooklyn-based writing group together. We were both so hopeful about getting a manuscript published. We celebrated when I got my first book deal." Constance then shuddered at a phantom recollection. "And she helped me regain my confidence bit by bit after the fallout from that dud. I'd moved away from the city by then, but we still FaceTimed or emailed pretty regularly."

Poppy swallowed a bite of muffin and asked, "When was the last time you saw each other in person? Before this visit, I mean?"

"Two years ago. I was on tour with my fifth Misthollow Mystery. During my NYC dates, I stayed at Margie's place, for old times' sake. We did some writing together and reviewed each other's work. Margie's new work-in-progress was good. It had promise."

"Was it the book that she has coming out?" I searched my mind for the title. "*Under the Red Barn?*"

Poppy suddenly jolted back from the kitchen counter, nearly knocking her coffee cup over. I opened my mouth to poke fun at her clumsiness when I noted her distressed expression. Her right eye twitched wildly, her gaze locked on Constance.

I turned back to our friend, wondering what in the hexes Poppy saw in her aura. But Constance's white knuckles and flared nostrils told me all I needed to know. She was piping mad.

"No," Constance seethed, her reply clipped. "It was *not* the same one."

"Okay," I said, stretching the word out to buy myself time.

Poppy drummed her fingers on the countertop. "Does this have to do with the argument you and Marjorie had?"

Constance didn't respond.

"If we're going to figure out who killed her, we need to understand what happened between you two," I reminded her. "We need to prove you *didn't* have motive to kill Marjorie."

Constance snorted. "Trouble is, I kinda did."

Poppy sank back onto her barstool, shooting me an anxious look. "Spill it, C."

"You can trust us." I reached for her unbandaged hand.

Constance pulled away from my touch. "Yeah, that's what Margie once said, too." She stared off into space before releasing a long sigh. "Sorry. That was unfair of me. You guys have been nothing but lovely since you interrupted my writing sesh to ask for advice on solving a murder."

We giggled softly at the outlandish memory from last summer.

"Okay, here's the deal." Constance reclined against the back of her seat. "That last time I saw Margie in New York, we did writing sprints together." She must have noticed our confused expressions, for she quickly added, "It's a method of timed writing. You write as much as you can in a set amount of time.

"Anyway, I was working on fleshing out a new idea in case the Misthollow Mysteries didn't get picked up for more books by my publisher. I wrote an outline and the opening chapters over the weekend to share with Margie. She tried to give me good feedback, but I could tell from her lackluster response that she wasn't impressed by what I'd written. I chalked it up as a bust. Since I'd handwritten the chapters and outline, I crumpled them up and tossed the project into her trashcan."

Constance paused to massage her temples. "After that, I didn't revisit the idea. I honestly forgot all about it. Until two weeks ago." Her brow furrowed and her gaze darkened. "You see, Margie had reached out to me this past December with news about her upcoming book, and she asked if she could visit me in Crucible to celebrate. 'We can do sprints like old times,' she said. A do-it-ourselves writing retreat." Constance motioned around her spacious home. "Of course, I was happy to host her and beyond thrilled about her release. It was a dream come true for her. So, we made plans for her to visit once we both had some downtime."

Constance rose from her seat and ambled over to her Nespresso machine, putting in a silver pod. "When she arrived, it was like we were back in college, having a blast. Until I convinced her to let me read her new book."

An unsettling notion began to bloom in the back of my mind.

"Well, I didn't convince her so much as snuck it out of her bag to read for myself." Constance pressed her fists against the marble counter. "Margie had an ARC with her since the publisher was getting ready to put the preorder links up. I read the back cover and was kinda surprised at how familiar it seemed. Then, I read the first two chapters, and…" Her words trailed off, her voice hoarse with emotion.

"They were the ones you'd written when you last saw her."

Constance nodded at Poppy's deduction. "Yep. She'd hardly changed anything."

"Omigosh." I wrung my hands. "That's awful. How could she do that to you?"

"Pretty easily, I guess." Constance sounded heartbroken and utterly betrayed. "Margie must have dug my work out of the trash when I wasn't looking. Using the first two chapters and my outline, she decided to write the rest of the book herself."

"That's intellectual property theft." Poppy's jaw clenched. "Did Marjorie think she could get away with it?"

Constance shrugged. "I have no digital receipts the book was actually my idea. Believe me, I've tried to find proof." Her defeated gaze dropped to her bandaged hand. "Some scrap of old paper, some note. But I have nothing other than my word."

I considered the troubling scenario. No wonder Constance had been so quick to accuse Marjorie of stealing her missing scarf. The woman had already stolen Constance's words and IP to get herself a book deal. And a lucrative one, at that. From my online research, *Under the Red Barn* had gone up for preorder this past Tuesday, and it was already trending with book reviewers on Instagram and TikTok. For Constance to find out that this buzzworthy book was actually *her* brainchild…Curses, no wonder she'd tossed Margie out.

"Have you told anyone else about this?" Poppy pressed. "What about your agent?"

"No way. I have no proof." Constance reached for her espresso. "All it would do is make me seem like a jealous literary rival trying to belittle a new and upcoming author."

I hopped down from my stool and brought my dirty dishes over to the sink. "What did Marjorie have to say for herself when you confronted her?"

Constance scowled. "She had the audacity to ask me to write her a blurb."

"What?" Poppy's eyes widened.

Constance bobbed her head. "Yeah, she said that I *owed* her after all the feedback and support she'd given me over the years, as if our friendship had been purely transactional." She hugged herself, growing more agitated with every word. "Margie said that since I already have Misthollow, couldn't I let her win, just once? As if her lack of success in the publishing world was *my* fault."

I wiped my hands clean of dish soap and scooped Constance into another hug. "You are not to blame. For any of this."

Poppy bounced over to join us.

"Thanks," Constance said as we broke away. "Margie made me feel like *I* was the one who'd betrayed *her*. I just couldn't with her. I told her to get out of my house and out of my life. She grabbed her bags and left. Or, at least, I thought she did."

"So, you really had no idea she was still in the area these past two weeks?" Poppy held Constance's gaze, no doubt searching for answers in our friend's aura.

Constance shook her head adamantly. "None. I was totally shocked when I saw her at the library yesterday."

Poppy shot me a sidelong glance accompanied by a barely imperceptible nod. Constance was telling the truth. She didn't know her frenemy had been hanging around Crucible.

I considered the strange situation. What had Marjorie been up to for those two weeks that had gotten her killed?

"When you saw her yesterday, did she tell you why she hadn't left town?" Poppy asked.

Constance's cheeks flushed with embarrassment. "Um, no. I really didn't give Margie much of a chance. I tore into her pretty hard."

The TikTok clip definitely supported that statement. "Did you introduce Marjorie to anyone she might have become friends with?" I dug my phone out of my pocket, ready to take down any names.

"Nope." Constance shook her head. "No one. Well, other than you guys when we ran into you at trivia night." She folded her arms across her chest. "We hung out at the house for the most part. Ordered in and such. We went for a daily walk around the lake, but we never ran into people."

Poppy blew back a wisp of her auburn hair. "Well, we can start by asking Bea if Marjorie booked a room with her." Bea Thompson was Poppy's good friend from high school and the proprietor of The Elderberry Inn. "See if Marjorie had any visitors during her stay."

I nodded. It sounded like a good place to start. "Anything else you can tell us?" I looked at Constance hopefully. We had so little to go on.

She stared at the floor momentarily, tapping her foot as she thought. "Her agent, Lauren, is based in the city. Margie's life was in New Jersey; she only moved there a year ago. I have no clue how she could've had another connection to Crucible beyond me."

I moseyed around the kitchen and paused at the archway that led into Constance's living room. With a massive stone fireplace, grand piano, and leather chairs, it looked like it belonged at a ski resort.

A vaguely familiar splash of red and yellow caught my eye. I narrowed my gaze on one of the end tables. "Is that Marjorie's book?"

Constance arrived at my side. "Yes. She left it behind. 'In case you change your mind about a blurb,'" she mimicked her friend's low, drawling speech.

I moved toward the end table, taking in the sinister yet bright, arresting cover. I'd seen the image when I'd Googled Marjorie last night. "A far cry from the cozy, inviting covers on your Misthollow Mysteries."

Constance folded her arms. "My vision for the novel was way darker than Jinx's storyline. That's one of the reasons why Margie told me she didn't like it when I pitched it to her." She clenched her jaw, her anger over the betrayal returning.

Poppy glided into the room, eager to see what we were doing. "Does an advanced copy contain an acknowledgments section? Maybe that will give us a clue." She answered her own question by flipping open the book and finding the ACKNOWLEDGMENTS header toward the front.

She mumbled as she read, *"Thank you to my tenacious agent, Lauren Johnson, for her belief in and dedication to this little idea of mine."* Poppy paused to mime gagging.

Constance giggled with appreciation.

"I will be forever grateful," Poppy continued, *"to Dorian and the editorial team at Griffinsmith for taking me and my manuscript under their wing. Together, we have created something special."*

I mulled over Poppy's dramatic reading. One of the words teasingly tickled the back of my mind.

"What is it?" My aunt nudged my side after she set the book down.

"Griffinsmith. Why does that sound familiar?"

"That's Margie's publisher," Constance spoke up.

I placed my hands on my hips. "I could have sworn I've heard that name before." But where? I may have been an avid reader, but I rarely ever checked where a book had been published. I mean, I knew Constance's publisher was Althorp & Altmer because it had come up in a previous case. As for Griffinsmith—

"They're Iggy's publisher, too!" I interrupted my own train of thought.

Poppy tilted her head. "Really?"

"That's why it sounded so familiar." While working the counter at A Wick in Time, Iggy always shared the latest and greatest about his publishing journey. My friend and colleague had definitely mentioned his editor to me before—"Clive from Griffinsmith" were his exact words.

"Do you think Iggy knows anything about Marjorie that could help us?" Poppy bounced on her heels.

Constance leaned against the back of a chair. "Publishers do encourage their authors to buddy up with one another. Usually, it's with folks who have release dates close to each other, and since Margie and Iggy would've both been debut authors..."

"They could've been in each other's orbit," I said, finishing her lingering comment. "It's worth a shot to ask him. Besides, I have to head to the store anyway." I checked my watch. I needed to clock in to cover the rapidly approaching lunch breaks.

Poppy clasped her hands. "I'll see what I can learn from Bea. I'll swing by A Wick in Time after I'm done."

Constance cleared her throat. "What can I do to help?"

"Rest assured, the Glenmyre Girls are on the case." Poppy swelled with confidence in our mission.

"We'll handle this, C," I pledged. "You focus on taking care of yourself and staying out of the police's way."

She opened her mouth to respond when a loud knocking echoed

through the house.

Curious as to who her visitor was, the three of us hurried toward the foyer. Our eager footsteps grew heavy with dread when we spotted what looked to be an officer in uniform, distorted through the window glass.

Constance let loose a nervous chuckle. "Hard to stay out of their way when they're literally at my front door."

Chapter 5

With a steeling breath, Constance grabbed the brass handle and pulled the door open.

Detective Declan Shroud's stern expression deflated the moment he noticed me and Poppy flanking Constance.

"Ms. Crane?" he asked in gruff greeting, evidently intent on ignoring us.

Constance nodded. "That's me." She hadn't had the pleasure of crossing paths with Declan before now.

"Detective Shroud with the New York State Bureau of Criminal Investigation. This is Officer Richards." Declan motioned to the taller, dark-skinned man beside him. It had been the trooper's crisp blue uniform we'd seen through the window. Declan wore a tailored gray suit, signaling his rank.

Constance held her head high. "What can I do for you, Detective?"

"We'd like to speak with you about Marjorie Zeller, ma'am," Declan responded curtly, his words measured. "We're currently investigating her homicide."

Constance flinched at his matter-of-fact remark. "I-I heard about her death. Terrible."

Declan raised an eyebrow, glowering at Poppy and me. Clearly, he thought we'd blabbed about Marjorie's death. Well, we had, but just the murder-y part.

"My agent called last night to tell me," Constance explained to fill the tense silence. "She didn't want me finding out through the news."

Declan nodded, although his expression revealed he didn't quite believe her.

"We came over to check on Constance," Poppy chimed in, her right eye twitching. "She and Marjorie were close."

"I'm aware." Declan acted like he'd barely heard Poppy. His stormy blue eyes were narrowed in on Constance's bandaged hand. "Did you hurt yourself recently, Ms. Crane?" His question was layered with suspicion.

Oh no. Declan probably assumed Constance had hurt herself while attacking Marjorie.

Constance flicked her wrist, showing no harm, no foul. "Hair straightening mishap."

Unfortunately, her innocent explanation didn't cause the distrust to evaporate from his eyes. "May Officer Richards and I speak with you? Alone?"

I didn't like the idea of leaving Constance to fend for herself, but our continued presence here would only annoy Shroud, and that was the last thing we wanted to do.

"Is this something my lawyer should be present for?" Constance answered in challenge.

'Atta girl. I hid a small smile. *She'll be fine.*

"Just some routine questions, Ms. Crane." Declan studied her intently. "Unless you think you *need* a lawyer."

Constance shrugged. "I don't, but having my lawyer here also won't hurt. I wouldn't want anything I say to you somehow making its way into the press."

Declan ballooned with indignation. "Ms. Crane. Our office treats its cases with the utmost confidentiality. If you're suggesting—"

"Come in, then, officers." Constance stepped aside to welcome them into her home. "Since I have your word." She winked at Poppy and me. "My guests were just leaving."

"Call us," Poppy mouthed as we gathered our things and waved goodbye.

We walked to our cars in silence, each casting wary glances back at Constance's colonial home.

"I hope Declan doesn't bully her like he did Iggy," Poppy muttered once we'd reached our vehicles.

I gave her a reassuring pat on the arm before going to open my driver-side door. "I like to think that Declan learned his lesson last time. He knows he needs to play nice." I swallowed before asking a gnawing question only Poppy could truly answer. "Did Declan believe Constance about her hand?"

"Nope. In fact, her explanation put him even more on edge." Poppy's nose wrinkled. "She was telling us the truth about the hair straightener." She paused to chew on her lower lip. "At least, I think she was."

"*Think*?" Her response had me spooked. My aunt was rarely unsure about her whim.

Poppy sighed. "Her aura was all over the place the entire time we were there. It was a tempest of betrayal, anger, and guilt over Marjorie being in Crucible." She pressed her palm against her forehead, as if to quiet her whim down. "So I can't be one hundred percent certain Constance was telling us the truth about her hand. But I'm definitely sure she's not a killer," she quickly added.

"That's a given." I folded my arms. "But why would she lie to us about the reason for her hand being hurt?"

"I don't know. Maybe she's too embarrassed to admit what really happened?" Poppy guessed with a half-hearted shrug.

What could that *be?* "Unless Constance says otherwise, I say we believe her. She's never given us a reason not to."

Poppy bobbed her head in agreement. "What do you make of the whole scarf situation?" she asked.

"I hate speaking ill of the dead, but if Marjorie was deceitful enough to steal a book idea, I have no problem believing she was devious enough to steal a scarf." I shivered as a gust of chilly wind washed over us. "It's not like Constance was wearing it yesterday when we saw her at the library."

Then again, for all we knew, the scarf *could* have been tucked inside her bag and we hadn't seen it. I shook my head to rid myself of that incriminating notion. No, Constance's certainty that the accessory had been in her closet proved otherwise.

"You're right. Taking the time mentioned in Holden's whim reading into account," Poppy theorized as she stroked her chin, "it would be nearly impossible for Constance to have driven home, grabbed the scarf, and then gone out and killed Marjorie with it."

I frowned at her wording. "*Nearly* impossible still allows for a shred of possibility, which I'm sure Declan will latch onto, what with Constance being Marjorie's only known connection to Crucible." We *had* to figure out what Marjorie was still doing in town and who else she might have encountered.

"Come on," I continued, "we'd better get a move on. Let's hope Iggy or Bea has some good intel on Marjorie."

Ten minutes later, I pulled into the parking lot reserved for Rosewood Lane business employees, nestled behind the row of shops that constituted downtown Crucible. I checked my watch and noted I had about twenty minutes before Iggy expected me at the shop. Plenty of time to swing by The Poignant Page and visit with my boyfriend.

Sunlight struggled to peek from behind the clouds overhead, casting a gloomy hue over the quaint storefronts lining Crucible's main road. With the piercing chill in the air, it sure didn't feel like April was right around the corner. I hugged my peacoat tightly to my five-nine frame, wishing I'd opted for my thicker winter parka.

There wasn't a lot of foot traffic along my walk. Crucible's central hub was quiet, though it was still early enough in the day. Once lunchtime came around, the sidewalk would be busier, so I enjoyed the peaceful atmosphere while I could. Ezra's bookshop was at the far end of the lane, and Lake Glenmyre glittered on my right as I strolled down the pavement. While the lake's surface was still covered in ice for the most part, I observed that a few more spots had thawed since yesterday. More importantly, it looked like Dom and Lamonte had retrieved their ice fishing shacks before havoc struck.

A welcoming blanket of toasty air settled over me as I wandered into The Poignant Page. The smell of new books filled me with peace, reminding me of the shop's handsome proprietor. Along with his pine and cedar aftershave, Ezra Walters always had a "novel" air about him.

The object of my affections glanced up from his workspace behind the glass counter. He'd been immersed in—what else—a book.

Ezra's hunter-green eyes sparkled. "Hey, Hazel." The smile that spread across his striking face never failed to make my knees turn into melted wax.

"Hello, yourself." I scanned the shop to make sure we were alone, then leaned across the countertop to give him a deep kiss. "How's your day going so far?"

"You just missed a busload of seniors that rolled into town from Binghamton." He motioned to the shelves. "Just got everything straightened up in here." Crucible, with its many shops and eateries, often served as a stop for recreational or community center outings.

"Straightened up?" I surveyed the pristine bookshelves. Not a spine was out of place.

Ezra chuckled. "It was like watching a slow-motion hurricane blow through."

I playfully knocked his arm. "Mind your elders."

The store's landline phone rang, interrupting our flirty banter. Giving me an apologetic wince for the intrusion, Ezra picked up the receiver. "Hello, The Poignant Page. This is Ezra speaking. How can I help you?"

He spent a few moments scribbling down some book titles on a monogrammed notepad, along with a phone number. "Great. I'll be in touch," he said before signing off the call. "Sorry about that."

I batted away the apology. "I know you're on the clock. I just wanted to swing by and say hi."

He reached across the counter and gave my fingers a tender squeeze. "Any news about the accident near your place?" he asked, changing the subject.

I tilted my head from side to side. "Er, kinda."

He raised a thick, dark eyebrow, his eyes glittering with intrigue. "And?"

I swallowed. Poppy and I had promised Holden we'd keep everything about the case to ourselves until more information was made public. While I wouldn't break my promise, I hated keeping secrets from Ezra. I already had to keep so much of my life hidden from him. No one outside our family knew about the Glenmyre whims.

Sure, throughout Crucible's history, it had been nearly impossible for the Glenmyres to keep all our uncanny abilities completely off the town's radar. Take our Great-Great-Great Uncle Harvey, who had the ability to predict the weather. Whenever he needed to convince the neighboring towns to prepare for a flood or bad storm heading their way, he always chalked up his warnings as "gut instincts." After all, the Glenmyre enchantment barrier shielded only Crucible from the dangers of the natural world, not the towns around us. In the early 1900s, we had a cousin who could read minds with her whim. Whenever Cousin Lily slipped up and revealed something she wasn't supposed to know, she blamed her Glenmyre instincts for the lucky guess.

Those "gut feelings" would be our saving grace for keeping our secret. The people of Crucible were either gullible enough or charitable enough to believe such white lies.

"I take it from your long silence that you can't tell me." Ezra, bless him, plastered on a look of understanding, but I couldn't miss the twinge of hurt in his gaze.

"Once the police make a formal statement, I'll fill you in on what I can," I promised.

"I get it. Don't worry." He came around the counter and pulled me into his arms. "You're all right, though, aren't you? I mean, I heard that it happened not far from your house. You didn't…see anything, did you?"

His concern made my eyes water with sudden emotion. Here he was, worried that I'd had some horrible encounter with death when my involvement in Marjorie's murder was completely of my own doing. Moreover, Ezra had no idea that without my glasses, I'd always be surrounded by death and its cruel hold over the living.

"Poppy and I saw the car on the side of the road, but that's all," I hurriedly reassured him. We'd rehash the scarf part later. "I'd better get going." I reluctantly extricated myself from his arms. "Any chance you're free for dinner tonight?"

Ezra's carefree expression returned. "I heard there's a band playing at Cold Cauldron. Want to hit it up? I think they go on at eight."

"Perfect." As I said goodbye and headed outside, a warm, tingling feeling flowed through me in heady anticipation. There was nothing better than date nights with Ezra. He made me laugh with stories about the silliest things and always had some fascinating new book to share. He also listened attentively and made me feel like I was the only person in the room. I loved him. That I knew. I wanted us to spend the rest of our lives together.

I just didn't want to know how long the rest of our lives would be.

Those warm, lovey-dovey feelings vanished as I retraced my steps along the sidewalk. The chill settling over me wasn't due to the fickle spring weather alone. It was the all-too-familiar grip of anxiety that seized hold whenever I thought about seeing Ezra's lifeclock. Up until now, I'd been exceedingly careful not to take my glasses off or let them slip in his presence. But my neurosis had ruined some intimate and beautiful moments. I couldn't keep it up forever.

You've seen your friends' lifeclocks before, Hazel, I chided myself. *It doesn't have to ruin things.*

There'd been an unfortunate incident last fall when I'd witnessed Iggy's lifeclock glowing eerily above his head. Thank goodness he had over seventy years ahead of him. Knowing my friend and co-worker would live well into his nineties made harboring the gloomy knowledge somewhat more bearable. But what if Ezra didn't have that kind of time left?

I shook the suffocating thought from my mind. *One life-or-death situation at a time,* I told myself. The news about Marjorie's murder would likely break soon. I needed to focus on our case. More immediately, I needed to get my butt to work.

My phone beeped just as I reached the crowded entrance to Bright Moon Café.

I fumbled for the device as I snagged a spot in the long line. Just the smell of coffee gave me a much-needed jolt of energy. The text Holden had just sent our family group chat gave me another.

Cpt Silva is announcing news about the vic at 10:30. She and

Shroud en route to the Crucible PD now. United front and all.

I replied with a quick thumbs-up emoji, heartened to learn that BCI would be coordinating with Holden and his team. I'd read one too many books and listened to one too many podcasts where county and state officials iced out the local police force. Despite living in Crucible for less than a year, Holden had become a pillar in our community, and he had a pulse on things "outsiders" didn't. I was glad Declan recognized Holden would be an asset to the case, not a hindrance. I was also surprised Declan was already done questioning Constance. That had to be a good sign, right?

I sent her a text in the group convo we shared with Poppy. **Everything all good on your end, C?**

Her response followed shortly. **As good as can be expected, I guess. Still getting my lawyer looped in. Detective Machismo made a big stink about my connection to Margie. Doesn't believe me about the scarf being MIA, either. Wish I had gone to dinner with you guys.**

Poppy chimed in with **Us, too. But don't worry. We'll get this sorted. You focus on reality TV marathons and taking care of yourself.**

Constance sent a GIF of *Schitt's Creek's* David Rose's deadpan expression in answer.

I giggled softly, happy to see her sense of humor on display. While I wasn't thrilled that Declan didn't believe Constance's account of her movements, I was relieved he hadn't arrested her on the spot. My unintended faux pas with the scarf might still be salvageable.

The line at Bright Moon moved along quickly, and soon, I made it to the front to place my order. Jolie Potter, the café's cheerful, chatty owner, wasn't out front. Instead, a group of teenagers manned the coffee counter with trained efficiency.

I listened for any mention of the TikTok video featuring Constance's argument, but given the mid-morning rush, none of the kids had much time for idle chitchat. I was out the door with coffee three minutes later without any local gossip. *Bummer*. Not only was I curious about the public's take on Constance's library spat, but I also wondered if anyone had discovered the more sinister nature behind

Marjorie's demise. Did anyone suspect murder, or was Crucible still under the assumption there'd only been a terrible car accident?

Mindful of the hour, I hustled toward my beloved candle shop, making sure not to spill the blood-orange mocha lattes I'd picked up. It was Bright Moon's new spring flavor, and I was eager to try the inventive pairing.

My small store was perched on the corner of Rosewood Lane and the side road leading up to Crucible Commons, the town park. Despite the tight, awkward-shaped layout, A Wick in Time had thrived for over four years in this spot, and I hoped it would flourish for many more.

"Hey, boss!" Ignatius "Iggy" Alewell waved from behind the counter as I entered the shop.

My newest hire, Quinn Quigley, tossed a quick smile over her shoulder as she arranged candles on a top shelf. "Morning, Hazel."

A menagerie of fragrances overwhelmed me, and I stifled a cough with my elbow. "Hi, guys. I know it's a bit chilly, but maybe we should let the place air out a bit."

Iggy reached underneath the counter and pulled out a sweater. "Go for it. I hardly notice anymore."

Quinn chuckled as she climbed down the short stepladder and unrolled her sleeves to cover her toned arms. "I will admit my first day here was a doozy on my sinuses, but I got used to it pretty quickly."

"Thank goodness for that." I'd hired Quinn two months ago in an ongoing effort to make work-life balance more sustainable for myself and Iggy. With Iggy's writing career taking off and my distaste for actually *working* retail, I knew A Wick in Time needed to make some serious business changes if the shop was going to continue to grow and prosper. Enter Quinn, a forty-something divorcee who'd moved to Crucible from Elmira, NY, a few years ago to put some distance between her and her onerous ex-husband. With Quinn's son graduating from high school soon, she'd decided to look for some part-time employment. While I could have hired someone with more retail experience, Quinn was a delightful human and an exceedingly hard worker. She'd made such a great impression on both Iggy and me that I'd offered her the job the same day she'd come by for an interview.

I propped the front door open, allowing the fresh air to permeate the strong smells wafting from my homemade candles. While I wanted customers to know my products packed a punch, I didn't need them getting knocked out of the shop.

"Quiet day so far?" I handed Quinn a latte.

She beamed with gratitude. "A few bursts of activity here and there."

"Just the way I like it," Iggy confessed as I handed him a drink. "Perfect for getting some more work done on my proposal. Speaking of work, why don't you take your fifteen now, Q Ball?"

"You sure?" Quinn motioned to the shelves she'd been arranging. "I can finish this up first."

Iggy waved her offer aside. "You said you forgot to eat breakfast. Why not pick something up to snack on?"

"You don't have to twist my arm. Can I get you guys anything?"

Iggy and I assured Quinn we were good, and once she'd collected her jacket from the coat rack in the stairwell, she was out the door.

"Best idea ever, hiring her. Besides hiring me, that is." Iggy nudged my shoulder.

"I'm glad you think so." I grinned happily at his comment. I had worried that bringing on a new person would ruin the fun, silly dynamic Iggy and I had. Thankfully, Quinn fit right in, as made evident by the nickname Iggy had already bestowed upon her.

I folded my arms and stared at Iggy's laptop. "Any progress on the pitch?" With one book deal under his wing, Iggy was hard at work creating a new manuscript proposal for his literary agent.

The dark brown skin on his forehead furrowed. "Not really. I'm stuck on the plot conflict. I want to write about a guy who buys a house rumored to contain buried treasure, but that feels a bit too on the nose."

I chuckled. "I'm sure inspiration will strike when you least expect it." I raised my own beverage in the air, and we cheers-ed.

Iggy took a thoughtful sip of his latte. "Well, with all the drama around here lately, inspiration certainly isn't in short supply."

"Drama?" I opted to play coy to see what Iggy would dish.

He began counting on his fingers. "Well, there's Renee and

Hugo's divorce being finalized."

I nodded. "I'm glad he didn't contest her. Renee might have her flaws, but she deserves way better than Hugo."

The Tarlings were one of Crucible's five founding families, and with Hugo Tarling's recent fall from grace, his wife had decided to leave him. Part of the settlement allowed Renee to keep their swanky manor up near the Finchaven estate. Renee and Philippa Tarling, Hugo's younger, whimsical sister, had bonded over the scandal, and last I'd heard, Philippa was rooming with her former sister-in-law to help her navigate the nightmare.

"Good riddance to bad rubbish, I say." Iggy snorted before continuing to list off the recent turmoil around town. "Then there's the nasty bidding war that happened over Renee's old office space. Not to mention Charlie Almsworth usurping Grant as LGBA treasurer. And that's just in the last month alone."

I blinked rapidly, temporarily distracted from my mission. I hadn't heard about that third item. "What's this about the boat club?" Grant Finchmore had been its treasurer for almost as long as I'd been alive.

The Lake Glenmyre Boating Association was one of the most exclusive clubs in the state. Many affluent Upper East Siders owned summer homes in the area so they could apply for membership.

Iggy rubbed his hands together, ready to divulge some juicy deets. "Ione told me that ol' Charlie staged a coup. He invited a bunch of members out to his Hamptons house to wine and dine them while Grant was out of the country on vacation. He then called for a new election, which, according to their fancy-schmancy bylaws, they can do. Charlie got the votes and took over last week."

"Wow." I recalled my encounter with Tula Sardolous at Lakeside Mulligan's last night. Despite her loyalty to the Finchmores, she was a notorious source of gossip about the family, yet she hadn't made any mention of Grant being concerned about losing the club position. "I didn't know Charlie had such a ruthless streak in him. He seems like such a nice, affable guy."

Iggy gave me a dubious look. "You don't get to be a tech giant by being *nice*, Hazel." Charlie Almsworth—one of Crucible's summer residents—had made his money in the cloud-based web services industry. Whatever *that* meant. He owned a big house on the northwest side of Lake Glenmyre and had summered here for several years.

"Well, I have some unfortunate news to add to your list." Before I shared the details of Marjorie's death, I closed the store's front door for some privacy now that the intense aroma from my candles had been mitigated.

"Uh-oh. How unfortunate are we talking?" Iggy straightened with alarm.

I checked my watch. The digital numbers glowed **10:35 AM**. "Pull up the local news, and we can watch for ourselves."

Chapter 6

Iggy had his laptop open and on YouTube TV by the time I was back behind the counter. He clicked our regional news station and jacked up the volume.

Captain Carmen Silva stood in front of a basic blue background, her sharp features narrowed with authority as she spoke to the camera. "We are investigating this matter as a homicide and encourage anyone with information about the victim to come forward. Or, if you happened to be in the area between five and eight PM, please contact either the Crucible PD or our county BCI office. You may have unknowingly seen something that could be of vital importance. Thank you." She stepped out of frame, and the broadcast cut back to our local anchors.

I cursed inwardly. We had logged on midway through Captain Silva's briefing and missed the vital details. "Can you rewind so we can listen from the beginning?"

Iggy didn't need me to ask twice, but all Captain Silva revealed was that thirty-four-year-old Marjorie Zeller had been found dead in her car, parked along the southeast road near Lake Glenmyre.

"Marjorie Zeller?" Iggy's wide brown eyes doubled in size once the segment ended. "As in *Under the Red Barn* author Marjorie Zeller?"

"What do you know about her?" I folded my arms. "She's with your publisher, right?"

"She sure is—was." He grimaced. "Our books are both due out in November." Iggy closed the lid of his laptop with a *snap*. "What the heck was she doing in Crucible?"

My hopes deflated with his comment. "You mean you didn't know she was in town?"

He tilted his head. "No. Why would I?" Iggy narrowed his gaze. "What are you up to, boss lady?"

I tugged at my long, dark locks with frustration. "Hitting a dead end, it seems." Since we were alone in the store, I quickly brought Iggy up to speed on Marjorie's death and Constance's connection, *minus* the whim-related content.

"Holy cow." His expression slackened as he slouched against the back wall. "I had no idea Marjorie and Constance even knew one another. Which, honestly, in this business, is kinda weird." He motioned to the notebook lying beside his laptop to indicate he meant the publishing industry.

"How so?"

"Not to sound cynical, but being a successful author these days is not only about being talented. It's about who you know, too." Iggy arched an eyebrow. "Constance is a *big* name. And a newcomer like Marjorie? She should have been name-dropping her friendship with Constance left and right."

I held my tongue. I hadn't shared with Iggy the news about Marjorie stealing Constance's idea. It wasn't my story to tell. But his comment revealed that Marjorie had purposely kept her distance from Constance within their writing circles.

"I'm bummed Marjorie didn't reach out to me while she was here." Iggy's shoulders slumped. "It would've been nice to chat with her in person."

"Had you talked with her before?"

He nodded. "The Griffinsmith PR department got us together via Zoom. Since we both were releasing psychological thrillers this fall, they thought we could do some tandem engagements together. You know, like signings and book events."

I swallowed the last sip of my velvety, sweet latte before tossing the compostable cup into our indoor recycling bin. "Did Marjorie know you lived in Crucible?"

"Hmm..." Iggy stroked his smooth chin. "I don't remember if I mentioned it. Honestly, she didn't seem very present during our meeting, if you get my drift. The PR guy had to repeat things to her several times."

"Interesting." I drummed my fingers against the countertop in contemplation.

"All right, I've answered your questions." Iggy lanced me with a shrewd stare. "Your turn in the hot seat. I take it Constance is on the police's radar because of their shared history?"

I sighed. "You guessed it. Given that Constance was Marjorie's only connection to the area, she's already in their crosshairs. It doesn't help that she and Marjorie got into a nasty debate yesterday in front of the entire library."

Iggy straightened his shoulders. "Oh, shoot. That was with Marjorie?"

I nodded.

He cringed in response. "When I was picking up food at Herb Garden after my shift last night, Mammie mentioned that Constance had lost her temper with someone. I assumed it was just an overbearing fan."

Mammie Lewis was our town's self-appointed matriarch. She lorded over the town's rumor mill from behind the checkout counter at the local produce market. And if Mammie knew about the library altercation, then everyone in town knew about it, regardless of whether they were on social media.

"I'm surprised you didn't see the video on TikTok," I said.

Iggy did a double take. "What video?"

I dug out my phone and showed it to him.

He stuck his tongue out after watching it. "My agent is after me to get on TikTok, but I just can't. Instagram is bad enough for my mental health."

"I get it." I didn't even have a personal Instagram account, just one for the store.

"Poor Constance. I can't imagine that video is doing her any favors." A haunted look floated across Iggy's face. He knew firsthand how terrible it was to have the police suspect him of a crime. "How can I help?"

I released a heavy breath. "At this point, I feel like I'm already stuck. When I realized you and Marjorie shared the same publisher, I hoped you might have an idea as to why she hung around Crucible after Constance kicked her out."

"Sorry to rain on your parade." Iggy patted me on the shoulder. "But consider me touched that you actually remember the name of my publisher."

The bell over the door jingled, indicating Quinn's return. My eyes immediately homed in on the gooey-looking chocolate pastry in her hand.

"Is that from Come Again Chocolates?" My stomach rumbled.

She nodded. "Moses is sourcing some new stuff from a bakery in Hyssop Falls. I hope he decides to stick with them. This is heavenly." Quinn offered us each a bite, and we gratefully tore off small, buttery pieces.

The dark chocolate went from bitter to sweet on my tongue. "Oh wow."

"Yum." Iggy's gaze went to the sky in mock ecstasy.

Moses Lloyd had won the bidding war for Renee Tarling's real estate office and converted the space into a cozy yet sophisticated chocolate shop. Moses and his husband Gabriel were new to Crucible, as Gabriel had been transferred to the area to assume the role of bank president, what with Hugo Tarling's departure.

"He made the chocolate ganache and everything." Quinn dabbed her lips with a napkin. "I didn't realize how deadly this town could be on my waistline."

I stilled at her off-the-cuff remark. *Crucible has become deadly in more ways than one,* I thought morosely.

A group of young adults wearing Ithaca College sweatshirts ambled inside the store, interrupting our little huddle. Iggy tapped on the screen of our iPad register to wake it up, and Quinn and I plastered on friendly smiles and asked if they needed assistance.

Ten minutes later, we'd sold fourteen candles to the group. It turned out the apartment they all shared was in desperate need of some spring cleaning, and burning candles was easier than taking the time to scrub down the space.

Iggy shuddered once they left. "I'm so glad I don't have to deal with roommates anymore."

I chuckled. "I just hope Lemon Drop Lollipop does the trick." I'd recommended one of the strongest and sweetest-smelling candles I made to cut through the stench of long-forgotten pizza boxes and empty beer cans.

"After that sales pitch, Hazel, I'm buying some to take home." Quinn placed two yellow candles on the checkout counter. "My son's room needs to be fumigated."

I took the two candles and placed them under the counter without taking her payment. "These are on the house."

The bell chimed again, summoning our focus to our next customers. While Quinn assisted an elderly couple with their browsing and Iggy helped a young man, I darted upstairs to grab some inventory that had been curing in my craft kitchen. After pouring the scented wax into my signature glass jars, I let my candles cure for a week, allowing the fragrance to fully permeate the wax.

I grabbed a padded wood crate that I used to transport goods and collected all the Sweet Vanilla candles I'd poured last Thursday. It was one of my signature year-round scents.

I arrived back downstairs and stocked the shelves with Quinn while Iggy rang up our customers. A steady stream of patrons kept us busy, and the store wasn't empty again until the pendulum clock hanging on the wall behind the counter chimed noon.

Aware of the time, I pulled out my phone to check my messages, wondering where Poppy was. As luck would have it, I had a text from her waiting to be read.

No dice with Bea. Grabbing lunch at Fitz's. Be over in a bit.

I frowned as I stared at my phone screen. What did Poppy mean? Had Bea not provided her with anything useful, or had she not even gotten the chance to speak with her?

My questions would have to wait until her lunch date wrapped. "Hey, Ig, Quinn. You guys hungry?"

"I brought some white bean chili from home," Iggy replied.

"Want me to take lunch now?" Part of the candle kitchen renovations had included a nice little breakroom on the second floor. "I can be done in fifteen."

I waved his offer aside. "Take thirty." As store manager, Iggy worked incredibly hard and often didn't take as many breaks as he was due.

"I don't mind watching the store by myself if you need to grab food, Hazel," Quinn offered.

"Did you bring lunch?" I asked.

She shook her head, her stylish, light brown bob swishing from side to side. "I was going to pick something up at Sip."

"Why don't you take lunch then, too? Any chance I can give you some cash to pick up a chicken Caesar salad for me?" I rooted around in my tote bag to find my wallet. Ione made the best chopped salads in the upstate area.

"Sure." Quinn shifted on the balls of her feet while she waited.

I handed her a twenty and thanked her. She put her coat on and headed out once more.

I didn't realize Iggy was staring me down until I turned around to check the time. "What?"

He leaned against the doorframe with crossed arms. "Don't do that weird thing again where you worry about giving Quinn too much responsibility." His words were curt.

I bristled at his sullen attitude. "What do you mean, 'again'?"

"Oh, come on, Hazel." Iggy sighed. "For like, the first *year* I worked here, you made me feel like I wasn't able to handle things on my own."

"I didn't—"

He held up his hand to stop me. "I know it came from a good place. You were concerned about giving me too much work and having it interfere with my writing. But until I figured that out, your actions made me feel like I wasn't good enough to work for you."

"What?" Shame and disbelief made my stomach twist into knots. "Omigosh, I'm so sorry. I never meant…" I was at a loss for further words.

Iggy came over and placed a hand on my shoulder. "I'm saying this with love because you're an amazing person, and you've grown into being a great boss. You don't have to feel bad giving Quinn work. That's what she's here to do. Trust me on this, okay?"

"I'm sorry I ever made you feel that way, Ig." I swallowed. "Quinn didn't say something to you about this, did she?"

Iggy shook his head. "No need to apologize. And no, she hasn't. But next time she offers to take on more responsibility, why not give her a chance?"

Embarrassment burned at my cheeks. Despite keeping the doors open for over four years, I still had a lot to learn about running a small business. "Okay, will do."

Iggy headed upstairs to enjoy his lunch, giving me some time alone with my thoughts. He was totally right. I tended to stress about putting too much on the shoulders of others. Deep down, I understood a significant amount of my fixation came from the guilt I had about my good fortune in life. My candle shop wasn't a critical source of income for me. With my family's trust fund, I was able to live a comfortable life, pursue philanthropic interests, and follow my passions. Most people in the world weren't ever afforded such luxury.

As I surveyed the fully stocked shelves and bright array of colors, I remembered the early days when it was just me, juggling the store alone. I was so lucky to be able to turn a hobby I loved into a thriving small business.

My pensive thoughts were interrupted by a familiar figure catching my attention outside the shop's big window. From the sidewalk, Holden peered in, spotted me at the counter, and reached for the door handle.

"Hey, cuz." He tipped his Crucible PD baseball cap in greeting. "Glad I caught you." Dressed in a white polo, khakis, and a windbreaker, Holden's casual uniform was a far cry from the sleek, formal suits of his BCI days.

I studied him closely as he hurried toward the counter. While his clothes may have been relaxed, his demeanor definitely was not. "What's up?"

"You alone?"

I pointed to the ceiling. "Iggy's upstairs having lunch, and Quinn will be back in a bit."

Holden scanned the room as if to confirm for himself. "Hmm, okay." He kept his voice low, clearly not wanting our conversation to be overheard. "Shroud just finished briefing our department about what's been uncovered so far."

"Anything you can share?" I wasn't really expecting an answer. I remembered Holden's earlier promise to keep his lips zipped about the official investigation.

"No. Except that his chat with Constance went exactly how we feared." Holden rubbed his temples. "Shroud told us that she was very cagey about her relationship with Zeller, had a suspicious wound on her hand, couldn't produce the scarf you mentioned, and eventually told Shroud he could direct all questions through her lawyer."

I sighed. "Smart move to get her lawyer involved, but I can see how that all puts her in a bad light."

Holden nodded. "Shroud also mentioned he ran into you and Poppy at her house."

I prepared myself to be reprimanded, but to my surprise, he asked, "Were you able to get anything from Constance that Shroud couldn't? What's the deal with this scarf?"

"She thought it was in her closet," I explained. "When Constance couldn't find it, she told us Marjorie must have stolen it from her."

Holden raised his eyebrows. "*Stole* it? That's a pretty intense accusation." He studied me intently. "Does it have anything to do with why she and Marjorie were on the outs?"

"Yes..." I let my answer trail off. Being Holden's Crucible informant was one thing, but I didn't want to betray Constance's confidence.

Luckily, he understood. "Okay, message received. I won't pry further. If it was relevant to the case, I'm sure you'd tell me." He held my gaze, and guilt started to bubble within me.

It *was* relevant in that it painted a less-than-scrupulous picture of Marjorie and her work ethic. If she was willing to stoop so low to get published, what other risks in life had she been willing to take? Who else had she betrayed? And had that someone followed her to Crucible in search of revenge?

"Marjorie and Iggy share the same book publisher," I offered in an effort to change the subject. "I asked Iggy if he had any additional info about her that might be helpful, but he said other than a lackluster Zoom call, he didn't really know her."

Holden's windbreaker crinkled as he folded his muscular arms. "Zeller didn't reach out to him while she was in town?"

"Nope." I absently straightened a small display of six-ounce candles on the countertop. "So we still don't know why she continued to stay in the area after Constance tossed her out."

Holden considered my words until his phone beeped. He unclipped it from his belt and read the screen. "It's Shroud. I'd better get going." He secured his cell before saying, "The BCI forensic team kicked off their official review of the crime scene a couple of hours ago, now that they have daylight." Holden gave me a wave and headed for the door. "He wants me to assist in another sweep of the area."

"Good luck!" I must have just missed the forensic team setting up shop alongside the road when I'd driven in to work. I hoped this latest search would reveal something that pointed police away from Constance.

Footsteps thudded behind me, and Iggy appeared in the back doorway just as my cousin disappeared outside from view. "Was that Holden? Did I hear that he and Declan are working the case together?"

I smiled at the surprising warmth that layered Iggy's voice at the mention of the gruff detective. Despite getting off to an incredibly fraught start, Declan and Iggy had become good pals over the last five months. So much so that Declan was now a regular at the weekly Dungeons & Dragons game Iggy hosted at his home.

"Yeah. BCI is lead, of course, but Declan wants to keep Holden in the loop. What happened to taking a thirty-minute lunch break?"

Iggy shrugged. "I'd rather spend the time reviewing my pitch with you and Quinn. Maybe we can nail down a spicy hook."

"Happy to lend an ear." I was always thrilled to be Iggy's sounding board and honored to help him with his creative process.

The passing thought made me contemplate Marjorie and Constance's relationship. I shuddered. I couldn't imagine stealing Iggy's idea and calling it my own. Moreover, it was hard for me to picture Marjorie doing such a thing. In the short moments I'd spent in her company, she'd done a masterful job at concealing her backstabbing side. Even Poppy hadn't caught it in her aura.

"Also, I *may* have done some snooping regarding our victim." Iggy gave me a sly grin. "Griffinsmith has an online forum for its authors. Mostly to share marketing opportunities and book events, but there's some networking stuff, too."

My chest hummed with anticipation. "Have they announced her death? Does the publisher even know?"

Iggy propped his laptop for me to see. "The CEO posted a meeting link this morning. Something about wanting to speak to the Griffinsmith family as a whole." He arched a suggestive eyebrow. "Sounds like they want to break the news over Zoom, rather than just posting or emailing it."

Iggy then pointed out the notice pinned to the top of the webpage. "It's in fifteen minutes," I said as I read the cryptic text.

"I'll log on so you can listen."

I beamed. "Awesome. Thanks, Ig."

"Helps to be friends with an industry insider, right?" He tipped an imaginary hat in my direction. "That's not all I found. Check this out." Iggy clicked another open tab. The page displayed the Amazon listing for *Under the Red Barn*. "I preordered a copy of Marjorie's book when it went on sale earlier this week."

I stifled a mock gasp of horror. "Not from Ezra?"

Iggy brought a guilty finger to his lips. "*Shhh*. Don't tell him. I had a gift card. Anyway," he said, motioning to the product information, "you know how Amazon has a preorder pricing guarantee? If you buy a book at a lower price, if it increases, you still get it at the lower cost?"

I nodded.

"Well, get this. I bought Marjorie's book for $18.99 on Tuesday." Iggy pointed at the current price listed on the site.

"This says to preorder for $26.99!" I narrowed my gaze as I suspiciously scanned the screen. "That's a pretty big price bump."

Iggy bobbed his head. "Almost as if the publisher is expecting there to be a surge of interest in Marjorie's book now that she's dead."

I trembled at the disturbing notion. "I know publishing is a cutthroat industry, but that's really gruesome."

"No kidding." Iggy folded his arms with a scoff. "Makes me reevaluate all of Griffinsmith's 'we are family' mumbo jumbo."

I continued to stare at the laptop, an outlandish theory simmering in my mind. "You don't think someone *killed* Marjorie to increase her sales numbers, do you?"

Chapter 7

"Good grief, Hazel, I hope not." Iggy tittered nervously. "I didn't sign up for that kind of guerrilla marketing."

I snorted at his joke. "I know it sounds ridiculous, but at this point—"

"It's the only theory you've got to go on," he finished my sentence. "Let me run with this for you. I'll see if anyone at Griffinsmith has connections to the Crucible area."

"I don't want to pile more work on your plate, Ig."

He cut off the rest of my protest. "It's no trouble at all. Besides, Constance got to play sidekick for you and Pops when I was on the hook for murder. Now, let me return the favor." He turned his webcam on and checked his appearance in preparation for the impending Zoom call. "I wish I'd worn a collared shirt," he muttered.

I pointed to the back staircase. "As much as I'd love some product placement with all your fancy author friends, let's take this upstairs. Quinn can watch the sales floor for us."

A triumphant smile stretched across Iggy's face as he realized I was taking his managerial advice. "Awesome. I'll go get set up."

Quinn arrived with my lunch not three minutes later. "Ione insisted you try her new Thai chicken salad." She chewed her lower lip as she handed me a Sip compostable takeout container. "I hope you don't mind."

I giggled. "No worries. Ione is always overriding my lunch order, and she's always right."

"Oh, good." Quinn swiped her hand across her forehead. "It sounded so yummy, I got one for myself, too."

I wrung my hands, realizing I was about to renege on my suggestion that she take her lunch. "Do you mind watching the register for fifteen minutes or so before going on break? There's some stuff I have to take care of upstairs." While I really liked Quinn and trusted her with my business, I wasn't ready to share my murder-solving exploits with her just yet.

"Oh, gosh, no." Quinn grinned. "Take your time."

"Thanks. You're a lifesaver."

Leaving the sales floor in Quinn's capable hands, I dashed up the stairs and into the cozy breakroom situated just off my candle-making kitchen.

I plopped down in a chair opposite Iggy and his laptop, giving him a thumbs up.

"Okay, logging on." He crossed his fingers for good luck.

I kept silent as Iggy launched the meeting and said hello to the current participants.

"All right, I'm on mute," he said out of the corner of his mouth so as not to move his lips too conspicuously.

We waited in tense silence until his laptop speakers crackled to life.

"Hi, everyone," a deep, feminine voice spoke with soothing tones. "Thank you for joining us on such short notice. We, here at Griffinsmith, wanted to share some very tragic news with our publishing family. Last night, one of our authors, Marjorie Zeller, was killed. We don't know much at this time, but the police have been in touch about her death and may be reaching out to our authors if their investigation requires it. Now, I know this is very shocking news, but the editorial team felt that it was important that this come from us, rather than you all hearing about it online. We've also invited Marjorie's agent, Lauren Johnson, to share a few words."

There was a brief lull before I heard a woman clear her throat and speak. "Thank you, Vera." Her voice was strong and animated. "Marjorie spoke very highly about the Griffinsmith community and all the wonderful people she'd connected with since signing her book. I'm simply devastated by her loss." Except Lauren's gushing tone didn't exactly convey believability.

"She was truly something special, but at least I'm comforted to know that readers will still get to meet Marjorie when her book *Under the Red Barn* launches posthumously next month."

"Next *month*?" Iggy snapped before quickly double-checking that he was still muted. "Her book was slated for a November release, like mine." He motioned me over to his side. "Don't worry, I turned off my camera."

I peered over his shoulder. We were back on the Amazon product page.

"Well, I'll be." Iggy sat back with folded arms. "Look at the date. I didn't notice that had changed, too. They're not wasting any time, are they?"

I read the release date for *Under the Red Barn*. It was scheduled for April 25—little less than a month away.

"Your idea about boosting book sales doesn't seem so farfetched now," Iggy grumbled.

I shushed him, eager to hear the rest of the Zoom call.

"I'm currently out of town, but once I'm back in the office, I'll be organizing a memorial for Marjorie. It would be lovely to have Griffinsmith authors attend and support one of their own."

Lauren Johnson's voice was sugary sweet, but even the pixelated Zoom frame couldn't hide the annoyance in her eyes. She was very beautiful, with light brown skin and curly dark hair. And despite her warbling words, she didn't look too broken up about Marjorie's sudden passing.

"Did you hear that?" I nudged Iggy's arm. "Lauren isn't in NYC right now."

He stroked his chin. "Think she could be somewhere near Crucible?"

"It's worth checking out." Perhaps it wasn't Griffinsmith looking to increase Marjorie's book sales, but her agent.

Once Lauren turned the call back over to the Griffinsmith team, a few other people spoke about Marjorie and her passion for *Under the Red Barn* before ending the meeting.

Iggy snapped his laptop lid shut, his mood visibly soured. "That sounded more like an infomercial than anything."

I couldn't blame him. The idea of being treated as a commodity rather than a person felt off-putting. I gave him an encouraging smile. "Why don't we join Quinn and go over your pitch?"

Iggy's expression was still a bit glum as we headed downstairs.

A familiar, bubbly voice chatting with Quinn caught my attention, and I hastened down the last two steps.

"Hey," I greeted Poppy as we arrived on the sales floor. "How was lunch?"

She beamed brightly as she waved to Iggy. "Good. Sorry for the wait. Fitz got to talking about some brewery tour he wants us to go on, and things lasted a lot longer than I anticipated." Poppy rolled her eyes for emphasis.

Quinn had her elbows propped on the register counter. "Hon, I would not be complaining if a guy as hunky as Fitz was planning a romantic weekend getaway with me." She flirtatiously batted her blue eyes.

I chuckled. "Poppy has a hard time letting other people do nice things for her."

Quinn flipped her hair. "Not me. After all the drama my ex put me through, I'm settling for nothing less than the royal treatment." As we laughed at her sassy jab, Quinn checked her watch. "Am I all set to go on break, Hazel?"

"Sure thing. Enjoy your lunch."

Once Quinn had retreated upstairs, Iggy and I turned our focus to Poppy. "So, a brewery tour? That sounds fun." I hoped my auntie would pick up on my hinting tone. She deserved to take a little vacation away from Crucible.

"Yeah. But now's not a good time." She shrugged her arms out of her plaid trench coat. "Maybe when we don't have another killer running around town." She nodded toward Iggy. "Have you filled him in?"

Iggy swelled with mock arrogance. "I'll have you know, I've already provided some instrumental clues."

As I giggled at Iggy's antics, Poppy's eyes widened with glee. "Ooo, do tell."

With Quinn on her break and the shop empty save for the three of us, Iggy and I brought Poppy up to speed on Marjorie, Griffinsmith, and Lauren Johnson.

"Diabolical." Poppy shook her head once we'd unloaded everything on her. "You really think boosting book sales is motive for murder?"

I shrugged. "Maybe Lauren wasn't feeling confident in Marjorie's debut. We all remember how poorly Constance's first novel was received. And given their close association with one another, perhaps Lauren didn't want to take a gamble on a potential dud."

"I'm still not quite sold." Poppy hugged herself.

Iggy grinned wickedly from behind his laptop. "What if I told you Lauren Johnson was photographed at Blackthorn Grove Winery two days ago?"

"What?" Both Poppy and I raced behind the counter to see what Iggy had found on the Internet.

"Lauren has her socials linked to her agency webpage. Check out her last Instagram post." Iggy slid the computer closer for Poppy and me to examine.

An image of Lauren sipping a glass of red wine filled the screen. Her surroundings were nondescript, but the tree-silhouette insignia on the glass was instantly recognizable to a Crucible local.

"That's Blackthorn Grove, all right." Poppy's brow furrowed as she studied the image. "Interesting."

"That's an understatement." My heart pounded with the thrill of the chase. While Blackthorn Grove Winery was a relatively new addition to the Crucible business scene, the Desjardins had been exporting their grapes to other winemakers for decades. The family had only recently launched their own award-winning label and opened their vineyard to guests.

"It puts Lauren in the area." Iggy folded his arms, a look of triumph written all over his face. "I get that the book sales theory is a little half-baked. Maybe it's as simple as her and Marjorie not being on good terms."

"It's worth exploring, for sure." Poppy's growing smile told me that she was beginning to come around to the idea.

I pointed out, "And it's someone *else* in town who Marjorie had a connection with. That's good news for Constance. Maybe Marjorie stayed in Crucible because her agent was visiting Blackthorn Grove."

"Speaking of staying," Poppy mumbled, her enthusiasm beginning to deflate, "I came up blank on that front. Bea had no idea who Marjorie was. She wasn't a guest at the inn."

I pondered our next move. Where else could Marjorie have been staying for the past two weeks? "Maybe she wasn't a swanky hotel kinda gal. Or maybe Marjorie couldn't get a room."

"She could have AirBnb'd something," Iggy suggested.

Poppy snapped her fingers. "Or maybe she booked one of Trae's cabins. Didn't he just launch some kind of special partnership with Blackthorn Grove?"

Waking Woods Cabin Rentals hadn't even crossed my mind, given that Lake Glenmyre had yet to thaw out. In the summer, Trae Longboat's cozy cabins rarely had a vacancy, but during the winter and spring, Trae usually spent his time fixing up the cabins and preparing for the upcoming tourist season.

Iggy tapped away on his keyboard. "Yep. Here it is. Fifteen percent off your entire stay with a Blackthorn Grove tasting package." He showed us the promotional banner running across the top of the Waking Woods website. "Nice deal."

Poppy glanced my way. "I've been meaning to stop by and ask Trae if he wants new bulbs to plant outside the cabins."

I knew where this was going. "And while you're talking shop, I'll see if either Marjorie or Lauren was a guest."

"Since you two are going to spend the afternoon Hardy Boy-ing it up," Iggy added, "I'll see what I can squeeze from my author pals. I can't be the only one who thought that Griffinsmith meeting was beyond gauche."

I checked the clock on the wall behind us. It wasn't even one o'clock yet. I winced. I was supposed to work until six, but with Quinn's help, Iggy at least had someone to cover breaks throughout the day. "Feel free to have Quinn work the floor solo while you're on the hunt. You didn't really take a full lunch."

"Please, I've been letting her man the floor solo since her third week." Iggy batted my comment aside with a carefree shrug.

Poppy giggled. "Your delegation skills are admirable, Ig. Way better than Hazel's."

I shushed my aunt's teasing. "All right, we'll head over to Trae's, but I'll come back to help close," I promised in an effort to alleviate my guilt for being the world's flakiest boss. All three of us were supposed to work Saturdays together, even if business hadn't picked up yet for the season. "Text me if you guys need anything."

"Will do." Iggy added a mock salute for emphasis.

Once Poppy and I said our goodbyes and were outside the shop, I reached for her arm. "I'm going to swing by the house to walk Noli. Meet you at Waking Woods?" I typically used my lunch break to speed home and check in on my fur babies.

"Of course. See you soon." Poppy waved her phone at me. "I'm going to give Constance a ring and update her on this whole Lauren angle."

"Ask if her agent can shed any light on our theory," I called over my shoulder as I took off toward my car. "They're friends, after all. Maybe Lauren complained about her client."

Twenty minutes later, I gave Noli air kisses and promised I would return home soon. We'd had a nice walk around my property, and I gave both her and Berg some treats before heading out.

It was nearly one-thirty when I buckled myself into my SUV. I made a mental note not to spend too much time at Waking Woods. Not only did I have to help Iggy and Quinn close the shop, but I also had to get myself ready for a night out with Ezra at Cold Cauldron. While the brewery wasn't a glamorous hotspot, I wanted to get a bit dressed up for the band *and* for my man.

I pulled out of my driveway and drove cautiously down the road toward where Marjorie's car had been found. There was a strong chance the area would still be blocked off, but my morbid curiosity wanted to catch a glimpse of the action. I imagined Holden, Declan, and the other BCI investigators still had to be combing the scene for evidence.

Sure enough, a blockade greeted me when I crested the bend.

Charlie Scott, another one of Holden's new officers, stood behind the bright orange blocks, directing traffic to turn around.

I slowed my Equinox and rolled down the window. "Hey, Charlie. Keeping warm?"

"Hi, Hazel." The young recruit motioned to his neon yellow jacket. "This is doing the job."

"Any idea how much longer the road will be cordoned off?" I asked innocently.

"Soon, I hope." Charlie snorted. "It's such a major time suck having to drive all the way around the lake to get to the highway. I've been reamed out by more than one commuter today."

"I'm sorry." I frowned at the inconsideration the young officer had encountered. "Folks should understand the seriousness of what's going on."

"No kidding. But it doesn't surprise me," Charlie huffed. "These days, the second someone is mildly inconvenienced, all you-know-what breaks loose."

I smiled at his candid response and scanned the tree line for activity. I saw plenty of police vehicles but no movement. *Drat.* So much for gathering any useful intel. "Well, I hope you aren't kept out here in the cold for too much longer." I waved and navigated away from the scene.

Taking the long way to Trae's, I drove through downtown Crucible and along Lake Glenmyre's peaceful northern edge before turning into the parking lot of Waking Woods Cabin Rentals. The main building looked like a miniature Aspen ski lodge with its sweeping gables and log exterior. Surrounded by budding trees and luscious evergreens, Waking Woods was a serene spot, even during this time of year.

My hopes that Lauren might be staying here dimmed as I took stock of the cars in the parking area. Trae's truck, with his business logo painted on the side, was only accompanied by Poppy's Subaru.

"Maybe she's spending the day at Blackthorn Grove," I murmured hopefully as I climbed out of my vehicle.

Poppy's voice chirped brightly as I opened the front door to the main lobby. "It'll be a nice pop of color for your guests. Now that you're working with the winery, you might want to consider glamming things up."

Trae laughed, his deep, velvety timbre as warm as his usual wide smile. "I'm not turning this place into a spa resort. Alan and Brigitte knew what kind of establishment I was running when we teamed up."

I hesitantly stepped inside to find an annoyed expression blooming across Poppy's face. Trae Longboat, standing behind a pinewood reception desk, had his muscular, tan arms folded with authority.

His kind, dark gaze darted toward the entrance. "Hey, Hazel! What a nice surprise. You looking for another piece?" He motioned to the paintings and wood carvings hanging all around the lobby.

In addition to his cabin rentals, Trae sold art on consignment. As a member of the Cayuga Nation, Trae wanted to share the beautiful creations of his people. I had several oil paintings made by Trae's extremely talented older sister hanging in my home.

"Hi, Trae. I'd love to take a look around." Inadvertently, he'd given me a perfect excuse for being there. "Hey, Pops. Didn't know you'd be here." I waved at my aunt to keep up the ruse.

Poppy rolled her eyes. "Tell Trae his cabins need a little zhuzhing."

Trae sighed. "As if I even know what *that* means."

"Some sprucing up!" Poppy threw her hands in the air as if she hadn't just learned the term herself on *Queer Eye*. "You're catering to *wine* people now. They'll expect a little glitz and glam."

Trae snickered. "Right now, they'll be lucky to get running water."

"Trouble keeping the pipes unfrozen?" I asked as I began to survey the artwork hanging around the lobby.

"I'm hoping the worst has passed, what with the temps beginning to level out." Trae ran a hand through his long, raven hair. "It's why I close down for the winter months. Too much hassle keeping everything heated."

"Got anyone staying with you now?" I tried to conceal the nervous flutter in my voice. "I heard there's some big event going on up at Blackthorn Grove this weekend." I hated lying to good people.

"Really?" Trae frowned. "Alan didn't mention anything to me."

Busted. I shot Poppy a panicked look.

Luckily, Trae answered my question. "I've had a few folks trickle in since I reopened at the beginning of March. It's been a good test run for the start of tourist season. A nice way to ease into things, what with the Big Melt kicking off next weekend."

About a hundred years ago, the Big Melt started as a simple town gathering at the beginning of April, aimed at commemorating the arrival of spring and the melting of Lake Glenmyre. But like most Crucible traditions, over the decades, the Big Melt had grown into a major upstate festival, this one featuring melted foods and themed crafts. Sandwiches, candies, blown glass, ironworks...you name it, the Big Melt had it.

"That's great to hear." Poppy smiled sweetly.

Trae leaned over his desk, his expression growing conspiratorial. "And, uh, have you girls heard about the woman who was murdered in her car?"

"We sure did." Poppy bobbed her head.

I was a little less enthused. "The police found her on the road outside my house."

Trae let loose a low whistle. "Dang, that's right. I forgot you were on the south side. Well, get this," he said, his voice dropping to a whisper, even though it was just the three of us in the lobby. "The woman, Marjorie Zeller? She'd been staying here. The cops came by this morning and checked out her cabin."

I resisted the impulse to high-five Poppy right then and there. We could always rely on humanity's friendly urge to gossip. "No way. Did you have to speak with them, too?"

Trae nodded. "That new detective, Renee Tarling's nephew, asked me how long she'd been staying and if I knew what her plans were. Unfortunately, I couldn't give them much. Ms. Zeller didn't exactly go out of her way to chat with 'the help.'" He made air quotes for emphasis.

"Sounds like she wasn't the best guest," Poppy mused.

"You got that right." Trae gave us a sheepish shrug. "She came in here about two weeks ago, demanding a cabin. I almost turned her away because she was so nasty, but then she broke down crying, and I felt bad for her."

I nodded in sympathetic agreement. "Did she say why she was so upset?"

Trae stroked his chin. "Not really. Just a lot of mumbling about being alone in the world and how she deserved better. I thought she was going through a bad breakup and had been kicked out."

Poppy and I shared a knowing glance. Trae hadn't been that far off the mark.

"While she was staying here, did you see Ms. Zeller interact with anyone?" Poppy asked. "Perhaps one of your other guests?"

Trae shook his head. "Not that I saw." He narrowed his dark gaze. "Why?"

I gulped. *Curses.* We'd worn out our welcome already.

Poppy, however, played the whole thing cool. "Well, the police are investigating her *murder*, Trae."

His eyes widened. "You think one of my renters had something to do with it?" His tan skin lost some of its luster. "Good gravy, I didn't even think of that."

I frowned at his naiveté. "Didn't the cops question you about her stay?"

"Well, yeah," Trae replied, "but they mostly asked whether I could account for her movements and if they could have the key to her cabin."

I gritted my teeth at this development. It seemed like Declan had yet to expand his scope beyond Constance.

"When did you last see her?" Poppy batted her eyes as if that act alone made her question entirely innocent.

Trae drummed his fingers on the top of the reception desk. "Honestly, I don't remember. Had to be a few days. She pretty much kept to herself."

His fidgeting brought my attention to a large ledger splayed open next to his computer. I squinted. At first glance, it looked like a handwritten guest log, but I couldn't quite make out the names.

"Hey, Poppy, I think that oil painting would look gorgeous in your sitting room," I said, speaking a little bit too loudly in the hopes my aunt would pick up on what I was *really* saying. I pointed to a landscape hanging on the far wall.

Poppy's right eye twitched, and a heartbeat later, she clapped her hands. "Oh, perfect, yes! I need something above the bookshelf. Trae, can you help me?" She eagerly waved him away from his spot behind the desk to assist her.

I smirked. Yep, Poppy had definitely seen the excitement and curiosity in my aura, and boy, was she good at thinking on her feet.

With Trae no longer hovering around the confidential guest information, I stealthily leaned over the counter and adjusted the ledger so I could read his slanted handwriting. Since Waking Woods had only been operational for a few weeks so far this season, there wasn't much noted, but two *very* familiar names practically jumped off the page at me: Marjorie Zeller and Lauren Johnson.

My heart raced as I skimmed the rental details listed next to each entry. Marjorie had been assigned to Spruce Cabin two weeks ago, and Lauren had checked into Cedar Cabin on Wednesday. Two days before Marjorie was murdered.

Chapter 8

"Holy hexes," I murmured to myself, carefully sliding the ledger back into place. With a covert glance over my shoulder, I found Poppy haggling with Trae over the price of the painting. Catching her eye, I gave her a thumbs up. I no longer needed her to run interference.

"Fine, ring me up for two hundred," Poppy said with an elaborate exhalation. It might have been a steep price to pay for the distraction, but the stylized watercolor *was* very beautiful.

Trae beamed as he hurried back over to the reception desk. "My cousin will be thrilled."

While he wrapped the painting for transport, we made idle chitchat about how talented his family was. Several of Trae's siblings and cousins had their work on display at Waking Woods.

"I'm basically the only one with no artistic talent." Trae chuckled as he loaded the canvas into Poppy's car out in the parking lot.

I motioned to the cozy cabins shrouded by woods around us. "Maintaining your rentals is an art form all its own."

A crimson flush spread across his cheeks. "You're too kind." With a wave goodbye, Trae jogged back inside the lodge.

Poppy whacked my arm lightly. "All right, dish. For two hundred bucks, this had better be good."

I shot a furtive look at the lodge windows, trying to picture whether Trae could still see us and our cars from behind his desk. I didn't want him to know we hadn't gotten into our vehicles and left. "Lauren checked in three days ago. She and Marjorie *must* have crossed paths with one another."

Poppy pumped a fist in the air. "Do you think Holden is aware that Marjorie's agent was in the area?"

"We can ask him." I pulled out my phone to type a message in our group chat.

Hey, Chief. We just found out the vic's agent was in Crucible at time of M's murder.

"Should we see if Lauren is around?" Poppy shielded her eyes as she scanned the stoic forest. "I can get a read on her."

I bit my lower lip, remembering the last time I had inadvertently confronted a killer. "Maybe we should let Holden take it from here."

"Hey, don't worry." Poppy nudged me in the side. "I'm here with you, Hazel. You're not alone this time."

I cursed inwardly. The "perks" of having a bestie who could practically read your mind. "There aren't any other cars parked here." I motioned to the empty lot.

"If Lauren took the train up from the city, she could have Ubered from the Syracuse station," Poppy countered. "Before you arrived, Trae mentioned that Blackthorn Grove has a shuttle to pick up and drop guests off here once their tasting concludes, so she wouldn't necessarily need a car."

Auntie Dearest was not going to let the matter drop. With a sigh, I told Poppy what she wanted to know. "Lauren's staying in the Cedar cabin. But let's make this speedy. No lingering."

Mindful to make sure Trae didn't spot us through the lobby windows, we hurried around the back of the building and toward the wooded pathway leading to the rental cabins.

The trees around us were mostly evergreens, so we couldn't see much through the dense forest beyond the path. From Trae's marketing efforts, I knew that each of his fourteen log cabins sat on its own quarter-acre plot, providing a tranquil sense of privacy for vacationers.

The walkway branched off about a hundred feet from the lodge with a marker for "Birch Cabin." A cobblestone trail cut through the trees, leading off toward the rental.

"This is not the cabin we're looking for," I muttered, tugging Poppy along the main path.

"Okay, Obi-Wan," Poppy giggled at her *Star Wars* joke.

We passed the Ash, Oak, and Elm cabins before finally spotting a familiar name.

"Spruce Cabin is where Marjorie was staying." I pointed through a thinning gap in the forest. Ironically, Spruce Cabin was surrounded by maple and poplar trees whose leaves had yet to sprout, giving us a clearer view of the modest property.

Poppy squinted. "No police tape." A cunning grin twitched on her lips.

I grabbed her elbow before she took off. "No way. We are *not* breaking and entering. If we get caught—"

"Yeah, yeah. It would reflect badly on Holden," Poppy finished my rebuke with a grumpy sigh.

I shuddered to think how it would look for the new Crucible police chief if his cousins were arrested for trespassing at a murder victim's temporary residence. Actually, now that the thought had entered my mind, if Poppy or I were caught interfering with *any* aspect of the case, it could spell big trouble for Holden. We weren't the only ones putting ourselves at risk here.

Great, one more thing to stress about…

A heart-stopping *crack* snapped through the air.

Chapter 9

Poppy inhaled sharply and reached for my arm. "What was that?" she hissed.

I took hold of her hand and glanced around. Were we being watched? Followed? Or were we merely overreacting to upstate New York wildlife?

My gaze darted along the main path, searching for the source of the sharp sound.

Another *crack* filled the air, followed by another.

"This way." Poppy mouthed her words and pointed toward the lake.

We inched along the trail, the noises becoming more frequent as we approached a bend. Yikes. It sounded like breaking bones.

As we rounded the corner and took in the scene, the tension building within me deflated, and Poppy let out a laugh of relief. "Hi, Cliff." She waved.

Cliff Parker straightened, waving the branch in his hand before snapping it into smaller pieces. "Hey, Poppy. Hazel." The fifty-year-old Crucible native wore work clothes and a flannel jacket. "What brings you girls out here? You're not staying at the cabins, are you?"

I opened my mouth, unsure what I was going to say, but Poppy had an excuse at the ready. "I'm considering having my birthday party here and wanted to see what kind of amenities we'd have to work with." With her quick thinking, she was like a modern-day Nancy Drew—Poppy's thirty-fourth birthday wasn't until the end of July.

Cliff motioned around the area he was clearing. "Well, I'm whipping the campfire pit into shape for the season. Usually, it doesn't take me this long. Guess we had a lot of downed branches from those crazy snowstorms we suffered through this winter." His exposed ebony skin glowed with perspiration, even in the chilly temperatures.

I nodded, doing my best to keep my expression neutral. With Grandmaster Jedidiah's shield no longer protecting us from the cruelty of Mother Nature, our winter weather had certainly been more erratic than previous years. "Looks like you're making good progress."

Cliff put his hands on his hips and surveyed his work area. "Would like to be further along but Trae and I got held up with the police earlier this morning."

"The police?" I gave him my most convincing spooked look. "What were they here for?"

"The woman who was murdered along south Rosewood Lane." Cliff's bushy eyebrows pinched together. "She's been staying here a while."

"Oh, wow." Poppy whistled.

He didn't need any further encouragement. "What a hassle. I can barely remember what I had for dinner last night, let alone what some Jersey girl got up to while she was renting from us." As the maintenance man for Waking Woods, Cliff didn't interact with visitors as often as Trae did.

I bobbed my head in understanding. "So you weren't able to tell them anything useful?"

"Nope." His reply came quickly. "I don't think I saw her beyond the night she checked in." Cliff puffed out his cheeks. "Boy, she was in a right state. Sobbing and whining about how life was soooo unfair." He rolled his eyes. "Life can't be too bad when you're driving an M3."

I tilted my head. "An M3?"

"The type of BMW she drove," Cliff replied. "*That* I do remember."

Poppy giggled. "Of course you would." When he wasn't doing maintenance work for Trae, Cliff could usually be found in his garage, tinkering away on classic cars. I was surprised we hadn't seen his shiny green 1970 Chevrolet Camaro out front, but perhaps his vehicle was parked elsewhere on the property.

Cliff grabbed another branch and began breaking it apart. As he tossed the pieces onto a large brush pile, he said with a shake of his head, "It's a real tragedy about what happened to her, though. Something's not right with the town. Peace and quiet for as long as I can remember, then *bam*." He smacked his gloved palms together, their sound muffled. "Makes you think."

I swallowed a surge of remorse, and I suspected Poppy felt the same. It was the Glenmyres' fault all this negativity and turmoil was happening to Crucible. Our dwindling numbers had caused Grandmaster Jedidiah's enchantment to deteriorate and leave the town vulnerable to the evils of the world.

"Well, ladies, I'd better go drag the woodchipper down here from the tool shed." Cliff motioned to the large pile of brush he'd collected. "I'll see you around." He tipped his hat and took the path back toward the lodge.

Poppy's brow furrowed as she watched him disappear through the woods.

"What?" My pulse quickened. "Something in his aura?"

"I got a strange reading. When you asked him whether he told the police anything useful, his reply was deceptive. There was some smugness, too."

I folded my arms across my chest. "So, he does know something about Marjorie."

"Or he *thinks* he does," Poppy murmured, more to herself than to me. "I wish I could have pushed him more on the topic before he took off."

I considered our brief encounter with Cliff. One of the perks of Poppy's whim was that she could tell when someone was being untruthful, but a big downside was that she couldn't outright accuse someone of deception without outing her own power.

"Don't beat yourself up about it. If we'd pried further, he'd no doubt get suspicious about why we were asking." While Poppy and I could trust our friends with our sleuthing exploits, we didn't need other residents getting wind of our efforts.

Poppy shrugged off my reassurance. "Come on, let's see if Lauren is around."

I checked my phone. No messages, and I still had about three hours before I had to be back to close A Wick in Time. "Lead the way."

We continued following the main trail, passing Sycamore Cabin before finally reaching a marker bearing the name Cedar.

"Together." Poppy held out her hand, and I gratefully took it. We were just here to do some fact-finding. Poppy could get a read on Lauren's aura, and then we could scoot. No confrontation required. I hoped.

We hurried up the cobblestones that led to the cabin's screened-in front porch. I scanned the windows for any signs of activity, but the curtains were drawn.

With a steeling breath, Poppy knocked on the front door and waited. And waited. *And* waited.

"Err, I don't think she's here." I shifted on my feet, relief and unease leaving me conflicted.

Poppy stomped her foot, her childish disappointment rearing. "Where could she be? You don't think she skipped town, do you?"

"If she did, I'm sure Holden and his team will find her." I patted my aunt on the back to calm her down. "Now, let's get out of here before Trae realizes we're still parked out front."

Poppy rolled her eyes. "Fine." She did not sound fine, but I'd let her have her little pity party. Poppy had more of a "sprint-not-a-marathon" mentality. She wanted our investigations to move a million miles a minute. I mean, I also wanted to catch a killer quickly, but I knew reality was against us.

We backtracked toward the main trail in silence, each lost in our own thoughts. I checked my phone again, wondering if Holden had gotten my text yet. Had the police already found out about Lauren's little visit to Crucible? Maybe that explained why she wasn't here. She'd been detained for questioning.

Footsteps and conversation floated from up the path, coming from the direction of the lodge.

Poppy turned to me, her hopeful expression practically screaming, "Lauren?" Our expectations were doused, however, by the appearance of an older white couple wearing sweatshirts with the Canadian flag on them.

"Oh, look, hon! New renters." The woman giggled with excitement and tugged on her partner's sleeve.

The gentleman waved at Poppy and me. "Enjoying the scenery, aye?" His Canadian accent was very apparent.

"Hi, there," Poppy greeted them warmly. "We actually live around here. I'm just scoping out the place to rent for my birthday party."

I forced a smile as the couple studied us. "Are you enjoying your stay?"

"We are loving it, aren't we, hon?" the woman gushed as she batted her husband's forearm.

"Sure are, and we've been to quite a few places on our retirement road trip. Nicest little town we've been to." He rocked back and forth on his heels. "Everyone is just so friendly."

I pointed to the path leading to Lauren's empty cabin. "Any chance you've seen our friend who's staying here?"

The woman frowned in concentration. "Nope, can't say we have. It's been fairly quiet at the campground. Haven't seen many of our neighbors lately."

"What about a woman with straight brown hair?"

I paused at Poppy's description. Lauren didn't have straight hair.

"Short, very pretty," my bestie continued. "Her name is Marjorie. She's another friend of ours."

I expected the Canadian couple to freeze at the mention of her name, but they just stared at one another.

"Marjorie...Doesn't sound familiar," the man murmured as he stroked his salt-and-pepper beard.

"Wasn't that young lady we saw at breakfast a few times named Margie?" His wife perked up, snapping her fingers.

"Oh, her. You might be on to something, Helen."

"Yes, I think it was." Helen turned her attention back to us. "Any chance they're the same person?"

"It must be our friend." Poppy beamed. "We've always called her Marjorie," she added, sounding slightly awkward.

"She was a sweetheart, wasn't she, Paul?" Helen sighed. "Seemed like she was here to decompress."

Her husband nodded. "The girl liked her privacy, for sure."

Since these two weren't Crucible locals and, therefore, not obligated to contribute to the rumor mill, I took a gamble. "Did you ever see Margie hanging out with anyone while she was here?"

If Paul and Helen thought my question odd, they didn't show it. "She was on her own most times we ran into her," Paul offered.

Helen tapped her foot on the earthy ground. "You know, a man did come by our cabin earlier in the week, thinking it was hers. Asked for Margie and everything." Helen held a hand to her chest. "I, of course, instructed him that she was in the cabin next door to us. I know because we walked to breakfast together with her once or twice."

Poppy and I shared eager looks. Helen clearly loved to dish. "Do you remember what this man looked like? Did you know him?"

"Well, we don't really *know* anyone here, besides Trae and Cliff." Paul chuckled at his own lackluster joke. "But he was a dapper-looking fellow. Trim, fit white guy. Maybe in his late fifties, early sixties."

I raised my eyebrows. The age caught me slightly off guard. Marjorie was thirty-four. I didn't want to sound too judgmental, but what was Marjorie doing hanging out with a man nearly twice her age?

Trim, fit white guy over the age of fifty-five? In Crucible, that hardly narrowed things down.

"Why so many questions, ladies?" Helen squinted at us. "Is everything okay with Margie?"

"We're just getting back from a hike. Collecting some kindling for our fireplace." Paul's gaze twinkled as he checked his wristwatch. "We didn't see her at breakfast this morning. Is she all right?"

Panic shot through me. I didn't want to break the bad news to them and raise their suspicions about our questions. But I didn't want to lie to these kind people.

"We haven't seen her," I blurted out. It was within the realm of truth, after all.

Poppy bobbed her head, although her right eye twitched as she assessed the couple. "We're trying to track her down. But I guess you haven't seen her today, either." She made a folksy *aw-shucks* gesture. "Oh, well. Thanks for your help." She waved and turned on her heel to leave.

"Enjoy the rest of your time in Crucible." I gave the couple a feeble smile before hurrying after my aunt. It wasn't the smoothest exit we'd ever made, but at least we hadn't given our neighbors to the north the time to ask further questions.

"I've never seen someone so excited to build a fire before," Poppy murmured with bemusement once we were out of earshot. I assumed she was referring to what she'd seen in the couple's aura about gathering kindling.

"A dapper, trim man in his late fifties," I repeated the description of Marjorie's visitor.

Poppy stroked her chin. "Who the hexes could that be?"

"And how did this mystery man know Marjorie?" I added as the parking lot came back into view. "What was their relationship?"

Poppy shrugged. "You don't come by someone's reclusive cabin rental for idle chitchat."

By now, we'd reached our cars. "What's our next move?"

Before Poppy could respond, my phone rumbled to life in my palm. Holden was calling via video chat. I clicked Accept, and his face filled the screen.

"Hey, sorry for the radio silence. I just got your message." His brow furrowed with anxiety. "Been in an afternoon briefing. What's this about Marjorie's agent? Do you mean Lauren Johnson?"

I nodded, and Poppy jostled her head into the camera frame. "Yep. She's the one. Lauren's been staying at Waking Woods since Wednesday."

"*What?* Really?" A scowl engulfed Holden's face. "She failed to mention that."

"When did you speak with her?" I pried.

Holden rubbed his temple with his free hand. "Shroud called her last night to inform her about the murder. Ms. Johnson was listed as Marjorie's emergency contact."

I remembered Constance telling us this information. "That's kinda weird, isn't it? Shouldn't it be a family member?"

"Marjorie had no next of kin," Holden replied. "Her mother died last year. She had no siblings or romantic partners, and it doesn't seem like her father was ever in the picture. He wasn't even listed on her birth certificate."

"That's sad." Poppy's eyes pinched with compassion.

I bobbed my head, understanding Marjorie's situation a bit better. Not only had I lost my incredible mother to cancer early on in my adulthood, but I also had a non-existent relationship with my own dad. "It puts what she said to Trae when she checked in here in a new light. Not to mention what Cliff overheard her saying about life being unfair."

"Wait." Holden narrowed his gaze at us through the video feed. "You guys are at Waking Woods right now?"

Poppy smiled innocently. "Yup. We're trying to track down Lauren."

"Well, that ends now." Holden's expression grew even more unyielding. "This woman failed to disclose she was staying in the very same town where her client was murdered. She must have a reason for that omission. This is a job for the police, cousins. I'll reach out to her after I hang up here and arrange another interview."

Part of me sagged with relief. While Poppy might not always listen to my protests, perhaps she would respect Holden's authority.

"This is the thanks we get for feeding you a big, juicy tip?" Annoyance flickered across my bestie's face.

Holden sighed. "Trying to keep you safe while still letting you play detective? Yes, it is."

I smiled at his loving frustration. "Message received, Chief. Let us know if Lauren cracks."

Holden gave a distracted wave and ended the video call.

Poppy folded her arms in a huff. "What a dweeb. No doubt, Holden will take alllll the credit with Shroud for what *we* dug up."

"As he should," I gently reminded her. "Otherwise, we'd be in hot water. Constance, too." Since when did Poppy care so much about getting recognition for our amateur sleuthing efforts?

She wilted on the spot. "I suppose you do have a point." She folded her arms and leaned against the side of her Subaru. "I still can't wrap my head around why Lauren would murder her own client. The book sale angle seems like such a big risk. What's to say the publisher wouldn't drop Marjorie's novel completely?"

I shrugged. Since we hadn't spoken with Lauren and knew so little about her and Marjorie's working relationship, I didn't have another motive. "I'm sure Holden will bring us up to speed once he chats with her. Now, I should get back to the shop." Since we had struck out at Waking Woods, I could at least be back at A Wick in Time by two thirty for some candle making.

Poppy straightened to attention but didn't get into her car. Her cerulean blue gaze widened as she stared behind me. "What in the— holy hexes, incoming!"

I turned to see a bright red convertible pulling into the parking lot with its top down. I immediately recognized the chic driver. She'd taken center stage on Iggy's Zoom call a little less than two hours ago. "That's Lauren!" I squeaked, my nerves flaring. Holden had told us to stay away from her, but how could we when she'd pulled into the vacant spot right next to my SUV?

Lauren untied the silky blue scarf protecting her gorgeous curls and tossed it into the glove box before grabbing an expensive-looking messenger bag and gracefully exiting her flashy ride.

When her sunglasses-covered gaze finally landed on Poppy and me, she jumped, clearly startled. "Oh, hi there. Didn't see you. You ladies checking in?"

I shot Poppy a panicked glance. *What should we do?*

My aunt's alarmed expression mirrored Lauren's. "Um, no. We live nearby."

Lauren nodded absently as if she were no longer paying attention.

"Are you enjoying your time in Crucible?" I blurted out. Now that Marjorie's agent was standing right in front of us, my curiosity overtook common sense *and* Holden's warning.

Lauren paused, then sniffed. "I was." The response trembled

across her perfectly glossed lips.

"Oh, dear. Did something happen?" I opted to play the nosy, concerned citizen since it didn't require too much acting on my part.

Lauren removed her Chanel sunglasses, revealing watery, red eyes. "Actually, yes. I just found out a dear friend died last night."

Before either Poppy or I could react, Lauren dissolved into a torrent of tears. "I-I can't believe it. I saw her only a few hours before it happened. And then all this business with work and now the police. Oh, Lord, it's like a waking nightmare."

I swallowed, totally taken aback by her sudden outburst.

"I'm s-sorry to unload on you like this." Lauren's sobs became more controlled. "I'm just—I don't know what to do. I was supposed to be on vacation, and now…" Tearful whimpers consumed her once again.

Poppy shook her head and sprang forward, wrapping an arm around Lauren's tall, quivering frame. "Oh, sweetie. Cry it out. What awful news."

I eyed my aunt cautiously. What was she doing, latching herself onto a potential murderer? I then remembered the confused, startled expression Poppy had on her face when she'd first assessed Lauren. *Of course*, I thought to myself. *Poppy's whim*. What had Auntie Dearest seen?

"This may be completely off the mark," Poppy cooed in Lauren's ear, "but you're not talking about that visiting woman who was murdered last night, are you?"

Lauren gasped before collapsing against Poppy. "Yes. Poor Margie. I can't believe she's gone. How could someone do this to her?"

As Poppy consoled the despairing agent, she held my gaze. It was there I saw the certainty in her eyes.

Lauren Johnson wasn't our killer.

Chapter 10

It took Lauren a few minutes to collect herself. "Gosh, you both must think I've got a screw loose. Here I am, a random stranger unloading all my problems onto you." She wiped her eyes. "I've been struggling to hold myself together all day. You're the first kind people to actually notice that I'm not okay."

I remembered her polished and poised appearance on Iggy's Zoom call. She'd done an admirable job of fooling me.

Poppy stroked her arm. "It's fine, honey. Here in Crucible, we look after one another."

I admired Poppy's ability to treat everyone as a lifelong friend. Even someone she'd suspected of murder not two minutes ago.

I cleared my throat, eager to emulate my aunt's genuine concern. "How did you know Margie?"

Lauren smoothed the sleeves of her cropped jacket. "Professionally, I was her literary agent. But we had become good friends in recent months."

Questions swirled inside my head, each fighting to be asked first. "Only recently?"

"Her mom passed away last year. She needed a shoulder to cry on, and we grew close." Lauren swelled with sudden pride. "My girl didn't have many people she could rely on in the world, but she had me fighting in her corner."

This aligned with Holden's explanation as to why Lauren was Marjorie's emergency contact. "Were you here vacationing together?"

Lauren shook her head. "Actually, no. I had no idea she was in the area until I ran into her getting coffee in the lodge yesterday morning." She dug out a tissue and blew her nose. "You see, a few weeks ago, Marjorie told me she was taking time off for a writing retreat, but I had no clue where. She went radio silent after our conversation. No socials, no emails, no nothing."

Lauren stared at Lake Glenmyre's icy top, shimmering through the trees. "I couldn't have been more surprised when I saw her at the coffee bar. What a small world…to think we were staying at the same place."

A small world indeed. I mulled over the suspicious scenario, glancing at my aunt to gauge her reaction.

"A writing retreat, huh?" Poppy twirled a strand of her auburn hair. "I heard on the news she was a soon-to-be-published author. Her first book is due out this fall, right?"

Lauren scoffed. "It was." She folded her slender arms, a scowl growing. "Now, Margie's publisher wants to launch it next month."

Poppy pretended to be shocked. "Why the change?"

"They're looking to ride the wave of public sympathy and intrigue surrounding her death." Lauren gritted her teeth. "Forget that Margie was a real person who mattered to people." She muttered the barbed remark more to herself than to us.

Broomsticks. It sounded like Griffinsmith was the driving force behind the book's new launch date, not Lauren. "That's awful." I didn't have to feign my disgust.

Lauren bobbed her head in agreement. "I've been in meetings with them all day. They're firing on all cylinders. The executive team is even making me arrange some publicity stunt memorial to spotlight their authors."

"*Making* you?" I repeated in disbelief. So, the memorial service Lauren had mentioned during the Zoom call was all Griffinsmith's idea? Iggy would not be happy to hear how his publisher was skillfully monetizing a woman's death.

Lauren glanced at the slim gold watch encircling her wrist. "Yes, and before I head down to the police station, I need to jump on yet another call with the publisher's PR team. They want to speak with me about doing Marjorie's book tour on her behalf." She swiped a hand across her cheeks again, ridding any lingering sign that she'd been crying. "Thank you for your kindness. I needed it." Lauren gave us a weak smile. "I'm sorry. I never even got your names."

We formally introduced ourselves, and Lauren shook our hands. Her polished professionalism had returned with a vengeance.

"Thanks again. I was having a lovely time visiting your town before all this happened," she said before excusing herself to her cabin.

Poppy and I remained in the parking lot, waiting until Lauren was out of earshot before speaking.

"Welp, she didn't do it." My bestie's shoulders sagged. "What's worse, I feel super guilty for suspecting her. Lauren's gutted." Poppy looked like she was debating something internally. "I'd even wager she and Marjorie were more than friends."

"They were dating?"

"Not dating," Poppy corrected me. "More like sisters. What's even weirder is that Lauren was telling the truth about having no idea Marjorie was staying in Crucible. What are the odds she'd take a weekend getaway up here?"

"It's strange, right?" I crossed my arms. "Maybe Marjorie mentioned Crucible at some point, and it wormed into Lauren's subconscious when she started looking for wineries to visit." My gaze trailed thoughtfully over to the Waking Woods lodge. "I'm also wondering why Marjorie didn't mention where she was doing her writing retreat. You'd think she'd want her agent to know she was hanging out with *the* Constance Crane."

Poppy tapped her chin. "So many questions. We still don't know why Marjorie stuck around Crucible so long, either."

She snapped her fingers as an idea struck. "Let's swing by the police station. I can fill Holden in on my reading. Since we know Lauren didn't kill Marjorie, maybe we can help him reframe his interview to figure out what Marjorie was up to."

I wrung my hands, wary of what I was about to ask. "Are we *sure* Lauren didn't kill Marjorie?"

I didn't want Poppy to feel like I was questioning the validity of her whim, but the topic had come up before during our previous investigations. If someone could be cold and calculated enough to take the life of another, would their aura really reflect the truth? Would a murderer have any guilt over their actions? Any remorse?

Poppy took my fidgeting hands and squeezed. "I recognize your concern, Hazel. I do. Every whim has its limits, but I think we can trust Lauren's aura. The killers we've encountered in the past…her aura isn't like theirs."

I nodded, relieved by Poppy's understanding. It probably helped matters that she could see my own guilt radiating around me. And if I was being honest with myself, I was probably projecting my own insecurities about my whim onto my aunt. Not just about how I was going to handle eventually seeing Ezra's lifeclock, but the fact that my whim wasn't infallible. While the lifeclock revealed the time a person was destined to die, whether from an accident, disease, or natural causes, my whim couldn't determine deaths caused intentionally by human will. It was how I'd realized Kevin Finchmore had been murdered rather than dying from a heart attack. His lifeclock had shown nearly fifty years when I'd inadvertently seen it, and yet, he'd been found dead the next day.

Poppy stared at me for a long moment, likely sensing I was at war with myself.

"I'm okay," I assured her with a weak smile. "Let's go give Holden a quick heads up, but then I need to get back to the shop."

Crucible's police station was currently located on the northwest side of Lake Glenmyre, near the town's historical society. While the museum resided in a sleek, state-of-the-art facility, the police station was still a work in progress. For the past five months, Mayor Kyla Mooney had been on a campaign to secure more funding for the fledgling department. In the interim, Holden and his team operated out of two doublewide trailers. Both Poppy and I had made generous donations to the Crucible PD project, using money from our Glenmyre trust fund, and word on the street was that Mayor Mooney was planning to break ground on a new permanent building soon, this one adjacent to the town hall.

Eight minutes later, I pulled into the dirt lot, followed by Poppy. Several cars were parked outside the temporary facility, Holden's black SUV among them.

"Do you know which one Holden's office is in?" Poppy murmured out of the side of her mouth as we approached the two trailers.

I didn't. I assumed one building had to house the admin offices, while the other contained makeshift holding cells and interrogation rooms. Observing the two austere structures, a pit of sadness filled me. Crucible had never needed this kind of institution before when Grandmaster Jedidiah's protection shield had been in place. It was sobering to see our town's new reality.

As Poppy and I neared, the words on a paper sign nailed to the right trailer became clear—*Crucible Police Department: Administration.*

We ascended the ramp leading to the metal door and hesitated at the threshold.

"Do we knock?" I didn't even know the proper protocol for entering a police station.

My bestie shrugged. "They don't in the movies."

I chuckled. "As if those get everything so accurate." Regardless, I followed Poppy's advice and grabbed the door handle to let ourselves in.

Thankfully, the inside of the station was much warmer and cozier than the gloomy, gray exterior. Two couches sat kitty-corner to each other, creating a small, comfortable waiting area. Watercolor paintings hung from the walls, and someone had installed metal panels and glass to section off the waiting room from the dispatcher stationed behind the front desk.

The woman on duty glanced up, a welcoming smile spreading across her face. "Well, I'll be. It's the Glenmyre Girls."

"Hi, Holly," Poppy and I chimed together.

Another one of Holden's recent hires, Holly Hanscom served as the community liaison for the station. I had known Holly since high school. She'd graduated a year before Poppy.

"It's nice to see you, Holls." I smiled as we arrived at the front desk partition.

"What are you doing out here?" Poppy leaned in as far as the bullet-proof glass panel would allow her. "I thought you'd be enjoying your swanky new private office."

I chuckled at Poppy's sarcasm. She had been hanging out with me at A Wick in Time when Holly came by last week. Poor Holls had been in dire need of lavender candles to help douse the weird smell permeating her temporary office.

Holly motioned to the analog clock hanging on the wall behind her. "I needed the fresh air, and Mellie needed a break." Mellie Bridges was one of the new dispatch receptionists. "Usually Chief takes over for dispatch, but he's prepping some reports." Holly pushed her wheelchair back from the desk and crossed her arms. "Mayor Mooney needs *another* write-up from him about his personnel plans for the new station."

Poppy feigned a gag at the endless red tape Holden and his team had been subjected to these past months. "Any chance we can chat with him?"

Holly swiped a strand of her buttery blonde hair out of her face. "About what, pray tell?" Her bright blue eyes sparkled with mischief. "This wouldn't have anything to do with a certain ongoing investigation, now, would it?"

Poppy and I shared embarrassed looks. As much as we had tried to keep our prior sleuthing on the down low, our involvement in two murder cases last year hadn't gone entirely unnoticed by the Crucible locals.

"It *might*," Poppy hedged, stretching out the word.

I cleared my throat. "We just learned something we think Holden should know."

Holly snorted before bursting into full-on giggles. "Relax, I won't read you the riot act. I'll leave that to the chief." She leaned forward and pressed a button wired to the front desk. A loud, short buzz was followed by an unassuming metal panel giving way. The inner sanctum of the administration building opened before us. "You're the only two people the chief has on his approved visitors list. Go on back. He's the last door on the right."

A burst of warmth spread through my chest at Holly's remark. I never would have thought the gruff, annoying detective we'd first met last August would become like the big brother I'd never had. I was so glad Holden was in my life *and* in my corner.

We thanked Holly and followed her directions, finding Holden's office door ajar. He sat behind a wobbling IKEA desk, typing at his laptop, a deep furrow etched into his forehead.

I knocked lightly before pushing the door all the way open. "Everything okay?"

Holden glanced up, his expression morphing into bemusement. "Shouldn't I be asking you two that question? What brings you by the station?"

Poppy herded me inside the small yet organized office and closed the door. "We've got some additional intel on Lauren Johnson. She didn't kill Marjorie."

Holden propped his elbows on the desk and studied us with dark eyes. "Oh? Less than twenty minutes ago you were telling me she's the killer. What's changed?" His words had an edge to them.

I winced, steeling myself for his disappointment. "I know you warned us not to engage with her…"

Holden slapped his desk with a balled fist. "Are you kidding me? I told you guys—"

"It couldn't be helped," Poppy interjected. "Lauren literally pulled into the spot next to us just before we left Waking Woods. I got a reading—" she held her hands up in defense "—so sue me."

Holden took a few calming breaths. "A reading?"

Poppy shot me a covert wink. She had him hooked.

"A reading," she repeated. "Lauren is devastated by Marjorie's death."

"She had no idea Marjorie was even in the area when she checked into Waking Woods," I added. "All the stuff I said about increasing book sales—it's being pushed by Marjorie's publisher, not Lauren."

From there, we gave Holden a quick play-by-play of our encounter with the distressed literary agent.

"You're sure she's not lying?" He stroked the dark stubble peppering his chin.

Poppy dragged a finger crisscross over her chest. "Positive. I swear."

"Then why didn't Lauren mention she was already in the area when Shroud called her last night to deliver the news?" Holden pointed out.

I shrugged. "Shock? Maybe she didn't think her vacation plans were relevant."

"That's one thing we'll leave *you* to find out." Poppy tapped her finger to her temple as she stared Holden down. "Lauren seemed under the impression that Marjorie was in town for a writing retreat, so I'm not sure she'll be able to shed any light on why Marjorie stayed in the area after getting tossed out of Constance's."

"We also have a lead on someone Marjorie may have met up with while she was here," I offered. "A trim, dapper white male in his late fifties/early sixties was seen asking around for her at Waking Woods. But that's all we know."

Holden's shoulders straightened at my description. "Where did this intel come from?"

"A Canadian couple who are staying at Trae's. Paul and Helen. They said a man came by their cabin one day looking for Marjorie." After I relayed what Helen had told us, I realized it didn't really amount to much.

"Hmm, okay. I'll let Shroud know. He can send some BCI officers to speak with these Canadians." Holden reached for a pen and scribbled on a nearby notepad. "Only Trae and Cliff Parker were on the premises when we visited this morning."

"Trae told us you guys stopped by," I prodded. "And that you searched her cabin. Did you find anything?"

"Other than Marjorie's belongings, no."

I pressed my lips at his blunt response. We weren't going to get any further case specifics from Chief Whitfield.

Holden noted my reaction and sighed. "Sorry to snap. I really do appreciate the info, and in turn, I'll share some of my own. But it isn't good, guys. Without Lauren in the picture, the spotlight is going to shift back onto Constance. She's Zeller's biggest known link to the area."

"Well, maybe Lauren can tell you more about Marjorie's unidentified visitor." Poppy's knee began to bounce nervously. "We didn't get a chance to ask. Perhaps Marjorie met someone worth sticking around for."

Helen's description of our mystery man flashed through my mind. Just who was he? And how was he connected to our victim?

Holden's phone buzzed next to his computer. He glanced at the screen. "Shroud will be here soon to lead the interview with Ms. Johnson. I'll see how I can work this new angle without causing too many raised eyebrows." He rose from his chair to escort us out of the station. "Meanwhile, keep up the good work." He winked.

My annoyance over his tight-lipped attitude melted. Our cousin was doing the best he could.

Poppy saluted. "You got it, Chief."

Holden rolled his eyes at her theatrics and laughed. "I heard there's a band playing at Cold Cauldron tonight. I'm hoping to catch a few songs. You guys planning on being there?"

My response caught in my throat. On one hand, I was really looking forward to a romantic, fun date night with Ezra. On the other, Holden might let some updates about the case slip if he had a few beers in him…

"I'll be there, helping Fitz behind the bar." Poppy rubbed her hands in anticipation. "Tonight, I'm learning the art of the pour." She enunciated her words with a jokingly posh tone.

"Nice. What about you, Hazel?" Holden asked as he ushered us out of his office and down the hall toward the front desk.

"Sounds like I'll see you guys there." I smiled cheerfully. I'd text Ezra the slight change in plans with hopes he would understand. He was a good sport when it came to dealing with my kooky, tight-knit family. Besides, once I brought him up to speed on our latest mystery, Ezra would be just as invested.

Chapter 11

No probs, luv. Will be fun to see everyone.

My heart warmed as I read my boyfriend's good-natured response. **Ok. Meet you there at 7:15 <3.**

With renewed excitement for the night ahead, I glanced at the pendulum clock hanging on the wall of A Wick in Time. Three-fifteen. I'd returned to the store less than five minutes ago, and yet, here I was, counting down the seconds until I could close the shop.

Quinn was passing the time Swiffering the wood floor when her phone buzzed. One look at her exasperated expression and I knew whom the text was from. Her son, Dylan.

"This kid. Thinks he can just drop a school bake sale on my lap?" Quinn rolled her eyes as she put away her phone. "As if I have the time to make eighty cupcakes this weekend."

I shuddered at her predicament. Dylan was involved in a lot of school clubs, which meant doing a lot of bake sale fundraisers. "Why don't you head home early then? It's a ghost town right now." I gestured to the nonexistent foot traffic outside the front window.

Quinn gnawed on her lower lip. "Are you sure?"

I waved away her obvious concern. "Of course. Hey, Ig?" I

nudged his side. He stood next to me behind the counter, typing away at his writing project. "Why don't you head home, too? Enjoy the rest of the afternoon."

Iggy snapped his laptop shut. "I won't say no to that. Gives me some more time to tinker with this plot before Cora picks me up. She's invited me to an art show over in Hyssop Falls."

I inwardly shushed myself to prevent any prying questions from spilling out of my mouth. I didn't know if Iggy and Cora Donahue were officially an item, but I figured Iggy would tell me when the time was right. After all, Cora had lost her fiancé last summer and was still working through her grief.

Quinn's eyes widened. "Ooo, is it their new perspective exhibit? I went with some girlfriends last week. It's mind-blowing."

She continued to gush about the exhibit while she and Iggy packed up.

"All right, now I'm more enthused." Iggy wiggled his eyebrows. "I thought I'd be looking at paintings of flowers all evening." He then lowered his voice so Quinn couldn't hear. "I'll also see what I can dig up about Marjorie from my author pals."

I nodded my understanding. "Thanks. Keep me posted."

"See you tomorrow, boss." Iggy and Quinn waved goodbye as they left to enjoy their weekend.

With my coworkers gone for the day and no clients to tend to, time continued to drag on. I loved making all kinds of candles for my customers to enjoy, but manning the sales floor was my least favorite part of being a small business owner.

I decided to use this downtime to do more online research about Marjorie. I scoured her social media for any signs of her mystery visitor but found nothing. Like Lauren had alluded to, Marjorie hadn't posted anything new in several weeks. She'd reposted content from other authors, but that was it.

"Bummer." I cast another desperate look toward the clock. Why wouldn't it move?

The fancy, Victorian pendulum clock may have looked a bit out of place in my shop, but it was the one piece of my dad I had left. My father, Leopold Wickbury, was a mystery I had yet to solve.

Leo and my mom, Iris Glenmyre, had fallen madly in love when he'd come to Crucible to conduct research. Researching what, Mom never knew. He always teased her that it was "top secret." Yet, during their whirlwind romance, Leo came across something requiring further investigation and told Mom that he needed to leave town to check it out. He promised he'd return to begin the life they'd planned together, so Mom simply waited. And waited. By the time Mom realized she was pregnant with me, Leopold Wickbury had all but vanished into thin air.

I stared at my dad's clock, the one possession he'd left behind, my mind a sudden storm of mixed emotions. Despite the anger I harbored over Leo deserting Mom without a word, I liked to believe that by hanging the clock on my store's wall, my dad was somehow watching over me. I had no idea if he had abandoned Mom out of malice or cowardice, or whether he'd been met with some horrible fate. Even with the wonders of technology, I'd found no trace of him. It was as if Leopold Wickbury had never existed.

The bell over the front door jingled as a customer breezed in. I turned to greet them, smiling with recognition. "Hi, Tula. How goes it?"

Tula Sardolous gave me an absent wave as she surveyed the display closest to the window. "Things will be much better if you can help, Hazel. Mrs. Finchmore is craving the scent of gardenias. Do you have any?"

I noted the stressed undertones in Tula's request. When the Finchmores wanted something, they got it. "I have just the thing, but I have to run upstairs." I took the back steps two at a time and found my Poppy's Patch candles where I'd left them curing on shelves. I'd been prepping the new product line for weeks in order to have enough inventory for my big launch.

I grabbed a gardenia-scented candle and inhaled the fragrance to make sure it passed merit. "Thank goodness I brought the labels Cora created for me." A box of custom designs sat on the table, ready and waiting. I sifted through the stickers until I found "Gardenia Serenade." With deft hands, I applied the label, excited to share the fruits of my labor with a patron in need.

"What do you think about this scent?" I asked Tula as I arrived downstairs and handed her the candle.

She breathed deeply, and her eyes rolled skyward. "Oh, Hazel. This is perfect. Just the right amount of sweetness without being knocked out by it. Mrs. Finchmore will love it."

"I'm thrilled to hear that." I clapped my hands with glee. "I'm getting ready to launch a new floral-themed line, so this is a bit of an exclusive at the moment." I winked conspiratorially.

"Even better," Tula replied. "Mrs. Finchmore will love knowing she's the first in on a new trend."

I was about to laugh, but Tula's expression read that she was dead serious. "Wonderful," I said, sparing myself an awkward moment. "How was your dinner with Tobias last night?" I asked as I headed back behind the counter to wrap the candle for protection.

Tula's lips curled downward. "Non-existent, I'm afraid. There was some emergency Grant needed dealing with, so my baby boy canceled on me."

"That's too bad," I sympathized. "I hope everything is okay?"

Tula flicked her wrist. "My Tobias gets things done." She then reached for her scarf and began to twiddle with the tasseled ends.

The action drew my gaze to the periwinkle-blue accessory, the pattern tickling the back of my brain. Why did the bow-tie pattern strike me as familiar?

"Constance's scarf!" I blurted the realization out loud before I could stop myself.

Tula tilted her head. "Excuse me?"

Curses, I needed to backtrack and cover my misstep. "My friend Constance has the same scarf in a different color." I pointed to Tula's neck. "I love it."

She glanced down at the item and smiled. "Why, thank you. Sofía has a big display of them, and I fell in love with the design. It's made by a local artist." Tula stroked the silky material. "It was a gift from Tobias since he forgot to bring me a souvenir from Turks and Caicos," she added with a motherly chuckle.

"How nice of him." I did my best to give her a calm, collected smile as my heart began to race. So, the scarf used to kill Marjorie was made by a local artist selling their wares at Sofía Perez's shop. With Constance's scarf currently MIA, we'd been operating under the assumption that Marjorie had stolen it from her, only to have the accessory used against her in the end. But there was also the slim chance that Marjorie had been killed with a *different* scarf that looked identical to Constance's missing one. As I rang up and finalized Tula's purchase, I made a note to swing by The Corner Store on my way home and chat with Sofía. Maybe Marjorie had purchased the scarf for herself after seeing how good it looked on Constance.

"Thanks again, Hazel. You've saved me a major headache." Tula waved goodbye and disappeared out the door.

As soon as I was alone, I texted Poppy. **Get this. Tula just came into the store with a scarf similar to Constance's. Sofía is selling them. Might be worth seeing if more have been sold.**

Poppy's reply came a few minutes later. **So, you think C's isn't the murder weapon? Kinda too coincidental that hers is also missing...**

While I agreed with my aunt, I felt in my gut that it was still an avenue worth exploring. **Just want to check all our boxes. Going to swing by The Corner Store on my way home and see if Sofía can shed some light.**

Okay, sounds good. Keep me posted. Poppy ended our exchange with a thumbs up.

I glanced once more at my dad's old clock, doing some mental math. I couldn't afford to dillydally at The Corner Store for long if I wanted enough time to prepare for my outing at Cold Cauldron.

With the shop empty again, I returned to my online investigation into Marjorie. I navigated away from her social media and shifted my focus to her book. I read through some early reviews on Goodreads, each praising Marjorie's pacing and character development. *"Zeller writes like a worldly veteran of her genre. What talent. I can't believe this is her debut work."*

I snorted at the irony, and my anger flared. What I couldn't believe was that Marjorie had the audacity to reach out to Constance and organize a writing retreat in the first place. Did Marjorie really think she could get away with stealing Constance's idea? Why had she been willing to take such a huge risk?

Chapter 12

I made the executive decision to close the store at four since I hadn't had a single customer since Tula. It also gave me more wiggle room to visit Sofía and check out this telltale scarf display.

The Corner Store, Crucible's one-stop shop for home goods, perched on the other end of the block from A Wick in Time, so it was a short detour. As I waltzed through the entrance, I took stock of the crowd perusing Sofía's wares. With a large and varied inventory, her shop had much more foot traffic today than mine, which meant it might be harder to pin the friendly proprietor down for a chat.

I combed through the aisles in search of either the scarves or Sofía. Luck must have been on my side; the big display rack was right next to the register.

Perfect, I thought to myself. I could chat up Sofía while I pretended to inspect the scarves.

The beautiful Latina woman working the counter waved to me as she checked out her paying customer. "Hola, chica. How's the latest book club read coming?"

I greeted Sofía Perez warmly. "I'm still working toward the big reveal, so no spoilers." Sofía was a notoriously speedy reader within our book group, and she often was the first to finish our pick for the month.

She mimed zipping her lips. "Consider me a vault. But it's soooo good!"

I giggled as I began sifting through the scarf offerings. A rainbow of colors shimmered before me, all bearing the same telltale bow-tie pattern. "These are gorgeous," I gushed.

Sofía thanked her customer and wished them a good day before acknowledging my remark. "Aren't they? A woman over in Hyssop Falls makes them. She dyes the material—all organic—and then hand-stitches the bow ties into the silk."

"They're all hand-stitched?" My eyes widened at the immense labor of love on display before me. "That must take ages."

Sofía nodded. "This is all the product I'll get for a while, I think. I told her how well they've been selling, though, so I hope she continues."

My heart skipped a beat. How was I going to play this? I couldn't very well come out and ask if Crucible's latest murder victim had bought one of her wares. Besides, what were the chances that Sofía remembered everyone she'd sold a scarf to? "I just saw Tula wearing one."

"Oh, that's nice. She'd been hemming and hawing over them a while. The price tag is pretty steep," Sofía admitted with a slight wince. "Glad to see she's showing off her purchases."

We were interrupted by another patron checking out, so I waited until Sofía's attention was free again. It gave me time to formulate my next investigative question. "Poppy hasn't bought one, has she? I'd love to get her one as a gift." I mentally winced at the white lie. "She's been admiring the coral one Constance got."

Sofía tapped her chin in thought. "I don't think I've seen Poppy in here since they arrived." She then released a little squeal. "It totally made the artist's day when I told her *the* Constance Crane bought one of her creations."

"I bet." I stroked the fabric of an amethyst piece. "Do you have any more coral-colored ones? That shade looks so good against Poppy's skin."

"Unfortunately, no." Sofía gave me an apologetic look. "The artist only made one of each color. I do have a peach one, though." She leaned over the counter and dug through the display tree before pulling out her selection. "I guess it's a bit on the orange side."

I ground my teeth in frustration, and not because of the vivid peach hue. There'd only been one coral piece sold, and it had gone to Constance. *Constance was right, I suppose. Not only had Marjorie stolen her book, she had plundered her wardrobe.* How else could the stylish accessory have fallen into the hands of Marjorie's killer? Marjorie must have had Constance's purloined scarf on her person when she was attacked in her car.

I quickly tried to cover my disappointment. "I'll take this one instead." I pulled the amethyst scarf free of the rack. Even though it was waaaay more expensive than I'd expected—Sofía hadn't been kidding—it was a small price to pay for valuable intel. Intel I *wouldn't* be sharing with Holden, as it further pointed the finger at Constance since we had no proof Marjorie had pilfered the hand-stitched silk.

And besides, I'd kinda fallen in love with the smooth, shimmering fabric the longer I stood at the display. Even though I'd told Sofía I was shopping for Poppy, I decided to treat myself.

I paid and bid Sofía goodbye before texting my aunt on the way to my car. **Bad news. Sofía only has one scarf of each color in stock. Meaning the coral scarf we saw at the scene *had* to be Constance's.**

By the time I was buckled in, I had a reply from my aunt. **Since we know Marjorie had no issue taking things that belonged to Constance, I'm inclined to believe she stole the scarf out of spite. Super dark karma, though, that she ended up being killed with it.**

I shuddered at the notion. **No kidding.**

Where does that leave us? Poppy typed back.

We really need to figure out who else in town Marjorie knew. What if someone saw her and Constance arguing at the library and decided to use it to their advantage? The perfect cover, so to speak.

Right. Everyone would automatically think Constance was the killer because of their public spat. And we don't even need to narrow it to being at the library. Her attacker could've recognized Marjorie from behind in that TikTok vid.

I mulled over the likelihood of the scenario. **If that's the case, they would've had to put a plan into place pretty fast. Maybe it's** really all some weird coincidence. I also don't understand how this all happened on the side of the road. Why was Marjorie there to begin with? Was it a meeting spot or something?

Good question. I'll think on it. Let's sync up later, k? I've got a bit of a headache, so I'm gonna nap before date night with Fitz.

Oh dear. Poppy wasn't prone to headaches. I wondered if the stress of the case was getting to her. **Feel better soon <3**

I drove home for some much-needed quality time with my fur babies. Noli and I went for a long walk along the lake, where I let her run around to tire herself out. Once we were back inside and Noli was enjoying her dinner, I snatched the latest book club selection I'd left lying on my coffee table. My chat with Sofía had reminded me to finish it before our upcoming meeting.

Berg and I cuddled on the couch while I squeezed in some reading time. The book was a true crime novel Ezra had recommended to the group about a podcaster who used her platform to solve cold cases.

"Maybe it will provide some inspiration." I scratched Berg under his whiskered chin.

With one eye on the time, I dove into the next chapter. It featured the podcaster retracing the victim's steps the day she died. I stopped halfway through a paragraph describing the restaurant where the victim ate lunch. "Other than Marjorie being at the library, we don't know much about what she did on Friday." *Gosh, was it only yesterday?* I gave my kitty companion a searching stare. "Adding that to my to-do list."

Eventually, I had to extract a purring Berg from my lap and hop into the shower. I wanted to wash off the strong scent of candles clinging to my skin.

Even though I had self-sabotaged a romantic evening for two with Ezra, I still wanted to put some effort into my appearance. I quickly blow-dried my long, dark brown hair before weaving it into a sleek braid. I then donned black leggings with a purple sweaterdress for cutesy warmth and paired them with ankle boots and some flashy gold hoops that once belonged to my great aunt Ruthie.

"Okay, sweetheart, you be a good girl." As I got ready to leave, I blew Noli air kisses before bending down to scratch her left ear. "I won't be out late." Since she'd had a long walk, Noli would be set for another several hours.

Before we'd parted ways at the police station, Poppy had offered to pick me up on her drive back into town, but I declined. Ezra lived within walking distance of Cold Cauldron, so I made the strategic decision to take my car, just in case he wanted to come home with me. And there was no way I'd survive the embarrassment of my aunt/bestie dropping me and my date off at my house for an overnight.

Downtown Crucible was already hopping when I rolled my SUV into an elusive parking spot. We were getting closer to the Big Melt festival and the official start of boating season, so weekend nights were becoming livelier. Soon, the days would be too. A quiet Saturday at the shop like today would become a thing of the past.

As I climbed out of the car, the evening sky sparkled overhead. It was a beautiful night, and I planned to enjoy it. While Marjorie's murder still gnawed away at me, I promised to appreciate the precious time I had with my friends.

You could know for certain how much time you had left with them. Especially Ezra.

The macabre, sneering thought floated through my mind as I walked along Rosewood Lane toward Cold Cauldron. I tried to bat it away, but the notion kept playing on an anxious loop. Should I just get it over and done with? What if Ezra only had months left? A year? A week? A day?

The onslaught of questions made my heart pinch tightly within my chest. How was I going to deal with this? I couldn't keep my glasses on or my eyes closed around Ezra forever.

"Tonight's not the night to figure this out, Hazel." Talking to myself out loud helped drive home the point. I was already dealing with enough, what with Constance being so intricately linked to Marjorie's murder. I didn't need to add another hurdle to overcome.

Cold Cauldron glowed with cheerful activity as I arrived, even though the band wasn't scheduled to start for another forty-five minutes. Its signature hoppy, pinewood smell washed over me as I entered and surveyed the bubbling crowd.

The band, Rose & Raven, was getting set up on the slightly elevated stage Fitz had installed to accommodate such performances. A cheerful crowd was gathered in front of the stage, and every table was filled.

A smile sprouted across my face as my gaze landed on a tall, pale figure with tousled dark hair. Ezra sat hunched over at a table near the bar, engrossed in yet another book. He had a beer in hand, and from the looks of it, he'd already ordered me my new favorite hard cider, Adept Apple.

I moved through the throng of pub-goers, greeting the familiar faces I saw along the way. Crucible was out in full force to support Fitz's latest entertainment endeavor.

"Hello, handsome." I swooped in and kissed Ezra unsuspectingly on the cheek as I reached our table. "Mind if I join?"

"Hey. Don't you look lovely." Ezra's green eyes brightened, and he shut his book with a resounding clap. "You're the only person who could tear me away from a cliffhanger."

I checked the title. He was reading the new Louise Penny mystery. "I was devouring the podcaster non-fic you recommended to our book club before coming here."

"Oh," Ezra said with a crooked grin. He pulled back the chair next to him and waved for me to sit down. "Comparing notes?"

I did a double take as I claimed my seat. "What do you mean?"

Ezra chuckled. "Come on, Hazel. I know you well enough by now." He lowered his voice. "There's a murder practically outside your front door, and you're not going to get involved?" His eyebrows wriggled devilishly.

I whacked him lightly on the arm. "Hush, will you?"

"I have my answer." He folded his arms with a triumphant smirk, but his expression quickly melted into concern. "I know asking you to sit this one out is useless. I just hope you and Poppy are being careful."

I kissed him tenderly, this time on the lips. "We are. But so far, our efforts haven't amounted to much." As we sipped our brews, I brought him up to speed on everything Poppy and I had uncovered about Marjorie, Constance, and Lauren. All non-whim-related info, of course.

Ezra placed his empty glass on the table. "So, your only viable lead at the moment is figuring out who Marjorie's mysterious cabin visitor is?"

His summation of our investigation left me feeling discouraged. Not at Ezra, but at our unimpressive progress. "Well, we've yet to retrace Marjorie's steps the day she died. I'm hoping that turns up something useful."

Marjorie's final moments in life floated through my mind as I recalled the chilling words Holden had shared using the power of his whim. *Please, no. I swear, I'm not here to cause trouble. I'm just so close. Stop. Please, someone help me. I need to find—*

Need to find what, I wondered. Had she stayed in Crucible to locate something? Someone? Was our mysterious cabin visitor the answer to all these questions?

Chapter 13

"Would you like some company on your fact-finding mission?" Ezra offered, unaware of my inner monologue. "I'm only open from eleven to three tomorrow."

I studied my eager boyfriend intently. "Where's the sudden interest coming from? Usually, you're trying to dissuade me from stuff like this."

He shrugged, a silly grin twitching on his lips. "What can I say? I had fun the last time we played super-sleuth together." Ezra reached for my hand. "And I'd rather be there at your side than hear *after* the fact that you'd come face-to-face with a killer."

While my independent streak wanted to protest his light rebuke, the lingering fear in his eyes silenced any retort. It wasn't fair for me to disregard how my actions affected the people in my life. "I'd be thrilled to have your help. Although, trust me—Poppy and I are playing it cool this time around."

"What finally made you reevaluate your methods?" Ezra teased.

"Honestly? We don't want to get Holden fired from his new position."

Ezra snorted. "Only the Glenmyre Girls would put someone's job and reputation before their *own* safety."

I giggled. "All right, enough shop talk. Why don't we order some apps while we wait for everyone to join us?" Ezra and I had decided to meet up earlier for some alone time, but Holden and Poppy would soon be here. Although Poppy planned to work the bar with Fitz, I highly doubted she'd stay there all night. My aunt might have been an enthusiastic helper, bless her, but she also had a short attention span when it came to manual labor not involving flora.

Ezra flagged down the attention of a server, and we ordered a round of our favorite Cold Cauldron appetizers: buffalo wings, fried mozzarella sticks, braised beef eggrolls, and spinach dip.

Holden showed up at ten of eight, although I almost didn't notice him. He was careful to keep his hat on and his head down as he made his way to our table. I suspected he didn't want to be besieged by questions about the unsolved murder afflicting the town.

"Hey, guys." He nodded a greeting my way as he clapped Ezra on the back. He took a seat, positioning himself so that his back was toward the rest of the brewery.

I raised an eyebrow. "Didn't you come here to watch the band?"

He chuckled. "I came here to forget about the day job. The band will just be a bonus."

"That bad?" Ezra offered his sympathies.

Holden rubbed his temples. "It's just a lot of annoying administration stuff right now."

"Oh." Ezra's brow wrinkled. "I would have thought Mayor Mooney would be all over you guys about the murder."

"Oh, she is. But BCI is still lead on homicide cases until our department is fully trained and operational." Holden folded his arms with a smirk. "So she's Shroud's problem, not mine. At least for the meantime."

I swallowed back my burning questions concerning Lauren's interview. Holden hadn't even ordered a beer yet.

Our conversation turned to more mundane topics, like the weather and the chances of the Knicks making the NBA playoffs. Our apps were delivered, along with a Silver Staff Stout for Holden.

"Haven't had this one before." Holden raised his glass in cheers before taking a long sip of the dark brew. "Dare I say the taste is otherworldly?"

Like its moniker suggested, Cold Cauldron was dedicated to celebrating the supernatural. Fitz had decorated the walls with framed pages from books about witchcraft, mythology, the occult, voodoo...anything having to do with mysticism or magic. Our family's Glenmyre Opus would have made an excellent addition to the brewery's décor—if he ever learned about it. I wondered if Poppy was having trouble keeping her whim a secret from him. A topic for our next girl's night.

Ezra and I laughed at Holden's silly joke. I was glad to see my cousin in a good mood. He deserved a break after how hard he'd been working to get the police station up and running.

"Hey, guys!" Poppy appeared behind Holden's chair, her eyes going wide as she took in the appetizers lining the table. "Those look yummy." She licked her lips.

Glad to see that her headache must have subsided, I glanced over at the bar. Fitz was there, dishing out beers left and right. "Isn't your shift starting soon?"

Poppy rolled her eyes. "If you can believe it, I've already been shooed away. Apparently, my pouring technique is *disgraceful*." She plopped down on the chair next to me. "I think it's just because Fitz is a terrible teacher." Despite the harsh words coming from her, Poppy seemed in happy, bright spirits.

"Or did you realize you'd have more fun hanging out eating junk food with us and messed up your pours on purpose?" Holden lanced her with a narrowed stare.

Poppy opened and closed her mouth a few times before sticking her tongue out at him.

"Case closed." Ezra reached over and fist-bumped Holden.

Poppy finally found her voice. "Actually, I was more interested in your conversation with Lauren Johnson." She turned to me. "I assume you've filled in Lover Boy?"

"Lauren's the literary agent, right?" Ezra looked my way to confirm.

Holden gritted his teeth. "Jeez, you guys. What did I tell you about keeping this all under the radar?" He winced. "No offense, Ez."

"None taken." Ezra held up his hands. "I don't want any trouble from the chief of police."

Poppy nudged Holden's arm. "Oh, come on. Can't you tell us anything?"

"No."

I gulped at the curt response. "Drop it, Pops."

My aunt's right eye twitched as she studied our cousin. "Fine."

Holden tipped his chin at her concession, but his expression grew more on edge. "Oh, great."

I followed his steely gaze and was surprised to see Constance leaning against the bar. I hadn't seen her come in. I was about to call out her name and wave her over when I noted her strange demeanor. She nervously tapped on the counter, her head swiveling as she scanned the room. Her shoulders were hunched, and her long blonde hair was tucked under a Yankees cap. Not only that, but she had the sleeves of a baggy sweatshirt pulled down so far that only the tips of her fingers were visible. From here, I couldn't even see her bandaged hand. Constance was the epitome of incognito mode.

I elbowed Poppy and tilted my head in the direction of the bar. Understanding the need for stealth, my aunt innocently turned in her seat to stretch, allowing her to seek out Constance in the crowd.

"Uh-oh." Poppy's rosy cheeks had paled by the time she righted herself around.

She didn't have to say anything more. I knew what she meant. Constance's aura was giving her bad vibes.

Our friend had told us her chat with Declan had gone as well as could be expected. If that had been the case, why was Constance doing her best to be invisible among the brewery's patrons? I supposed she didn't want to be asked about her ties to Marjorie, and I couldn't blame her. I wouldn't want people asking me about my former houseguest's murder, either. But her mannerisms gave the impression of something much more unsettling. Constance seemed scared. Had she lied about the seriousness of her police interview to spare our feelings? Knots tightened in my stomach at the possibility that things were worse for Constance than we feared.

"Uh-oh, what?" Ezra, clueless to the silent communication happening between us Glenmyres, surveyed the area himself. "Hey, isn't that Constance? Should we ask her to join us?"

Holden cleared his throat abruptly. "I'm not sure that's a good idea."

Ezra's lips turned down, his expression one of confusion. "What? Why—oh. Probably not the best optics for our police chief to be seen having fried cheese with his top suspect."

"She's not *my* top suspect." Holden sounded a little defensive.

Poppy's eyebrows rose with intrigue, but she didn't follow up on the comment. "I would invite her, but she looks like she just wants to get out of here and go back home."

I nodded my understanding. That was Poppy-speak for *her aura told me so.*

"It's probably smart for her to keep a low profile, anyway," I added. "We don't need anyone else pointing the finger at her because she was seen arguing with Marjorie."

"It's more than that pesky quarrel, luv." Ezra's brow furrowed. "People saw them around town together. Folks here knew Constance had a visitor staying at her place. Even if she and Marjorie hadn't gotten into a fight, everyone would still be suspicious of her."

I took a long drink. *Great, Ez, way to make me feel better.*

We all watched as Constance collected the takeout bag Fitz handed her. She thanked him and pulled the hood of her sweatshirt over her hat. With her food tucked under her arm, Constance headed for the front door and disappeared out into the night.

"I feel so bad for her," Poppy murmured.

Not knowing what else to say, our table fell into contemplative silence as we munched on our appetizers. I'd send Constance a message later to check in on her. But for now, I trusted Poppy's aura reading that she wanted to be alone.

Our server came by to take our dinner order, and before long, the lights dimmed. Rose & Raven took the stage with youthful energy I hadn't been able to summon in years, and for the next fifty minutes, we vibed along to their upbeat set.

"We'll be back in ten, folks!" the lead vocalist and bassist announced as the lights came up.

"Need another refill to wash all that food down?" Fitz appeared at our table, balancing a tray of drinks on his shoulder.

Ezra bobbed his head as he swallowed a bite of his BBQ chicken tender entree. "Perfect timing." He gratefully accepted another beer.

Fitz doled out what was now our third round of drinks, handing the last glass to Poppy. "As you can see, this is how it's done, dear." He pointed to the thin layer of foam floating on top of her stout.

"Yeah, yeah, yeah." She batted him away but ended up grabbing his hand and squeezing it with loving affection.

He kissed her fingertips in return. "You guys excited for the Big Melt next weekend?" Fitz asked Holden, Ezra, and me.

Holden scratched his head in bemusement. "Crucible really seizes the chance to celebrate everything, doesn't it? Hard to believe this big ol' festival started because of some melting lake water."

"I heard the Finchmores are flying in a chef whose restaurant has *two* Michelin stars to serve on the judging panel." Ezra raised an eyebrow toward Fitz. "Are you ready?"

Fitz rolled his eyes. "Grant Finchmore and his fancy judge can't knock me off my game. I've got my eye on the prize." One of the more popular events during the festival was the Big Melt Off, a cooking competition. Contestants were tasked with creating the best-tasting melted sandwich, with the winner taking home a generous eight-thousand-dollar prize.

"He's so paranoid about someone stealing his idea, he won't even tell *me* what he's making." Poppy folded her arms with a huff.

"You might only be dating me to get the recipe," Fitz teased as he tickled her side.

I chuckled. "Talk about playing the long game."

Fitz spent a few more minutes at our table before scooting back to the bar. People milled around the room as the intermission stretched on, and I spotted a familiar, glamorous couple chatting a few tables over.

The twinkling overhead lights shimmered across Yvonne Finchmore's enviable blonde waves. Her skin was tanned from her family's recent trip to Turks and Caicos, and she looked happy for a change. Yvonne had a habit of being annoyed by everyone and everything around her. Why the heiress of a billion-dollar clean energy empire would view the world with such disdain was beyond me. But I could guess the reason for her smile tonight. She sat right next to Yvonne.

Blair Vanderfeld had been a close childhood friend of mine before our very different lives had forced us to grow apart. She'd attended a fancy private school and spent most of her adult life lighting up the NYC society pages. When she'd returned to Crucible a few years ago, there had been a lot of curious rumors swirling around Blair, and her unpleasant demeanor hadn't made it easy to be nice to her. However, the motive behind her move to Crucible had been anything but nefarious. She'd moved back home to be with her love. Ever since Blair and Yvonne had gone public with their romance, the two had become somewhat more endearing.

Yvonne caught me looking their way and wiggled her fingers in a minuscule wave. I smiled at the gesture. A year ago, she would have only given me one finger in particular.

To my further surprise, Yvonne tugged at Blair's elbow and pulled her toward our table. "Well, if it isn't the Glenmyres." She folded her arms as she assessed our group.

Throughout Crucible's history, our clan had done its best to get along with the Finchmores, and we considered ourselves the peacemakers among the five founding families. On the contrary, the Finchmores didn't really concern themselves with maintaining good relationships with the community, other than by opening their wallets and funding town projects.

"Hi, Ez." Yvonne's frosty exterior finally melted when her gaze landed on my boyfriend. Ezra had let Yvonne and Blair spend quality date time at The Poignant Page before the couple was ready to take their relationship public. "Everyone enjoying the band?"

Wondering where this uncharacteristic kindness was coming from, I answered hesitantly, "Yeah, they're really good."

"I'm representing them." Blair beamed as she tossed her luscious brunette curls over her shoulder. "This is their first paid gig."

Poppy's eyebrows raised, and she asked curiously, "Representing? Are you a talent manager now?"

Blair bobbed her head. "Music has always been a passion of mine, and with everything that happened with my dad…" She trailed off, her enthusiasm dimming.

My heart filled with sympathy. While Blair had never shared anything outright, the gossip over her fallout with her father had spread around town like head lice. Allister Vanderfeld hadn't taken the news about her relationship with Yvonne well. In a cruel, bigoted, and callous move, he'd cut her off from her trust fund.

"Well, I think you've made a great discovery." Ezra gave her a thumbs up.

I gave his thigh an affectionate squeeze under the table. Ezra had been a great support system for the couple. His own brother had come out to his parents when he was fifteen. Ezra's folks hadn't reacted kindly at first, and it'd taken them a long time to repair the damage they'd caused. Ezra being the kind of guy to give Yvonne and Blair a safe space to be themselves was just one of the many reasons why I fell in love with him.

Once the topic of the band had been exhausted, I searched for a new subject. "How was your family trip to Turks and Caicos?" I asked Yvonne.

Her smooth brow wrinkled. "I'd like to still be there."

"You guys aren't usually home so early," Poppy noted as she sipped her beer.

Yvonne shrugged. "Daddy thought it would be good for FPT to be more involved with the Big Melt planning, given that we are its major benefactors."

I stopped myself from rolling my eyes. Both at her elitist comment and at her clipped, frosty use of the word "Daddy."

"You mean for *Tobias* to be more involved with the planning," Poppy countered. "He's the one who's been showing up to all the event prep meetings." She would know, as she was a festival volunteer.

Yvonne brushed off her remark. "Daddy has been preoccupied with other matters."

"I bet. I heard Grant got ousted as boat club treasurer." Poppy looked like she was enjoying dropping truth bombs on the conversation.

I shot her a pleading glare to stop being so antagonistic. After the friendly way Yvonne and Blair had approached our table, my aunt's surly attitude didn't sit right with me. *What gives, Pops?*

Unaware of our silent exchange, Yvonne balled her fists at her sides. "As if. Daddy has a lot on his plate right now, so he *graciously* stepped down because he couldn't give the club finances the focus they deserve. He was the one who suggested *Charlie* take up the position in the first place." The seething emphasis that flew across her lips made her frustration evident.

Poppy's right eye gave a telling twitch. "How nice of him."

Blair patted Yvonne's back, trying to ease the tension in her girlfriend's shoulders. "Why don't we check on the band, Vonnie? It's almost time for them to go back on." She turned to our table, her smile a bit less genuine. "See ya around."

Once Yvonne and Blair disappeared into the crowd, I unleashed my disapproval on Poppy. "What was that about? Why'd you have to rile Yvonne up like that?" My bestie was usually the friendliest person around.

Poppy hunched forward, her voice lowered. The rest of us had to lean in to hear her. "Well, think about it. The Finchmores arrive back in town earlier than expected, and a woman turns up dead soon after? It's curious timing, that's all."

Holden frowned. "Curious or coincidental?"

"Yeah," I agreed. "How would the Finchmores even be connected to Marjorie?"

Poppy held up her hands defensively. "Hey, I'm just considering another angle."

I held her gaze, wondering what she'd seen in Yvonne's aura to send her down this obscure route. But the band's arrival onstage distracted us from the topic.

I listened to Rose & Raven for another half hour before my eyes grew droopy. It had been a long day, and thoughts of Marjorie's murder had kept me up the previous night.

Ezra squeezed my shoulder. "Ready to call it?"

I glanced at my watch. It wasn't even ten o'clock. "I'm such an old lady."

"Hey, mind your elders," Ezra playfully whispered in my ear. "Why don't I walk you to your car?"

I nodded, my hope for a romantic tryst snuffed out. It didn't seem like Ezra was up for an overnight. And based on how weird I'd been in the past about being intimate, I couldn't exactly blame him. The last time he'd tried removing my glasses for a more passionate kiss,

I'd yelped and jumped back, tripping over my coffee table in the process and scoring several bruises.

We said goodnight to Poppy and Holden, with promises to touch base in the morning. Hand in hand, Ezra and I strolled toward my SUV, enjoying the peaceful, quiet night.

As he opened my car door, he said, "I'll swing by A Wick in Time after three tomorrow once I close up shop. Got any ideas about how we should start retracing Marjorie's steps?"

I thought back to one of my earlier text conversations with Poppy. "Well, we know she spent some time at the library. Maybe we should start there and work our way back."

"Sounds like a plan. Until then, be careful." Ezra kissed me goodnight.

I didn't need reminding. Poppy and I may have been doing our best to keep our investigation quiet, but in a town like Crucible, secrets didn't stay buried for long.

Chapter 14

"Oh wow, this smells so fresh and bright." Quinn's eyes lit up as she inhaled my latest creation, Peace Lily Peony.

I smiled at her praise. "You like it?"

"I think that'll be a big seller," Quinn gushed. "I love this new floral line you're doing. It's got just the right balance."

I pressed one of Cora's handmade labels onto the glass jar. "It's tricky to get the fragrance right. A drop too much, and you get the wind knocked out of you."

Quinn giggled as she collected some other candles that were ready for the sales floor. "Wouldn't that be funny to see? Maybe you should do a line of gag gifts."

"I'd have to wear a hazmat suit while making them." I gave an exaggerated shudder. "How are things downstairs?"

"Busier than yesterday, surprisingly," Quinn replied as she gathered her crate full of inventory. "Is that normal for Sundays to have more foot traffic than Saturdays?"

"Only when a farmer's market is up at Crucible Commons." I pointed out the window facing the town's sprawling park. "Today's the first one of the year."

"How fun. I'll have to swing by and check it out." She sighed. "I know I sound like a broken record, but I'm so glad I moved here."

I smiled. "Me too. I'm happy you're happy, Quinn. You deserve a fresh start."

"Thanks, Hazel. You're the best."

Quinn headed downstairs to stock shelves before going on her lunch break, and I returned to applying labels to my Poppy's Patch collection. It had been a productive morning, and I'd been able to spend most of my time in the craft kitchen. Iggy and Quinn managed the steady stream of customers like seasoned pros, and I only had to come downstairs to help out while Iggy took his lunch.

My phone buzzed with a text from Poppy.

Can't join you for the library outing. Emergency FoC meeting re: Big Melt. One of the judges dropped out. Maggie is freaking, obvs.

I chuckled at the drama-laden message. I could practically hear Poppy's eyes rolling at Maggie Sherwin's antics. Maggie had appointed herself Poppy's rival back in high school, and, as the president of Friends of Crucible, she loved asserting her power over my aunt. The community volunteer group spearheaded the Big Melt festival and oversaw the event logistics.

Bummer. Your whim would be helpful. I quickly typed back. **Will keep you posted.**

Be careful, little niece.

I will. Promise.

I placed my phone back on the counter, a frown growing. Ezra and I would be at a severe disadvantage without Poppy's aura-reading abilities. Not that Ezra would know the difference. I sighed as I resumed my candle labeling. We'd have to rely on our good, old-fashioned sleuthing abilities.

I also hadn't heard from Constance today. I'd checked in on her after I got home last night, and she assured me she was doing fine. But my messages to her this morning had gone unanswered. I hoped she was okay.

By the time I finished applying the new labels, I saw on the closed-circuit feed that Quinn was back from her lunch break, carrying a cloth bag full of goodies she'd no doubt picked up at the farmer's market. I used the security video system to monitor the sales floor from upstairs in case Iggy or Quinn got overwhelmed and needed some extra help.

I headed down to join my friends. "Looks like a successful shopping trip," I concluded as I arrived at the register counter.

Quinn pulled out a jar of honey from a local bee farm. "Doesn't this look yummy? I can't wait to drizzle it on toast."

"Speaking of honey," Iggy began, "any chance you made some Sweet Green Tea candles recently? I think we'll need a new batch by week's end."

I nodded. "They're curing now. Should be ready by Friday." I used honey-scented oil to cut the bitterness of the green tea fragrance.

As Quinn showed us her other purchases, Iggy and I oohed and aahed appropriately. I hadn't been up to the farmer's market yet, and now, I wished I'd carved out time to stop by.

Customers milled in and out of the store as the afternoon wore on. Most were from out of town, but a few familiar faces graced us with a visit.

Philippa Tarling, the owner of Crucible's yoga studio, blew in like a radiant hurricane. "Hazel, I need your help. I left my compost bin in my office too long, and now my serene oasis smells like sour milk." She shuddered in horror. "I need to cleanse it, stat."

"Of course. Let's get you taken care of." I hurried to her side, directing her toward my Calm Seas display. The salted-ocean candle was designed to cut harsh smells without being overwhelming in its own right.

Philippa inhaled deeply as she held the candle up for examination. "Oh, yes. This will do nicely." She grabbed two more jars. "Now if only you had a candle to ward away bad juju."

"Bad juju?" I raised an eyebrow.

Philippa lowered her voice so as not to alert the other customers. "The murder that's all over town? When did Crucible become such a den of iniquity?"

I pressed my lips together, thinking it best not to respond. Instead, I occupied myself with straightening my Enlightening Eucalyptus display.

"I knew the poor woman, too." Philippa shook her head. "What a tragedy."

"Knew her?" I whipped my head in her direction, much too quickly for my glasses frames to catch up. They slid traitorously down the bridge of my nose, and before I could close my eyes to adjust them, Philippa's lifeclock glowed brightly over her head.

Twenty-two years, ninety-five days, three hours, sixteen minutes, four seconds, and counting.

A wave of sorrow and heart-wrenching pain assailed my senses. Oh, gosh. Philippa Tarling wouldn't make it to her sixty-fifth birthday. What could possibly extinguish this fit, vivacious forty-two-year-old woman so early in life? Tears pricked at my eyes, and I hurriedly blinked them away.

Philippa continued to chatter on, oblivious to the emotional storm raging within me. "Yes, Margie came by Peace of Mind for a few sessions last week. She confided in me that she had a lot of stress in her life and needed some tips on how to unwind. I knew the minute I saw her, she was in need of my expertise. I could just see the tension radiating from her. Her chakra was a mess."

I swallowed the suffocating lump in my throat. Poppy and I had often joked that Philippa's many career paths had given her the opportunity to live a bunch of lifetimes in one. Given the limited time she had left, that thought took on a more sobering tone now.

"Did she say why she was under so much stress?" I finally croaked out.

Philippa's brow wrinkled. "Margie said it was family drama, but she didn't elaborate from there." Her eyes widened as she let loose a sudden gasp. "You don't think it has to do with her death, do you?"

Still struggling to get that eerie lifeclock image out of my head, I puzzled over what Philippa had shared. Family drama? Hadn't Lauren and Holden both said Marjorie had no living family?

Philippa carried on, despite my lack of response. "Maybe I should have a talk with our hunky new chief of police about my interactions with Margie." Her tone turned oddly sultry. "Your cousin isn't dating anyone, is he?"

I choked at the personal change in topic. "U-um, not that I know of," I sputtered.

Philippa's lips curled into a smile. "You continue to make my day, Hazel."

My attention was thankfully diverted by another customer entering the shop. Tobias Sardolous had his cell phone pressed to his ear, his expression one of annoyance.

"All right, all right, Mom. I'm here. What did you want me to pick up again?" He listened momentarily, his dark gaze scanning the room before landing on me. "Got it. Okay, have fun with your knitting circle. Hey, Hazel," Tobias greeted me as he ended his call. "Hoping you can help. We've got a bit of a situation."

I excused myself from Philippa's side and glided toward Tobias. "Oh dear. What kind of a situation?"

"Mr. Finchmore has been asked to attend a banquet for the new hospital in Ithaca. A thank-you to the donors and such." Tobias waved his hand dismissively. "Since he's a table host, he has to provide a gift for everyone sitting with him. I've already compiled the goodie bag essentials, like an iPad, cashmere blanket, champagne, and Bose headphones, but suddenly, *Mrs.* Finchmore wants to add something more personal, more *local* to the mix. My mom suggested your candles to her, and Mrs. Finchmore jumped on the idea."

I blinked as Tobias rattled off his wild story. An iPad and Bose headphones? Goodie bag essentials? We ran in *very* different circles. "Well, is there a particular fragrance Mrs. Finchmore is leaning toward? Tula was in here yesterday to pick up gardenia candles for her."

"No, no, no." Tobias shook his head. "That will be too folksy for this crowd. How about something more luxurious? This is a *gala*."

Too folksy? I stifled a scoff and went back to the drawing board. "Well, you mentioned champagne in the gift bags..." I scooted over to my selection of Bubbly Bliss. "This is champagne and strawberry scented."

Tobias snapped his fingers in triumph. "Absolutely perfect. I'll take ten, please."

I gathered the candles and brought them to the register right as Iggy finished ringing up Philippa's purchases.

"May your day be filled with good vibes." Philippa beamed as Iggy handed her a shopping bag.

I tried to force a happy smile, her lifeclock reading still burned into my memory. "You too, Philippa."

Tobias arrived at the counter as the flighty yoga instructor waltzed out of the shop. "This is a great little establishment you've got going, by the way." He scanned the sales floor, clearly impressed. "I like what you've done with the place. Though I'll admit," he added with a blush, "I had more reason to come here back when Linus owned it."

I chuckled at his friendly banter. Before A Wick in Time, this space had housed Wizards of the Lake, where Linus Richards sold the Magic: The Gathering card game. "I haven't seen Linus around town for a few months." Since retiring, the gamer could often be found at Cold Cauldron. Fitz even let him host MTG tournaments every now and then.

"I think he goes to Florida for the winters now. He should be returning soon." Tobias glanced at his phone. "He's one of the vendors we have on the list for the Big Melt."

"Oh, right. Poppy mentioned you were involved with the festival this year."

He reached for the back of his neck. "Eh, I'm just acting more on behalf of the Finchmores." Tobias surveyed my shelves again. "Speaking of the Big Melt, I'm wondering if I could commission some of your candles as thank-you gifts for our volunteers."

I winced. The Big Melt began this coming Friday. To have candles fully cured for the volunteer goodie bags, I would've needed to start the order at least two days ago. "I'd love to help out, Tobias, but I'm afraid I couldn't have a batch ready in time." I then explained to him the week-long curing process.

Tobias waved away my reservations. "We're not going to give the gifts out until the end of the festival on Sunday, so the timing is actually perfect."

Perfect for who? I suppressed a frown.

"I'd happily pay you double for the trouble," Tobias offered with a blasé shrug. As if money could solve the issue—although, for people like the Finchmores, it usually did. "Or, if you'd rather, the Big Melt Festival committee could donate to a charity in A Wick in Time's honor?"

Curses. I couldn't pass on the chance to help an organization in need. Silver Linings, the rescue where I'd adopted Berg and Noli, jumped to the forefront of my mind.

From the calculated grin on his face, Tobias knew he'd made an offer I couldn't refuse.

"How many do you need?" I sighed in resignation.

Tobias smacked his palms together. "Excellent. Glad to have you on board." He hurried over to a display shelf and picked up one of my smaller, six-ounce candles. "Forty of this size would be perfect. And don't worry about labels or anything. The festival committee will take care of that."

I jotted down the tall order. "Do you have a scent preference?"

"Something spring-like. Flowers, maybe honeysuckle."

I mentally began to tally my workload. "I'll have them ready by next Sunday."

"Great, thank you."

I noted that Tobias's gratitude didn't quite reach his eyes. I suppose, as Grant Finchmore's right-hand man, he was used to getting what he wanted.

I left Iggy and Quinn to manage the downstairs while I hurried up to my craft kitchen to begin melting two hundred and forty ounces of coconut wax to serve as the base for the honeysuckle candles.

I checked my watch as I fired up my six-range stove. There was no way I'd be done by the time Ezra and I were supposed to go to the library.

I sent him a text. **Huge candle order for the Big Melt just came in…gonna take me a while to get them all poured.**

A response from Ezra buzzed a few minutes later. **Want another set of hands?**

I smiled at his thoughtfulness. Even with Ezra's help, we still wouldn't make it to the Sherwin Memorial Library by closing. **Thank you for the offer but you should enjoy your afternoon off!** With a sigh, I dropped my phone into the pocket of my apron and got to work.

The first batch of coconut wax had just smoothed into a silky wax soup when a *rat-tat-tat* sounded against the hallway door.

Neither Iggy nor Quinn ever knocked, and I could see them both downstairs on the closed-circuit video feed. "Who is it?" My voice warbled with hesitation, suddenly afraid of who might be on the other side. Had word gotten out that Poppy and I were on another case? Had Marjorie's killer come to silence me?

Chapter 15

"Surprise." Ezra peeked into the room, the sight of his wild dark hair putting me at immediate ease.

Hexes, Hazel. Paranoid much? "Hey!" I quickly recovered from my flurry of panic. "What are you doing here?"

"Well, you said I should enjoy my afternoon off," Ezra said as he came around to give me a one-armed hug, "so obviously, that means spending it with you."

Giddy butterflies danced in my stomach. "Well, that's the sweetest thing I've ever heard."

"It took me the entire walk here to think of it." He chuckled as he peered into one of the double boilers I had going. "Where'd this mega order come from?"

I explained how A Wick in Time had come to be involved in the Big Melt.

"Yikes. We'd better get cooking, then." Ezra offered to stir the wax while I set out the first round of glass jars and prepared their wicks.

I kept the cotton wicks upright with small wooden dowels. "It would've been nice if Tobias hadn't dropped this in my lap so last minute. I really wanted to check the library today."

"Anything else pop up in the case?" Ezra asked.

I shook my head. "And we have so little to go on as it is," I admitted before remembering my earlier encounter with the town yogi. "Well, actually, Philippa Tarling mentioned something that struck me as odd when she was here. She said Marjorie had attended a few of her classes last week, talking about how she was stressed from family drama."

Ezra's brow furrowed. "I thought Marjorie didn't have any family."

"Same. So what family drama could she have been talking about?" I murmured, concentrating on making sure the wicks were perfectly centered. As I did so, the latter part of Holden's whim reading bulldozed its way into my thoughts. *Stop. Please, someone help me. I need to find—*

In the moments before her death, Marjorie had been thinking she needed to find something or someone. Was she searching for something related to the Zellers? Or was I reading too much into things, and she was just begging for help against her unknown attacker?

Unable to share what I was thinking with Ezra, I focused on the crafting work at hand.

It was nearly five when Ezra and I placed the last of the Big Melt volunteer candles on their shelves to cure. I'd let Tobias know he could swing by next Sunday to collect them.

"They smell great." Ezra inhaled the wafting aroma of honeysuckle and sage that permeated the air.

I dusted off my hands. "They look great, too." I patted Ezra proudly on the back. He'd done an admirable job pouring with a steady hand.

He swiped his arm across his forehead. "That was quite the unexpected workout. Requires more upper body strength than I possess."

I giggled at his self-deprecating humor. "Why don't I treat you to dinner as a thank you after I close the shop?"

"I won't say no to that."

At five-fifteen, I locked the front door, waving as Iggy and Quinn set off to enjoy the beginning of their "weekend." With the store closed on Mondays and Tuesdays, our precious free time had commenced.

Hand in hand, Ezra and I strolled toward Herb Garden to grab ingredients for chicken enchiladas.

Ezra's phone hummed in his pocket. He quickly dug it out. "Hmm, it's my brother." His frown grew. "Let me take this real quick."

I bobbed my head, hoping everything was all right.

"Hey, Caius, what's—whoa, hold on, little bro. What's the matter? Are you okay?"

Ezra's tense questions had my heart racing. However, his stance soon relaxed, and his expression softened. "Caius got dumped," he whispered to me softly. Into the speaker, he said, "Take a deep breath, will you? Or you're gonna pass out and hurt yourself. No guy is worth going to the ER for." Ezra glanced up and down the sidewalk as he gnawed his lower lip.

I, too, surveyed the area. Rosewood Lane was relatively quiet on a Sunday evening, but there were a few pedestrians out and about.

"Yes, yes, of course. Hold on, I'm with Hazel. Yeah, sure thing." Ezra pressed the mute button. "Caius says hello, or at least I think that's what came through his blubbering. Sorry to bail on dinner, luv, but—"

"Go comfort your brother." I squeezed my boyfriend's arm, wordlessly telling him I understood.

He kissed my cheek. "Let's hit up the library tomorrow morning, okay?"

"What about your shop?" While Ezra was in the market for another employee, he didn't have one to run the shop in his absence.

His face grew flushed. "Ah, darn. I'd meant for this to be a surprise. I'm officially adjusting my hours so that I'm closed on Mondays." He brushed a finger against my cheek.

I understood what he'd left unspoken. Ezra was making big changes to his professional life so we could spend more time together. It showed just how much I meant to him.

"I'll see you tomorrow then." I kissed him, already wishing for Monday. "Tell Caius I'm sending him hugs." While I'd yet to meet the twenty-six-year-old graphic and web designer in person, I'd been introduced to him via FaceTime calls numerous times.

Ezra waved and hurried in the direction of his home while I continued toward Herb Garden. I still needed to feed myself, so instead of enchiladas, I opted to get ingredients for a homemade taco bowl, my go-to.

Herb Garden had several shoppers milling about its aisles. The old converted monitor barn offered a wide variety of fresh produce and cooking essentials. I gathered my items and headed for the checkout counter, where Kit Peakes greeted me.

"Hi, Hazel."

"Hiya, Kit."

"Nice to see you." He tipped his Herb Garden baseball cap before he began scanning my items. Kit had worked at the market for several years now and bagged everything with speedy efficiency. "Heard about that nasty scene outside your house on Friday."

I did my best not to snicker. Besides knowing nearly everything about Mammie's store, Kit had also picked up his boss's love for gossip while working here. "Terrible." I decided to keep my contribution to the rumor mill to a minimum.

"Did you know Margie?"

His use of her nickname surprised me. "Not really." I narrowed my gaze at him. "Did *you*?"

Kit shrugged. "Saw her a few times at Roadside Station. Got to chatting with her."

Roadside Station? What had Marjorie been doing at Sterling Ildrich's grimy dive bar in neighboring Hyssop Falls?

I evaluated Kit as he bagged my ground beef. He couldn't be older than thirty-seven, if that, but he was a tall, white guy with very light blond hair. The description of the mysterious visitor looking for Marjorie at Waking Woods entered my mind. Had the Canadians mistakenly assumed Kit's leathered skin was a sign of age rather than the result of cigarette smoking?

I decided to pursue my fledgling hunch. "I can't believe someone killed her. It's not like she had any ties to the area, right?"

Kit tapped his cashier screen to finalize my order. "Dunno about that. For someone not familiar with the area, I saw her at some pretty random places. Roadside Station, Field & Farm, the town hall…"

I frowned at the odd collection of local establishments. Was Marjorie researching something for her next book? "Did you know where she was staying?"

"She told me she *was* staying with that author friend of yours before getting tossed out." Kit eyed me, and from his snarky tone, it sounded as though he wanted to add a rather unpleasant adjective before "author friend."

Anxiety brewed in the back of my mind. I'd never heard anyone speak about Constance with such malice before. If others in town felt this way, no wonder she'd gone incognito at Cold Cauldron last night. "Why was Marjorie still in the area, then?" I asked as I paid with Apple Pay.

Kit shrugged. "She told me she had some unfinished business to resolve." He handed me my receipt.

Unfinished business…regarding her book? Was Marjorie worried Constance would out her for plagiarism? Or did this have to do with the family drama she'd mentioned to Philippa?

"Sounds like you two got pretty close." I knew my time for questions was rapidly drawing to an end.

"Nah, just blowing off steam together at Roadside."

I nodded, wondering if those drinking sessions had led back to Marjorie's cabin. Kit might have been a little rough around the edges, but he was an attractive enough guy. "Well, whatever the case, it's gotta be hard, knowing what happened to her. I'm sorry." I gathered my grocery bags and offered a sympathetic smile. "Take care of yourself, Kit."

He waved me off, his cheeks going a bit pink. *Curses*, I wished Poppy had been here to get a reading on him, because he certainly seemed more affected by Marjorie's death than he let on.

As I lugged my provisions to my SUV, I mulled over the intel Kit had shared. Roadside Station and Field & Farm were not exactly renowned tourist destinations. How had they even gotten on Marjorie's radar?

Maybe it was worth taking a drive over to Roadside Station and having a chat with Sterling. Sterling Ildrich, a locally infamous member of the Ildrich clan, didn't get along well with his influential family. According to stories told by my mom, Sterling had gotten himself into quite a bit of trouble in high school—outside Crucible's borders, of course—and became exasperated with his family's meddling attempts to control his life. By the time he was twenty, he'd moved away and into self-imposed exile. Sterling hadn't strayed too far, however. He lived and worked in Hyssop Falls, one of our neighboring towns.

Just as I reached my SUV, I reconsidered the idea of going on my own. Given its history of drunken brawls and dustups, Roadside Station was the type of place that warranted having backup.

An apprehensive thought entered my mind. *I wonder if Marjorie learned that the hard way.*

Chapter 16

Ezra was waiting for me outside his apartment when I pulled up to the duplex at ten o'clock the next morning.

"How's Caius?" I asked after he kissed me.

Ezra grimaced. "Poor guy is taking it hard. He thought Deleon was the one."

"Aww, that's too bad." I couldn't imagine the kind of heartbreak Caius was feeling. I'd always severed ties with relationships before they got too deep. That is, until I met Ezra.

"I told him to come up for a visit to take his mind off things." Ezra loosened his plaid scarf since the SUV's heat was on full blast. "He made a fuss, saying he couldn't bear to leave the city, but I think he'll eventually cave."

"I hope so. I'd love to meet him in person." We then chatted about my animals and how good it felt to sleep in on a Monday when everyone else was off to work.

Ezra stretched his arms. "Is Poppy going to be joining us for our sleuthing adventure?" he asked, switching to the task at hand.

I shook my head. "She wanted to, believe me. But she's got too much planting work to get done before the Big Melt. March and April are the busiest time of year for her, getting bulbs situated in her greenhouse and then transplanting them outside once the weather warms up." I shot him a coy smile. "So, you have me all to yourself."

"Music to my ears." Ezra grinned.

We pulled into the Sherwin Memorial Library parking lot a few minutes later. Only a handful of cars peppered the gravel, indicating there wouldn't be too many patrons milling about.

"How do we play this?" Ezra's brow wrinkled with sudden worry. "If we go in there questions blazing, won't that raise suspicion?"

"There's a fine line between gauging the rumor mill and investigating a murder." I chuckled as I gathered my bag. "If we're lucky, Janet Gibs will be the librarian on duty and ready to spill what she knows."

"But won't she think it odd we're just showing up to chat?" Ezra asked as we climbed out of my car.

I patted the side of my tote bag. "As if I wouldn't come prepared. I've got books to return, silly."

Ezra jokingly slapped his forehead. "I forgot I was dealing with a seasoned investigator."

Arm in arm, we entered the stately library, a hush falling over us. I scanned the spacious first floor, my gaze skimming the various displays and bookshelves before landing on the circulation desk. My heart plummeted at seeing Miles Lolliman behind the counter. Not because Miles was a bad guy or anything. He just wasn't as tapped into the Crucible grapevine as the affable Janet.

I scrambled to devise a plan that might help loosen Miles's tongue. He'd been a grade above me in school, but I honestly had more in common with his grandmother, Dottie Lolliman, than I did with the extroverted, athletic Miles. Other than a love of books, I supposed. He did make for an enigma of a librarian.

"I got this," Ezra whispered in my ear before saying, "Hey, bud. I didn't know you were working today." My boyfriend broke out in a big grin as he sauntered toward the front desk.

Miles glanced up from his computer monitor, his pale, bespeckled face morphing instantly from solemn to goofy. "Hey, Ez. What brings you into the enemy's lair?"

Ezra chuckled at his teasing. Bookstores versus libraries. A tale as old as time. "The only person who could." He motioned to me. "My lady."

Stunned by the bromance on display, I managed a sheepish wave in Miles's direction. "Hi, I have some books to return."

He held out his palms. "Hit me with 'em."

As I dug out the stack of romance novels I'd taken home with me during my last library visit, I shot Ezra a questioning glance.

He instinctively read my mind. "Miles is one of my pickleball pals." Ezra had taken up the popular sport last fall and played regularly at the town rec center.

"Our duo name is Returns & Receipts." The librarian chuckled as he began scanning my books.

I smiled at the pun. "How clever." With Miles's attention diverted by work, I elbowed Ezra in the side with a "the ball's in your court" look.

He took the hint and leaned casually against the counter. "So, you covering for someone today?"

"Nah, bro. I finally got a new schedule." Miles put his hands together like he was praising a higher power. "Janet's daughter broke her leg—bad news, I know, I know—so Janet needed to give up most of her weekday hours to help care for her grandkids."

I frowned at the giddy way he reveled in someone else's misfortune.

Ezra snorted. "You sound real torn up."

"Hey, you know how long I've been asking to move off weekends." Miles ran a hand through his shaggy, ash-brown curls. "Now I can actually have a social life."

"Watch out, ladies." Ezra released a low whistle.

Miles turned to me. "You got any single gal pals, Hazel? Poppy still dating Fitz?"

"They're going strong." I smiled apologetically. "I'm afraid I can't help you on that front."

"Hmm, what about Constance Crane?" Miles prodded. "You seem tight with her. She's a total babe. Could you put in a good word?"

Well, at least he doesn't think she's a killer, I thought with relief.

"Although," Miles continued, "I guess she's got a bit of a scarlet letter on her at the moment. Probably should steer clear of that trainwreck."

Those feelings of brief relief came crashing down.

"Scarlet letter?" Ezra frowned. "What do you mean?"

Miles stared at him like he'd sprouted another head. "Where've you been, dude? Constance and that murdered girl got *into* it." He almost sounded entertained by the whole incident. "Happened right here."

"Were you working on Friday?" I asked.

Miles nodded. "I was the one who asked them to take their catfight outside."

"What the heck happened?" Ezra scratched at his dark, tousled hair. "I mean, it's not every day a world-renowned author gets into a brawl right before your eyes."

I winced at the garish way in which Ezra posed the question, but I had to admit, it got results.

"I know, right? So surreal." Miles shook his head in disbelief. "I didn't even know Constance was in the building, to be honest. Margie came in and was doing some research when Constance exploded on her out of nowhere."

Margie? *Interesting.* Even Miles was familiar enough with our victim to know her by a nickname. "Did you hear what they were quarreling about?"

"At first, they kept it pretty hush-hush because, duh, library, but I could totally tell they were arguing. Then Constance called Margie a backstabbing you-know-what, and that's when I stepped in." Miles swelled with importance. "Wish I didn't have to be the responsible one, though. I would've loved to know what was going on. I mean, what could a veteran writer like Constance have against a newbie like Margie?"

"Margie's the woman who was killed, right?" Ezra played coy. "Sounds like you got close with her."

Miles shrugged. "I knew her for, like, a week or so. She said she was a soon-to-be-published author and wanted to do some research in our archives. It was just a bonus she was cute and friendly."

"Not to mention, her book has been gaining traction online.

Totally buzzworthy," I pointed out. "Was she here researching her next novel or something?"

"I honestly didn't know she was a fiction writer until I read about her death online." Miles's cheeks grew pink. "If anything, I assumed from her work she was some type of historian or genealogist."

I scrunched my nose at his surprising observation. Genealogist?

"What was she researching?" Ezra asked, skillfully trading off our covert interrogation.

Miles snorted. "The term 'research' might be a stretch. She was looking at old Lake Valley yearbooks."

Ezra and I shared confused looks. What in hexes did Marjorie Zeller want with our local high school yearbook?

Miles must have noted our reaction, for his pale blue gaze narrowed. "Why all the questions, you two?"

I'd already prepared an answer to use on Janet. I hoped it worked on Miles. "She died right outside my house. I can't help being a little curious about what the woman was doing here in Crucible."

"Wow." Miles's eyes doubled in size. "Way to sugarcoat it, Hazel."

"Sorry." I shrugged. "Inquiring minds want to know."

"I see." He nodded thoughtfully.

Ezra cleared his throat. "We on for Thursday night?" he asked about what I assumed to be an upcoming pickleball match.

"Can we push the game until eight?" Miles pointed to the small sandwich board sign propped next to his computer that displayed the library hours. "I'm now on the clock until seven."

Ezra checked his phone. "Sure, no problem. Hazel, you wanted to check the stacks for that new thriller, right?"

I was about to respond with, "What new thriller?" when I caught the twinkling glint in Ezra's eyes. "Yeah, you bet. Thanks, Miles." I waved and pulled Ezra away from the desk, pretending I needed to hang onto my boyfriend to function.

Once we put a few shelves between us and the chatty librarian, I whispered, "Quick thinking there, changing the subject. Miles was getting suspicious about our questions."

"Yeah, he might not always act like it, but he's a pretty astute guy," Ezra muttered. "Wish we could have asked him more about who else was in the library around the time of the argument."

"There might be a way..." I paused, digging my phone out of my bag.

Ezra leaned over my shoulder to check my screen. "The library events page?"

"I'm seeing if any groups might have met here Friday afternoon during Constance and Marjorie's fight." The library's community rooms were free resources for local clubs to use.

I scanned the website for info, surprised by how many clubs routinely booked time in the rooms. "Looks like both the Crucible Crocheters and the Puzzle People were both here until five thirty."

"Puzzle People?"

I giggled at Ezra's confusion. "Seems clear enough to me what they do." My amusement faded as I continued to study the two club names. "I've heard about the Crocheters before, but I have no idea who their members are."

Ezra was already on his phone. "Looks like they have a private Facebook group. I can't tell who's involved without joining."

I checked my own social media. "Same with the Puzzle People." *Hexes.*

Ezra folded his arms. "The community rooms are all the way in the back. We can't be sure anyone using them even heard the argument." He eyed me warily. "If someone followed Marjorie from the library, they would have been out in the main area, keeping tabs on her."

He made a valid point. What's more, the Puzzle People and Crucible Crocheters were both in session until five-thirty. According to Holden's whim reading, Marjorie was attacked at five twenty-six, so it would've been impossible for a member to be involved. "What do we do now?"

At my question, Ezra cocked an eyebrow. "Might be worth checking out what Marjorie was researching."

My pulse raced at the brilliant suggestion. "Any idea where high school yearbooks are kept?"

He craned his neck around and pointed to a sign hanging a few aisles away. "Town records. Sounds promising."

I led him forward by the hand. Maybe Marjorie had left a clue behind in her research. "Let's just make sure Miles doesn't see us. That would definitely raise more questions we don't want to answer."

Luck must have been on our side, for I heard the front doors slide open, accompanied by a windfall of footsteps.

"Ladies," came Miles's suave greeting, "how is my favorite crossword group doing today?"

A chorus of cooing women floated through the aisle. "Oh, Miles. Always the charmer," one said with a giggle.

"That must be the Wordplayers." Ezra looked like he might break out into laughter himself. "Miles was telling me about them last week at the rec. It's a group of septuagenarian women who come to do their crosswords together. He thinks they come to flirt with him."

I recalled seeing them listed on the community room schedule. "Let's hope he's right." I tugged my boyfriend down another aisle, putting as much distance between us and the circulation desk as possible. "We could use the distraction."

We heard Miles shush the Wordplayers multiple times as we neared the Town Records area, but the ladies' chatter kept echoing throughout the large space. It didn't sound like they were eager to leave the front desk. Maybe they were here to flirt with him after all.

Grateful for the cover, I stopped before a huge bookshelf containing the classic teal and white spines of the Lake Valley High School yearbooks. The high school served five communities, including Crucible, and was a few towns over. "Here we are."

Ezra let loose a cursing exhale. "Yikes. How are we ever supposed to figure out which ones Marjorie might have been using?"

"Good question." My brow furrowed. We had no idea what period Marjorie had been focusing on. There had to be at least eighty years of history on these shelves. How could we narrow it down? It wasn't as though the spine was more worn on one particular tome, and the shelves had recently been dusted, so nothing seemed like it had been disturbed.

Ezra, who had several inches on me, stood on his tiptoes. "Hey, what's this?" He reached for the shelf that contained yearbooks from the seventies and eighties and slid one volume out from the stacks. As he brought it down to eye level, I noticed what must have caught his attention.

"It's got a bookmark in it." My body thrummed with anticipation as I stared at the wide piece of paper sticking out from the top of the yearbook.

Ezra handed it to me. "You do the honors. But don't get your hopes up too high, Hazel. This could've been left by someone else."

While his reminder could very well be true, I also doubted the yearbooks section was a high-trafficked area of the library. Turning so he could see over my shoulder, I cracked open the spine.

The bookmark, which turned out to be an old photo, slid down a glossy page filled with headshots of smiling students. The year's graduates.

I examined the aged, blurry photo. The warm, beige hue wasn't an Instagram filter. It had been brought on by time. "This wasn't taken with a digital camera, that's for sure." I gently picked up the Polaroid pic to study it further.

The image captured what looked to be an outdoor event. A group of young adults, possibly teens, gathered around a picnic table. Two boys looked like they were wrestling each other, while one of the girls laughed at their antics. The other, darker-haired girl stood with folded arms, not looking as amused. Beside her, another young man hunched over a bucket of beers sitting on the table while an attractive couple ignored everyone else and posed for the camera. They looked very glamorous with their dark shades and yacht-like attire.

"Who are these people?" Ezra murmured as he inched his nose closer to the photo.

I flipped it over to see if the back contained any hints. My pulse raced as I tried to decipher the looping handwriting smudged in the corner. *"Senior Year Summer…showboat—no, Blowout with the Crew."*

I turned back to the front. "Looks like a great group of friends."

"But what does this have to do with Marjorie, if anything?" Ezra raised an eyebrow.

I gnawed on my lower lip, unsure. I studied the yearbook pages the photo had bookmarked, surprised to find a thin, pink sticker tag wedged in the binding. "What's this?" I gently handed the Polaroid over to Ezra before reaching for the tag. However, just before I removed it, I noted how it perfectly underlined the name of one of the LVHS seniors: Joshua Sherwin.

Joshua Sherwin? The first name didn't ring a bell, but something about the friendly smile and warm eyes struck me as familiar.

"Hey, don't these two look similar?" Ezra suddenly exclaimed in a low hush. He pointed to the guy shielding the bucket of beer bottles in the old Polaroid and then to Joshua's yearbook headshot.

The weathered photo made it hard to see the details of everyone's face, but the wavy haircuts both boys had did resemble each other. But that wasn't why Joshua's yearbook photo struck a chord in me.

"Call me crazy, but doesn't this kid remind you of a young Jared Sherwin?" Jared worked at one of the many family businesses the Sherwins owned in town. As one of Crucible's founding clans, the Sherwins had, over the centuries, excelled in cultivating the land, as was made evident by the numerous farms the family maintained up to this very day. Jared, though, managed the local agricultural store, Field & Farm.

Ezra tilted his head as he examined the images. "I guess so. Who's Joshua? His dad?"

"Nah, the dates don't match up." I wracked my brain for any memory of the name Joshua but couldn't find one.

Ezra held the Polaroid up to the overhead light. "The other people in this shot must be in the yearbook then."

I began to flip through the senior class pictures. "But what does this have to do with Marjorie?" I mumbled but stopped myself from saying anything further as another flash of pink caught my eye. "Here's another kid flagged."

Despite the black-and-white photo, I could tell this guy had blond hair, pale skin, and light-colored eyes. I didn't need to read the text beneath to know who it was.

Sterling Ildrich.

I cross-referenced the Polaroid, spotting blond hair on one of the wrestlers. Despite the grainy nature of the image, the shape of the young guy's chin sure looked an awful lot like Sterling's square jaw.

"So, we've got Joshua Sherwin and Sterling Ildrich...is anyone else marked?" Ezra tapped on the yearbook.

I thumbed through the pages, my pulse racing. When I'd attended Lake Valley High School, there'd been about three thousand students in total, with the graduating class capping at seven hundred and fifty. If this particular year was similar, we had a lot of pages to scan.

I could feel Ezra bouncing with impatience as page after page went by without any telltale sticky tags. As I reached the students with last names beginning with Y, I began to wonder if we were even on the right track. What was to say these tags or even this photo had been left by Marjorie?

My heart leaped into my throat as I flipped the page and another pink Post-it marker caught my eye. The student it flagged had me sucking in a stunned breath.

"*Jane Zeller*?" Ezra's palm gripped my shoulder with tense excitement. "Now we're getting somewhere!"

Indeed, any thoughts about coincidences vanished in the blink of an eye. Jane Zeller. Marjorie Zeller. There *had* to be a connection.

I placed the Polaroid next to Jane's photo. She'd been a pretty girl with curly brown hair and a great smile. A smile that matched the young woman laughing at the two wrestlers in the *Summer Blowout* shot. "What are we thinking? This could be Marjorie's mom, right?"

Ezra nodded. "Or another relative. I know you've mentioned she didn't have any family, but what if Marjorie was on the search to locate some?"

I considered the possibility. After all, Holden had done the same thing after the death of his mom, which was how he'd found his way into our lives. "Whatever the case, it looks like Marjorie came to Crucible with an ulterior motive." But if that was really the case, why had she kept her ties to the town a secret from Constance?

I held the Polaroid for closer inspection. Without the yearbook picture references, I would never have been able to decode who these individuals were based on the poor photo quality. Why had Marjorie cared about the other people in this old Polaroid so much? Had she hoped they could give her information about Jane Zeller?

The conversation I had with Kit Peakes last night suddenly came to mind. He said he'd run into Marjorie at the town hall, Roadside Station, and Field & Farm. Roadside Station, which Sterling Ildrich owned, and Field & Farm, a Sherwin family business. She must have been searching for answers. To what questions, I didn't yet know.

"I think we need to have a chat with Jared Sherwin." I glanced toward Ezra, a plan forming. "Maybe he can tell us who Joshua is and why Marjorie stopped by his store." I closed the yearbook and slid it back onto the shelf. Whoever the other four people in the Polaroid were, they weren't marked among the Lake Valley graduates.

Ezra raised an eyebrow as I dug my tablet out of my tote bag and slipped the Polaroid into its protective case. "Shouldn't we give that photo to Holden?"

I winced at his beseeching reminder. "Yes, you're probably right." As I took out my phone to text my cousin, a harsh reflection outside the nearest window caught my attention. My gaze shifted, and I was surprised to find the chief of police's SUV pulling into a library parking spot. A second later, Holden stepped down from the driver's side, accompanied by Detective Shroud.

I swallowed. What were they doing here?

I pointed to the scene out the window. "Looks like we can do curbside service." I tried to smile, but my nerves got the better of me. Holden already knew I was meddling in his investigation, but how was I going to explain away our findings to Declan?

Ezra's lips pressed into a thin line. "Why don't we see what they're doing here first?"

Relieved by his coy suggestion, I led the way toward the front of the library, careful to keep out of view. Luckily, the bookshelves provided us with the perfect cover.

Holden and Declan soon sauntered across the threshold, momentarily examining their surroundings before heading for the circulation desk.

"Mr. Miles Lolliman?" Declan began, his tone full of authority.

From our hiding spot, I saw Miles cower a bit, even though he had several inches on Declan. "Y-yes? Can I help you?"

"I'm Detective Shroud with the New York Bureau of Criminal Investigation. I'm sure you're familiar with Chief Whitfield. We have a few questions about your relationship with Marjorie Zeller."

Ezra and I turned to each other, wide-eyed. *Relationship?* Miles had certainly failed to mention *that*.

Chapter 17

"Whoa, Detective." Through the breaks in the stacks, I could see Miles holding his hands up defensively. "Relationship? I don't know what you're talking about."

Holden folded his arms, his expression stern. "Miles, I'd suggest you cooperate with us. Otherwise, we'll have to take this conversation back to the station."

"But Hold—Chief, I wasn't in a relationship with Margie Zeller. I barely knew the woman."

Declan reached into his suit and extracted a folded piece of paper. "Then care to explain these text messages? That is your number at the top, is it not?"

Miles grabbed the paper and read it. "Whoa, okay, fellas, you've got this all wrong."

"You sure about that?" Declan yanked the sheet from Miles's grasp and pointed. "'Can I come over now' seems fairly suggestive. Especially since Ms. Zeller texted you this numerous times during her stay in Crucible."

The librarian winced. "I get what it looks like out of context, but I swear, Margie was just texting me to see if the coast was clear here at the library."

"Why?" Holden pressed.

Miles ran a hand nervously through his curls. "Margie didn't want to run into her pal Constance Crane. They had a falling out, and Margie didn't want to cross paths with her. I guess Margie discovered Constance has been using our library to work on her edits, so she asked if she could get my number and check whether Constance was here or not."

My stomach curdled at how damning Miles's explanation sounded. Margie was so afraid of running into Constance that she texted the librarian on duty?

Declan's eyebrows rose as he glanced at Holden. I didn't need Poppy's whim to tell me he was simmering with suspicion.

"If that's the case," Holden began, his words drawn out and slow, "why did you tell Ms. Zeller she was free to come over on Friday if Constance was already working here?" He pointed to the paper, which must have been a record of Miles's response.

The librarian's cheeks grew even more flushed. "I honestly didn't know about Constance. She must have come in without me realizing. We had a children's story time event that afternoon, and it gets kinda crazy in here, what with all the community groups in the building. I swear, I didn't intend to mislead Margie."

Holden let his words linger in the air before asking, "When did you last see Ms. Zeller?"

Miles glanced over his shoulder, his gaze going to the clock on the wall behind him. "She stormed out of here shortly after she returned from their altercation outside. So, around five? She looked pretty shook up, too. Her workspace was a total mess. Usually, Margie put back the reference books she borrowed, but on Friday, she left them strewn all over the table. I had to get one of our volunteers to put them all back."

I shot Ezra a knowing look. If Marjorie had been frazzled by her encounter with Constance, it explained how the Polaroid of Jane Zeller had come to be left behind.

"Did you see her leave the premises?" Declan spoke up.

Miles shook his head. "I saw her go outside, but it's not like I watched her get into her car and drive off."

Holden scanned the cavernous library. "Do you have security camera footage we can review?"

Miles gulped. "That's above my pay grade, Chief. You'd have to ask our library director. But I'm pretty sure the footage overwrites itself every forty-eight hours."

"Figures." Declan's fist balled on the top of the circulation desk. "We should've moved quicker on this."

Holden patted him on the shoulder. "I'll give Rebecca a call and see if we can track anything down. We might get a lucky break." To Miles, he said, "Anything else you can tell us about Ms. Zeller? Do you know what she was researching here at the library?"

"Sorry, Chief. Not really." Miles motioned in our direction. "She spent a lot of time in town records, looking up yearbooks and old newspapers and such."

Old newspapers, huh? Miles hadn't mentioned that to us, either.

"I see." A tight smile spread across Holden's lips. "Well, thank you, Miles. If you think of anything else that might be helpful in our investigation, please reach out to Detective Shroud or give the station a call."

Declan slid a business card toward Miles as Holden spoke.

"Um, okay." Miles picked up the detective's contact info as if it were covered in germs.

Holden tipped the brim of his baseball cap and followed Declan as he stormed outside. Ezra and I didn't move from our hiding spot until the two got into Holden's SUV and drove off.

"What now?" Ezra murmured, his expression a mask of unease.

Anxiety boiled within me, too. The conversation we'd overheard hadn't painted Constance in a flattering light from an investigative standpoint. "We need to give Holden Marjorie's Polaroid."

Ezra glanced at his watch. "Want to head over to the station and then grab some lunch?"

"Sure." I threaded my fingers through his and stepped out from behind the shelf into Miles's line of sight. However, the poor guy was hunched over his desk, looking so shell-shocked that he didn't even acknowledge us as we left through the sliding door.

Ezra leaned close to whisper, "I'll see if I can get him to open up more during our Thursday game. Kinda weird Miles didn't mention the texting thing to us."

I bobbed my head in agreement. "She sure got close to him fast." I remembered Kit's comments about Marjorie and the time they had spent together. Perhaps she was just a much friendlier person than I was and warmed up to people quickly.

But if that were the case, why all the subterfuge about her reasons for being in Crucible? What was she hiding, other than the fact that she'd stolen her friend's manuscript? "I wonder what Marjorie was looking up in old newspapers. Perhaps tracking down any mentions of the people in the Polaroid?"

"Could be," Ezra murmured. "Holden's going to have his work cut out for him."

Once we were back in the car and on the road, I mused over everything we had learned during our very informative trip to the library.

"Hey," Ezra's voice cut into my thoughts, "isn't the turn-off for the police station that way?" He pointed over his shoulder.

"I want to make a pit stop real quick." I gave him a guilty smile.

He surveyed the road we continued down, a big, rustic sign coming into view. "I should have realized you'd agreed to respect authority too easily." He chuckled.

"Well, your comment about Holden having his work cut out for him got me thinking." My cheeks grew hot as I turned into the dirt lot in front of Field & Farm. "I just want to see what information we can gather before handing things over to him."

I wasn't a frequent shopper at the agricultural center. The only times I ever stopped by were to help Poppy with her fertilizer orders. Regardless, I was familiar enough with the layout of the store and its employees.

The odor of tangy, potent earth wafted through my nostrils as we crossed the threshold. A cement floor and rows of metal shelving gave the space an industrial feel despite the warm Mason-jar lights hanging overhead. Patrons milled about, and a productive hum emanated from the scene. I hoped Jared was working and that he'd have time to speak with us.

Ezra let me take the lead as I headed for the back of the store where the service counter was stationed. Jared could usually be found there or in the business office.

Sure enough, the handsomely burly fifty-something-year-old rocked back and forth as he chatted with a customer. He waved his hands around, clearly in the midst of telling an entertaining story. Or at least, what he perceived to be entertaining. The recipient of the tale, Garrett Lewis—Mammie's husband—didn't seem as amused as Jared was with himself.

"And turns out, it was the cow all along!" Jared clapped his forehead, his laughter booming.

Garrett managed a polite chuckle as he grabbed the large pair of pruning shears on the countertop. "Imagine that. Well, thanks for putting in the order, bud."

Jared's chest swelled in preparation to expel a hearty reply, and I seized the moment to intervene before he took off on another storytelling tangent. "Hi, Garrett. Hey, Jared. Got a moment to help Ezra and me with a little project?"

Garrett sent me a grateful look and muttered his goodbyes before darting toward the exit. He was a sweet man but the complete opposite of his social butterfly wife.

Jared tugged at the straps of his Field & Farm overalls. "A project? Did Poppy finally inspire you to create your own garden?"

"No, I'll leave that work to the experts." I giggled at the joke to help soften him up. He used it on me every time I came here. "I'm actually hoping you can help us with an old photo Ezra and I found." I opted to share a modified version of the truth. "It was tucked in a library yearbook, and we want to return it to its owner."

Jared stroked the tanned skin of his cheeks. "What makes you think I can help?"

"Well, it was bookmarking a yearbook page featuring Joshua Sherwin, and I was wondering if he was related to you?"

The moment the name sailed across my lips, Jared's demeanor morphed before my eyes. His shoulders curled, and his friendly smile faded into sadness. "Sure was." His voice grew heavy with emotion. "Josh was my big brother. Two years older. My hero, really. Taken too soon. Died in a hit-and-run."

"Oh my goodness." My hand flew to my mouth as sympathetic murmurings tumbled out. "I'm so sorry. I-I had no idea."

"Not a lot of folks remember Josh." Jared reached for the back of his neck, his cheeks growing red. "My fault, probably. I was in a bad way after he died, and it just became easier for the rest of the Sherwin clan if Josh's name didn't come up." He cleared his throat. "You said you found an old photo?"

I nodded and reached for my tablet case. "Here." I slid it gently across the counter.

Jared's gaze widened the second he laid eyes on the Polaroid. "Well, I'll be."

"Do you recognize anyone?" Ezra asked, his tone soft and gentle.

"You bet I do. Me, for one." Jared pointed to the young man wrestling with Sterling Ildrich. Seeing the grainy resemblance, it now made sense why we hadn't found him among the senior pages of the yearbook. Jared would have only been a sophomore at the time. "And, of course, my brother." His finger tapped lightly on the figure we'd assumed to be Josh Sherwin. "He was so mad that I crashed their little graduation party. But how could I not? He and Jane were going on and on about it for weeks."

My heart skipped a beat. "Jane?"

"Jane Zeller." Jared motioned to the young woman with long brunette curls. "Josh's girlfriend at the time."

Ezra tilted his head. "Zeller? That's not a local name I recognize."

"Her family wasn't from around here," Jared explained. "They bounced around a lot for her dad's work. She spent her senior year in Crucible and moved away shortly after my brother was killed."

The phrases "killed" and "hit-and-run" echoed in my ears. Such a tragedy couldn't have occurred within Crucible's borders, not while Grandmaster Jedidiah's protection shield had been intact. "Do you mind me asking what happened to Josh?"

Jared's hands balled into fists. He then jabbed a finger at Sterling's smiling face in the photo. "Yeah, that guy."

Chapter 18

I gulped. I knew Sterling was a bit of a black sheep in the Ildrich clan, but Mom had never said he'd had a hand in someone's death.

Jared didn't need additional prompting. "SJ—Sterling—was Josh's best friend. A bit rough around the edges, but I think that's why my brother took him under his wing. Looked after him a bit. A whole lot of good it did him."

Jared's jaw tightened as he continued studying the Polaroid. "I thought those two were closer than brothers. Goodness knows I was forever trying to get Josh to acknowledge me the way he looked after SJ. But that all changed once she came to town." Jared made an invisible circle with his finger around Jane.

"SJ was crazy about Jane, but she fell hard for Josh. The three of them were always together, despite SJ's envy of their relationship. I could tell things were tense between my brother and SJ, although neither of them wanted to admit it."

Jared's eyes grew glassy as he stared at the Polaroid. "This was probably the last good day the three of them had together. Not long after, Josh moved into his new dorm a few weeks before the term started. Student athlete and all. Well, he came back to Crucible one weekend to surprise Jane and found her with SJ."

I flinched, able to picture where this story was going.

"Josh was so angered by the betrayal, he turned right around and drove back to school in the middle of the night. A drunk driver blew a red light when Josh was a block away from campus." Jared paused as he took a deep, fortifying breath. "The police told us he died instantly from the impact, so there was some comfort knowing he hadn't suffered. But to know he spent his last minutes on earth likely thinking about his best friend stabbing him in the back..." His fingers balled into a fist once more.

"How awful." I placed a palm on Jared's forearm. "I'm so sorry."

He patted my hand and gave me a fatherly smile. "Haven't talked about Josh in a long time. I should do it more often. He deserves a better legacy. He deserved a lot of things, like a better friend." Jared's tone turned to a growl. "At least SJ had the decency to leave town a year or so after Josh died. My family hated seeing his traitorous mug strolling around without a care in the world. Although, since it was no secret what he did to my brother, most of Crucible turned their back on him anyway."

An awkward silence settled over the three of us, as neither Ezra nor I knew what else we could say.

"Good grief. Why the long faces?" A chipper, bright voice interrupted our melancholy. "Dad, you aren't boring poor Hazel and Ezra with your cow story again, are you?" Keelie Sherwin sidled up to the counter, her hands flying to her hips as she gave her father a stern glare.

At her arrival, Jared broke into a proud smile. "Now, sweetheart, just because you don't find it funny—"

"No one finds it funny besides you, Dad." Twenty-two-year-old Keelie rolled her blue eyes in exaggerated exasperation. "Sorry, guys. Did you need help with something?" She looked expectantly at Ezra and me.

"Your dad was just telling us about the people in this photo," Ezra hurriedly explained. "We're trying to track down who it may have belonged to."

Keelie did a double take at the Polaroid. "Hold on, I've seen this pic before."

"Really?" Ezra and I parroted.

Keelie took a closer look at the Polaroid for confirmation. "Yeah, last week. Some woman brought it into the store." She jabbed a finger into her dad's chest. "It was the lady I told you about. She wanted to speak with you."

"Me?" Jared seemed genuinely surprised. "I don't remember this."

"Ugh, Dad! I wrote a note for you on the message board." Keelie disappeared through the doorway behind the counter, returning a second later. "See?" She shoved a Post-it note into his outstretched palm. "What good is the message board system if you don't use it?"

Jared shrugged off his daughter's berating. "I hear ya, I hear ya. So, a woman named Marjorie came in with this photo?" He then held the scribbled note out for Ezra and me to read.

All it said was *Marjorie Z., Photo Questions*, and a phone number.

Keelie nodded, her blonde ponytail swinging aggressively. "Yeah, she wanted to ask you some questions regarding our family. Kit was with her and thought you'd be the one to help clear some things up."

"Kit?" The name was out of my mouth before I could stop it. "Kit Peakes?"

Keelie's gaze narrowed suspiciously at my tone. "Yes. So, what's the deal with this old picture?"

I ignored her question as I dug out my phone. "Is this the Marjorie you met?" I held up the screen, revealing the headshot Marjorie used for her book jacket.

Keelie studied the image. "That's the one. What about her?"

Had she been living under a rock for the past four days? "Um, that's the woman who was murdered on Friday."

Keelie squeaked. "Omigosh, are you serious?"

Ezra sucked in a breath. "Well, then. I guess that explains why no one has been missing this photo." He tapped the Polaroid, playing his part to a T.

Jared's jaw fell slack. "Wait, wasn't the dead woman's last name Zeller?" His gaze dropped to the photo. "I didn't think anything of it when I heard the news, but...you don't suppose she's somehow related to Jane?"

I shrugged, doing my best to appear clueless. Keelie's story was the confirmation we needed about Marjorie's connection to the Polaroid, but it was her appearance with Kit that had me reeling. What were they doing together? Kit hadn't mentioned being the one to take Marjorie on her Field & Farm excursion.

Jared stroked the stubble on his chin. "Jeez, this has me all in a tizzy."

"Agreed. It certainly is bizarre." Ezra wrapped an arm around my waist. "I guess we'd better take this photo to the police, then, Hazel. It could be evidence."

I knew he was giving us the out we needed before Jared and Keelie started asking more questions. "Right. Chief Whitfield will want to see this." I swallowed my nerves. "But before we go, can you tell us if you recognize anyone else in the photo, Jared? It might be helpful for us to pass on to the police."

"Sure thing. I remember this party like it was yesterday." From left to right, he named, "Sterling, me, Jane, Josh...this here is Tula Dukakis, well, Sardolous, now." He pointed at the dark-haired woman who wore a sour expression. His finger then hovered over the glamorous couple on the opposite end of the picnic table. "And then there were our surprise guests, Grant and Monica Finchmore."

I shook my head, clearly having heard Jared wrong. "I'm sorry. Who?"

"Grant and Monica Finchmore," Jared replied. "Well, Monica was still a Lauder at that point. The two had decided to mingle with us common folk." He snorted at his own joke. "Tula's father worked for Grant's dad, so that's how they learned about our gathering."

I studied the attractive albeit blurry duo, trying to wrap my head around their identities. Grant and Monica Finchmore? Dressed in shorts and polo shirts, the two looked like normal, albeit well-dressed, teenagers. Nothing like the uptight one-percent darlings they were today. "Grant and Monica came to your brother's graduation party?"

"I know, hard to believe, right? Royalty among peasants. But honestly, Grant was a nice guy back when he was a kid. Before his dad really drove a stick up his...you-know-where." Jared wiggled his eyebrows. "I think those two had recently graduated from their fancy prep schools and came down to the lake to hang out with Tula. One last hoorah before college and internships at Finchmore Power Technologies began."

I nodded absently as I continued to study the photo. *What an odd crowd.*

"Thanks for all the info, Jared," Ezra said, reaching his hand out for a shake. "Is it okay if we tell Chief Whitfield to follow up with you if he has questions?"

Jared smirked. "You two working for the new police department or something?" But before we could struggle through a panicked answer, Jared flicked back his hand. "Nah, I'm just teasing. Of course you can. Happy to help."

We thanked both Jared and Keelie for their time and bid them goodbye. With hurried steps, Ezra and I retreated to my SUV to speak in private.

"Yikes, Haz. Talk about drama." Ezra released a low whistle once we settled in.

I held the photo gingerly in one palm, capturing it with my iPhone camera so I could keep a copy for our amateur records. "Now it all makes sense why Sterling was driven out of town at a young age. I had no idea Crucible practically blamed him for Josh Sherwin's death. That's terrible."

Yes, sleeping with his best friend's girlfriend was rotten and all, but it took two to tango. Jared clearly held Sterling responsible—not Jane—for the circumstances leading to Josh's hit-and-run. Maybe Jane had escaped scrutiny because she'd left shortly after Josh died.

"Yeah. I feel for the guy." Ezra took the Polaroid from me as I prepared to drive to the police station. "But given everything we've learned, we still have no clue why Marjorie was chasing down the people in this photo."

"You're right." I gripped the steering wheel as I made the turn onto the main road. "But it definitely sounds like Kit knows a lot more than he let on when I ran into him at Herb Garden last night."

"Sure does." Ezra stroked his chin. "He's never struck me as the 'do it out of the goodness of my own heart' type of guy, so what would he be helping Marjorie for?"

"Damsel in distress?" I suggested.

"Maybe." Ezra sighed. "I was thinking something less chivalrous and more carnal, if you get my drift."

My cheeks heated at the current of innuendo running underneath his words. "It's possible he was trying to get into Marjorie's...good graces." *If it weren't for my stupid lifeclock, I would have let Ezra into my good graces a long time ago...*

We spent the remainder of the drive in contemplative silence and soon found ourselves in the police station's makeshift waiting room.

Holly Hanscom greeted us with a warm smile. "Hi, Ezra. Long time no see, Hazel." She winked at her joke.

"Escaping the smell again?" I smiled in greeting as we approached the reception desk.

Holly rolled her eyes. "We cannot move into the new building soon enough. Chief says the admin offices will be ready by the winter if all goes according to plan."

"Fingers crossed for you," I said, making the sign with my hand. "Any chance we could speak to Holden? We may have stumbled across something at the library regarding Marjorie Zeller."

"Stumbled?" Holly's expression turned dubious, but she quickly broke into a laugh. "Sure thing. He's taking lunch out back." She pointed out the doublewide's rear window. "It's probably easiest just to go around the building rather than through our breakroom."

"Awesome. Thanks!" With a wave, Ezra and I turned around and headed outside.

We found Holden sitting at a patio dining set, eating one of Ione's signature Sip salads.

"Hey, guys." Holden swallowed a choke-worthy bite of kale with ease before motioning us to take the chairs opposite him. "What brings you by?"

Ezra handed Holden the Polaroid while I explained the events of our morning. "We found something at the library regarding Marjorie."

Holden listened intently as I recounted finding the photo, the yearbook tags, and our trip to Field & Farm.

"So, it seems like Marjorie stayed in Crucible to figure out who the people were in this group shot," I concluded, trying to get a read on Holden's grim expression. No doubt, he was recalling Marjorie's final thoughts in life that his whim had dredged up. *I need to find—*

Having wiped his hands with a napkin, he studied the Polaroid intently. "So, we've got Sterling Ildrich, Jared Sherwin, Tula Sardolous, Grant Finchmore, Monica Finchmore, Josh Sherwin, and some woman named Jane Zeller." He pointed to each person as he named them.

"That's right," Ezra confirmed.

Holden adjusted the brim of his cap. "And I'm assuming you believe there's a tie between Marjorie Zeller and Jane?"

I nodded. "Both Constance and Lauren mentioned Marjorie's mother recently passed away. If Jane was Marjorie's mom, maybe she was on some mission to learn more about her."

"It makes sense to me." Holden sat back in his chair. "But the real question is whether this has anything to do with Marjorie's murder."

Ezra's shoulders slumped. "Learning about your mom's childhood sounds pretty harmless. Especially since it doesn't sound like Jane spent a whole lot of time in Crucible."

"What?" My jaw dropped open. "But this has to mean something! What if—"

Holden cut me off. "I'll have a chat with the people in this photo, Hazel. Don't worry. But it's not exactly a smoking gun."

"You mean it's not enough to take the heat off of Constance." I folded my arms in a huff.

He sighed. "No, it's not." He lowered his voice despite the three of us being alone outside. "Look, you didn't hear this from me, but Shroud has already received preliminary results back from the DNA found on the murder weapon. There were only two profiles found on the scarf." Holden held my gaze. "Both female."

A sharp, stabbing pain erupted in my gut. "That doesn't mean anything if the killer wore gloves. We all know Marjorie stole Constance's scarf before she got kicked out. Of course Constance's DNA would be on it!"

Ezra reached for my hand and squeezed.

Holden slipped the photo between the pages of the crime novel he'd been reading to keep it secure before packing his lunch. "We only have Constance's word the scarf was stolen." He held his palm up to silence my sputtering protests. "I know, I know. I believe her.

But criminal cases deal with proof, not gut feelings. Until other motives come to light, the official investigation will have to continue following the evidence."

He dipped his chin. "I appreciate you stopping by. Be careful out there." And with that, he left.

I stared at the chipped paint on the flimsy table, my mind a storm of activity.

"Hey, I know that didn't go as planned." Ezra draped a supportive arm across my shoulders. "But cheer up. I'm sure something will come of the photo we found."

I shot him a sneaky smile. "Actually, it went much better than I anticipated."

"Huh?" Ezra's nose wrinkled with confusion.

"I was worried we were going to get reamed out for tampering with evidence or something," I admitted. "But we basically got the go-ahead from Holden to keep digging into Marjorie's time in Crucible." I chuckled at Ezra's bewildered expression. "Didn't you hear him? The police need other motives to surface." My smile grew. "Who better to shine a light on Marjorie's life than a candlemaker?"

Chapter 19

Ezra snorted at my bad pun before breaking into full-body laughter. "I guess I shouldn't be surprised. Okay, Sherlock. What's next?"

I grew a bit sheepish. "Well, I actually need to put a pin in investigating for a few hours and run some errands." Mondays may have been my day off from A Wick in Time, but that didn't mean it was a day off from adulting. Noli needed a refill on her prescription kibble, which I had to pick up from our local vet before they closed at four.

I glanced at my watch. "Besides, Poppy would murder me if we did anything more without her. She said she would be done by three today, so let's sync up then?"

Ezra shrugged. "I'd be happy to tag along on your errands. Or do you need some time to yourself?" As a fellow introvert, he understood our frequent desires to decompress.

I leaned into his chest. "I'd love your company." And I meant it. Maybe this was what finding your person felt like. You had no wish to be away from them.

"Then I'm all yours." He pressed his lips into my dark hair for a tender kiss.

The memory of Holden eating a salad from Sip made my stomach rumble, so I suggested having lunch back at my cottage before hitting up the vet, craft store, and market to stock up on supplies for the week.

We ate homemade chicken salad wraps on the back porch, enjoying the sunshine and the beautiful Lake Glenmyre view.

Given the refreshing temperature, I opted to let Noli tag along with us on our errand run, as I could leave her in the car—windows open—without the risk of her overheating or being too cold.

I had just tossed a box of homemade pasta into my Herb Garden shopping basket when Ezra's cell rang.

"Hey, Caius." He answered my unasked question about who was calling. "What's going on, bro?"

I continued selecting my grocery items while Ezra listened intently.

"Seriously?" His eyebrows disappeared underneath his windswept bangs. "Well, of course. Sure, that will be fine. When were you thinking—*what*?" Ezra pressed his palm against his forehead. "Well, geez, dude. Would have been nice to get a little more of a heads up."

The conversation wrapped soon after.

"That kid." Ezra shook his head as he pocketed his phone.

I studied him with concern. "What's wrong?"

"Oh, nothing's wrong, per se." Ezra ran his fingers through his hair. "It's just that Caius decided to take me up on my offer to visit, and he's already at Port Authority booking a bus ticket to Ithaca."

From Ezra's anxious demeanor, I could tell this was throwing him for a bit of a loop. He loved his brother dearly, but remember that thing I mentioned about introverts needing time to ourselves? Well, extroverted Caius didn't exactly understand that.

"I'm sure you two will have a great time." I rubbed Ezra's lower back to help relieve some of his budding tension. "Is there anything you want to pick up here?" I motioned to Herb Garden's well-stocked shelves. "I can drop you off at home."

"Yeah, good idea. I think all I have in my fridge are almond milk and ketchup." He chuckled sheepishly.

"Take your time," I reassured him. "I'll check out and wait for you up front." Ezra's predicament had presented the perfect opportunity for me. Kit Peakes had been behind the register when we'd strolled into the store, and I wanted to have another chat with him about Marjorie.

While Ezra scurried away to grab his own shopping basket, I headed toward the checkout area. Mammie and Kit were working separate registers, and luckily, Kit's line was shorter. If his had been longer, it would have been weird if I'd chosen him over Mammie, and Mammie surely would have noticed.

Kit did a double take when my turn came. "Back so soon?" He began scanning my groceries.

"Getting my shopping done for the week." I smiled, trying to figure out how to innocently bring up what we'd learned from Keelie at Field & Farm. "Gotta love errand days. I just came from Jared's, and I'm off to The Corner Store next," I fibbed.

"Cool." Kit didn't even try to sound interested.

"Keelie Sherwin cornered me while I was at Field & Farm," I plowed ahead. "You know, asking me if I knew anything about the dead woman found on the road outside my house. She told me you and Marjorie stopped by last week, wanting to ask her dad about a photo…" I trailed off, hoping Kit would take my clumsily placed bait.

He did not. "That will be one hundred forty-three dollars and seventy cents."

I grimaced, both at his reaction and the pricey grocery bill. As I held my phone up for Apple Pay, I added, "Have you chatted with the police, Kit? Telling them about your relationship with Marjorie might help them with their case."

"I didn't have a relationship with her, Hazel." Kit's tone was sharp and pointed. "Look, I overheard her peppering Sterling with questions about the Sherwin family one night at Roadside Station. Sterling was having none of it and even told her to leave." He ripped my receipt from the printer and handed it to me. "Seeing how put out she was, I told her Jared might be able to answer whatever questions she had. I was going to Field & Farm the next morning to get some chicken feed, so I offered to have Marjorie meet me there and introduce them. That's all. Turns out, Jared wasn't even working, so we went our separate ways."

Was Kit telling me the truth? He seemed sincere enough, but his nostrils were also flared with annoyed anger. Curses, I wished Poppy was here to get a read on him. I made a mental note to tell her to come by and use her whim on Kit's aura. "I see. Did she tell you what was so important about this photo?"

"Nope. Next guest, please." Kit waved the person behind me forward, indicating he was absolutely done with our conversation.

Bristling at his curt attitude, I gathered my groceries and waited for Ezra by the newspaper rack. I absently scanned the titles while replaying my encounter with Kit, only to have a headline in the *Ithaca Interpreter* catch my eye.

"Does the Big Melt Spell Big Trouble for Crucible?"

The title raised all kinds of alarm bells, so I grabbed a copy and skimmed the article for details. By the third paragraph, my heart had sunk into my stomach.

> **Given the rising crime rate in once-idyllic Crucible, concerns are bountiful regarding the security of this year's springtime festival. Newly installed police chief Holden Whitfield has assured reporters that the public and vendors have nothing to worry about. "Our priority is keeping Crucible safe, and we continue to work alongside the New York State Bureau of Criminal Investigation on any pertinent matters."**
>
> The most recent pertinent matter, of course, being the murder of the up-and-coming novelist, Marjorie Zeller. Zeller was vacationing in Crucible when she was strangled and left for dead by the side of the road in her broken-down car. BCI Detective Declan Shroud stated that "this was a one-off tragic incident. Crucible is not, nor has ever been, at the mercy of a serial killer."
>
> Despite these reassurances from law enforcement, several longtime vendors are passing on this year's Big Melt Food Festival. The committee is even struggling to

secure judges for the Melt Off cooking event.

I ground my teeth as I tossed the newspaper back onto the shelf. "What a load of fearmongering." The issue with the Big Melt judges had nothing to do with Marjorie's murder. And what in holy hexes was Declan thinking, mentioning the possibility of a *serial killer*? Perhaps the quote had been taken out of context by the sloppy reporter.

The only interesting item of note was the mention that Marjorie's car had broken down before she was attacked at the side of the road. Was this the killer's doing? Or did it mean Marjorie's murder had been a crime of opportunity? Had some random person been passing by and seized the chance to take a life? The thought chilled me to my soul.

"Everything okay?" Ezra sidled up beside me with his purchases. "You only scowl that badly when you've burnt a pot of wax."

I rubbed my temples to alleviate the building anxiety. "I was just reading some irresponsible article about the Big Melt that's basically painting Crucible as a crime den." I shuddered at the mental image that the details about Marjorie's death brought about. How had the reporter learned she'd been strangled and that her car had broken down?

"Makes you worry about the place, huh?" Even though he didn't know about our whims or the Glenmyre family motto of *"With our whims, do good,"* Ezra understood that protecting Crucible's reputation and legacy was important to me.

What the article really made me want to do was catch Marjorie's killer even more. "Got everything?" I asked, changing the subject.

Ezra lifted his paper bags. "I think so. Caius is always on some fad diet, so who knows if this will satisfy him."

We chatted about activities his younger brother might enjoy in the area as we made our way back to Ezra's duplex.

"And, of course, I'd love for you to come over for dinner one night and meet him in person." Ezra reached for the passenger-side door once I slowed my SUV to a stop. "Maybe tomorrow?"

"Sounds great. You guys have fun catching up tonight." I leaned over to peck him on the cheek.

Ezra turned and kissed me on the lips. "Let me know if anything comes from your chat with Poppy about the case."

"Will do." I smiled as I watched him head inside. While I was bummed our day together had been cut short, it warmed my heart to know Ezra was willing to drop everything to help his brother. He was such a great guy. I was lucky to have him in my life.

My phone chirped with a message.

How did your visit to the lib go? Got any new leads?

Realizing how much I had to fill Poppy in on, I called her as I drove back to my cottage.

"I take it that's a yes," Poppy answered with a giggle. "What'd I miss out on?"

"A lot." I turned onto Rosewood Lane and navigated along the eastern shore of Lake Glenmyre. "Can you come over for a brainstorming sesh?"

"Be there in twenty." She disconnected without saying anything further.

~∞~

From the backyard, I caught sight of Poppy's Subaru pulling into my driveway. I waved at her, hoping she'd spot me, as Noli and I were on our afternoon walk.

"How's my favorite furry niece?" Poppy cooed as she jogged toward us and knelt down to accept Noli's wet kisses.

Noli's nubby tail wiggled her entire body as she whimpered with excitement.

"Want to walk and talk along the lake?" I suggested once Poppy straightened and dusted off her jeans. Maybe the fresh spring air would help us gain a fresh perspective on the case.

Poppy motioned toward the worn walking path that bordered my property. "Spill."

It took the length of our routine stroll for me to bring Poppy up to speed on everything that had transpired since my visit to the library with Ezra.

"Hexes. So Constance isn't the only connection Marjorie had to Crucible after all." Poppy stared at the whiteboard hanging in my kitchen. We'd added the new case details once we'd returned from our walk with Noli. "Jane Zeller seems to be the reason why Marjorie stuck around town after Constance tossed her out."

I poured fresh water into Noli's bowl before joining my aunt at the board. "But why? What is Marjorie hoping to gain by tracking down Jane and the people in an old photo?"

"The million-dollar question." Poppy tapped her chin with a capped dry-erase marker. "Can I see the snapshot again?"

I held out my phone, displaying the image I'd captured of the Polaroid to have on hand.

"I cannot get over that those kids are Grant and Monica." Poppy shook her head in lingering disbelief. "I never would have guessed."

I chuckled sheepishly. "I never would have recognized anyone— not without help from the yearbook images."

"Yeah, photo technology sure has come a long way." Poppy squinted as she zoomed in on Sterling Ildrich's face. "I also can't believe everyone in town blamed him for Joshua's death. That's gotta be rough."

I nodded my agreement. "Did Mom ever mention the circumstances around the hit-and-run to you?"

"I don't think so." Poppy's forehead wrinkled as she searched her memories. "I can't remember Iris ever mentioning the fact that Jared had an older brother." She handed me back my phone. "I know Sterling wasn't willing to talk with Marjorie about the incident, but maybe I can get a read on him."

I reached for a red dry-erase marker and drew a star by Sterling's name. "We can at least find out if Marjorie told him why she was tracking down her mom's friends."

"Do you think Marjorie figured out that Tula, Grant, and Monica were also in the photo?" With her marker, Poppy put stars by the famous Finchmore couple and their estate manager.

"I guess we can ask Sterling." I shrugged. "I'm inclined to think not, but only because she was still searching through yearbooks the day she died."

Poppy pointed to another item on our whiteboard. "What about the older gentleman the Canadian couple encountered at Waking Woods? Where does he fit into this picture?"

I furrowed my brow. "Well, if we're going off the individuals in Marjorie's photo, I don't think it could be Jared, and certainly not Josh."

"I've never heard Sterling described as a gentleman before, but there's a first for everything." Poppy stifled a giggle, but then quickly sobered. "Jared, on the other hand, I could believe. Is there a chance he could have been lying to you about not knowing Marjorie? Maybe Jared *did* see the message Keelie left for him and arranged to chat with Marjorie in person?"

My stomach flipped at the very real possibility. "I don't know, Pops. I didn't get a sense that he was being dishonest." Curses, if only she had been at Field & Farm when Jared had shared his story. "Kit Peakes, on the other hand…"

"Yeah, his demeanor certainly sounds cagey. I'll try to get a read on him without causing too much of a fuss." Poppy sighed as she made marks by Kit's and Jared's names. "I hate thinking such terrible things about people I've looked up to and respected my whole life."

I pulled her in for a one-armed hug. "Same. But if we're going to clear Constance's name and help Holden figure out why someone wanted Marjorie dead, we have to tackle these tough questions."

"You're right, little niece. As usual." My aunt glanced at her watch. "Roadside Station opens at four. I say we confront Sterling about Marjorie being overheard pestering him for information."

"Do we mention the photo?"

Poppy hesitated a moment. "Not at first. Let's see how much he shares without us showing our full hand."

Chapter 20

With a plan in place, Poppy and I spent some rare downtime just hanging out in my living room watching silly Netflix shows. It had been a while since we'd had some fun girl time. As much as we'd promised each other that our boyfriends wouldn't come between us, managing our busy schedules had been hard.

Poppy also filled me in on the latest drama afflicting the Friends of Crucible community group.

"Maggie Sherwin has gone full tyrannical mode now that we've had two longtime vendors drop from the Big Melt." Poppy folded her arms in a huff. "And then there's a hit piece in the *Interpreter* that isn't doing us any favors."

I winced in sympathy. "I skimmed it while I was at Herb Garden. It makes it sound like folks aren't safe to visit Crucible."

"Right? Totally taken out of context." Poppy began counting reasons on her fingers. "One vendor can't make it due to their restaurant flooding. The other, their promoter is going through chemotherapy and can't stretch themselves too thin. Terrible situations that have nothing to do with Crucible."

"Did the drama with the Melt Off judges get situated at least?"

Poppy rolled her eyes. "Sure did. Tobias pulled some strings using Grant's connections and got someone. The whole panel is now being bankrolled by Finchmore Power Technologies."

I frowned at her reaction. "Is that a bad thing?"

"No, not necessarily." She pouted. "I just hate the idea that money is the only thing that can solve problems these days. What happened to people helping out of the goodness of their heart?"

Her pessimistic view of the world surprised me. Poppy was normally a glass-half-full kind of gal.

I reached for her hand and squeezed. "The world needs more Poppys."

"I agree. There isn't enough of my goodwill to go around."

We both broke into laughter at her teasing sarcasm. "Speaking of help, should we fill Constance in about what we've uncovered?" I checked the time. We still had an hour before Roadside Station opened.

Poppy reached for her phone. "Good idea. I'd like her take on Marjorie's newfound ties to Crucible. Maybe something will stand out to her that didn't before."

Thirty seconds later, Constance answered the phone. "Hi, Pops. Everything okay?"

"All good," Poppy chirped. "I've got Hazel here with me to give you an update on the case."

Constance snickered on the other end of the line. "Should I be paying you guys for your services? You sound like professional PIs."

"No payment required. Just your brainpower." I leaned closer to the phone, which Poppy had placed on my coffee table. "We have a bunch of intel to share about Marjorie."

We then took turns divulging our latest finds.

"You said the photo featured Jane Zeller?" Constance repeated. "That's definitely Margie's mom. Wow…" Her voice trailed off for a moment. "She never mentioned that her mother lived in Crucible. But then again…"

"What is it?" Poppy prodded her to share what she was thinking.

Constance sighed. "Well, now that I think back on things, Margie did seem really adamant about visiting me once she learned I'd moved to Crucible. She'd never taken an interest in staying with me before." The sound of papers shuffling caused a burst of static over the phone. "At the time, I chalked it up to her needing an escape after her mom died. Guess that wasn't the case."

"Marjorie never mentioned wanting to learn more about her mom?" I asked.

"Nope. Nothing."

Poppy's brow furrowed. "Why the clandestine behavior, I wonder. I mean, it's a common coping mechanism for dealing with grief. I dug up everything I could about my mom and dad." Having lost her parents—my grandparents—at a young age, Poppy spoke from experience.

"I wish I could shed some more light on things, but I've got nothing." Constance sounded disappointed.

"No worries. We're tracking down the folks Marjorie talked to about her mom and this old photo." I nervously chewed on my lower lip. "How are things on your end with the police?"

Constance scoffed. "I've been asked to give a DNA sample, but my lawyer is having none of it without a court order. If Margie was killed with *my* stolen scarf, of course, my DNA would be on it. Other than that, my lawyer is doing a good job at keeping Detective Shroud and his minions in check. However, the online community hasn't been too kind. Word got out that Marjorie was here visiting me, so of course, vile rumors are swirling like a flushed toilet."

Poppy feigned a gag at her vivid imagery.

"Sorry you have to deal with stuff like that." I couldn't imagine sounding as calm and collected as Constance did. I stressed out when one person was miffed at me. There was no way I could handle the entire Internet.

"All in a day's work." Melancholy lingered in Constance's words. "At least it's giving me inspiration for a new novel. Something different. Grittier. The book I wanted to write before Margie stole it from me." The anger in her comment sent a small shiver up my spine.

"Yeesh, don't let Declan hear you talking like that." Poppy chuckled awkwardly.

I cleared my throat. "We'll let you know how our chat with Sterling Ildrich goes. See if he connected with Marjorie outside of his dive bar."

"Good luck, girlies." Constance brightened before signing off.

Poppy slid her phone back into her sweater pocket. "At least we now have confirmation that Jane was Marjorie's mom."

"It still strikes me as so weird that Marjorie hid her ties to the area from Constance." I propped my elbow on the arm of the couch. "I mean, they were supposed to be friends, right?"

"I don't know. Would you steal an entire book plot from your friend?" Poppy pointed out. "I'm getting the vibe that Marjorie had just used Constance whenever it was convenient for her. Especially since she never had an interest in visiting Constance prior to her move to Crucible."

"But why all the pretense?" I challenged. "If Marjorie was really coming here to get to know her mom better, why did she need to involve Constance?"

Poppy rose from the couch and stretched her arms above her head. "Let's hope Sterling has answers for us."

I nervously twirled a strand of my hair. "Me too, because at this rate, we're racking up more questions than I have candle orders."

After saying goodbye to Noli and Berg, Poppy and I hopped in my Equinox and headed for Roadside Station. The drive to neighboring Hyssop Falls took us all of fifteen minutes, and it was four on the dot by the time we pulled into the dirt parking lot.

I studied Roadside Station with a wary gaze. "Maybe we should have enlisted Fitz or Iggy to help us."

"*Psshaw.*" Poppy batted my concerns aside. "We're capable, kick-butt women. We can handle this crowd."

"But do we *want* to handle them?" I cast a disgusted glance at some of the rude and downright chilling bumper stickers adorning the trucks and cars in the parking lot.

Poppy must have finally clued in on my concerns, for her cheeks paled slightly. "Let's make this quick."

The stale smell of tobacco assaulted my nostrils as we entered the dive bar. A statewide ban on indoor smoking had taken effect in the early 2000s, meaning the stench that greeted us had to be from the tough-looking crowd smoking outside on the bar's back deck.

Poppy stifled a cough. "Who knew amateur investigating could be so hazardous to one's health?"

Since I'd had a gun pointed at me more than once, I chose not to comment.

"You lost, ladies?" a grating, gravelly voice came from the shadows behind the bar.

I squinted, trying to make out who'd spoken to us. "Um, we're here to see Sterling." Obviously, we didn't look like Roadside Station regulars.

A tall, muscular man stepped into the bar's dim overhead light. "Don't recall having a meeting on my schedule."

I sucked back an astonished gasp. Sterling Ildrich had changed drastically since I last remembered seeing him. He looked as though he had shed a hundred pounds or more, and his signature bushy gray beard was gone. In its place were chiseled, tanned cheeks and a strong chin. Sterling's shock-white hair was neatly trimmed. In a black Roadside Station polo and khakis, he looked like a golf pro, not a dive bar owner.

I shot a quick glance at Poppy, seeing the same surprise wash over her face. I didn't need a mind-reading whim to know what she was thinking. With his total-body transformation, Sterling Ildrich could very well have been the distinguished gentleman visitor looking for Marjorie's cabin.

Poppy found her voice first. "Hi, Sterling. Poppy Glenmyre. I did the flowers for your Aunt Tabitha's memorial service." She waved in a meek greeting. "Long time no see."

Sterling's upper lip twitched into a slight smile. "I don't need reminding who you are. The reputation of the Glenmyre Girls precedes you."

I gulped back a ball of nerves. What did that mean? Did Sterling already suspect we were here to talk to him about Marjorie? Had our cover been blown?

He motioned to two empty bar stools. "Can I get you anything?"

"Got any hard ciders?" I summoned the courage to speak up.

He responded by reaching under the counter and producing two bottles from a local cider house.

Poppy and I gingerly perched on the stools, smiling our thanks for the drinks.

Sterling drummed his fingers on the worn, scuffed wood. "So, you gonna ask me about that woman who turned up dead?"

I nearly choked on my sip of hard cider. Yup, Sterling knew why we were here.

"What makes you think that?" Poppy asked, the picture of innocence.

Sterling barked out a gruff laugh. "Come on. I might not live in Crucible anymore, but I don't live under a rock. I know you ladies had a hand in solving that string of murders last year." He shrugged. "I can put two and two together, you know. What other reason would you be gracing my establishment for?"

My cheeks burned with embarrassment. We hadn't given Sterling nearly enough credit. "Well, if that's why we *were* here, would you be willing to chat with us?"

"Of course. Trading stories is part of my job." Sterling tossed a bar towel onto one of his broad shoulders. "Marjorie, right? She seemed like a nice enough kid. Shame to hear what happened to her."

Marjorie was hardly a kid, I thought to myself. But I wasn't about to call out Sterling's patronizing behavior and cause him to clam up. "We heard that she came here a few times to talk to you about something."

"You heard right." Sterling began clearing away some nearby glasses. "Don't see what that has to do with her death, though. It's not like *I* killed her." He actually chuckled.

His flippant response threw me for a loop.

Poppy swirled her bottle of cider. "We've also been told by witnesses that they saw you visiting Marjorie at Waking Woods."

Sterling straightened and set the soapy glassware down in the sink. "Well, that can't be right." He folded his toned arms. "I did go to Waking Woods to speak with her, but she wasn't around. Marjorie ended up coming by Roadside later to speak with me."

"About what?" I pressed.

Sterling studied us for a moment. "About my relationship with her mom. Poor kid had convinced herself I was her long-lost father."

Chapter 21

This time, I really did choke on my cider. "What? Her *father*?"

Poppy's hand flew to her mouth as her right eye twitched. I yearned to know what Sterling's aura revealed.

Instead, I continued forging ahead with my windfall of new questions. "Why on earth did Marjorie think you were her dad?"

Sterling sighed. "Sounds totally harebrained, doesn't it? Seems Marjorie found an old photo in her mom's diary. Came across it while she was settling the estate. Jane had written in the journal that the photo was the only one she had with Marjorie's father." His expression grew pinched. "But, as luck would have it, Jane didn't indicate which person in the photo her dad was."

"Holy hexes," Poppy mumbled.

"Marjorie was on a mission to track down her dad." Sterling placed his palms on the counter. "Her mom had kept pretty tightlipped about him her whole life, and she wanted answers."

"Why were you so certain you weren't her father?" I asked, unable to find a way to approach the matter tactfully. "Jared told us you had an affair with Jane."

At that, Sterling's hands balled into fists. "That was a mistake I made when I was a kid. Believe me, I never repeated it. After Josh died…I never saw Jane Zeller again."

If Sterling was being straight with us, it would be impossible for Marjorie to be his daughter. She couldn't have been conceived the summer Jane graduated, or Marjorie would have been much older than thirty-four.

Poppy nudged me in the side, her expression pained. *He's telling the truth.*

I gave her a slight nod to show I understood. "How did Marjorie take the news?"

Sterling seemed somewhat surprised that we readily trusted him. "Not well. I tried letting her down easy, but she kept after the matter. She clearly didn't believe me. Accused me of shirking my responsibilities. I eventually got tired of telling her no." He grew remorseful. "The last time she came here, I said some things I regret. I should have been more understanding of her situation. Believe me, I know what it feels like to have no family."

Compassion swelled within me for the seemingly tough-as-nails man. While the Ildrich clan may be alive and well, they had all turned their backs on Sterling for his youthful misdeeds.

"What do you think Marjorie meant by shirking your responsibilities?" Poppy asked.

Sterling's expression turned sour. "Oh, she made it quite clear. She thought she was due financial compensation for her dad being absent all these years."

I cringed. My empathy for Marjorie waxed and waned with each new twist this case took. I could very much sympathize with wanting to find her father. I had tried doing the very same with my missing dad for years. But to want to track him down only for money? Was Marjorie really that hard up for cash? Or was it just greed, plain and simple?

"Did Marjorie ever show you the photo she referenced?" Poppy asked as she dug out her credit card to pay for our drinks.

Sterling shook his head. "I asked to see it, but instead, she insisted on peppering me with questions about Josh Sherwin. I'll bet you already know why I didn't feel like talking about him." He reached for the back of his neck, shamefaced. "After that, I kinda blocked

Marjorie out. She came by a few more times, offering to show me the photo, but I refused. Told her to leave or I would toss her out."

I extracted my phone from my bag. "Would you like to see it? We found the photo tucked in an old yearbook at Sherwin Memorial Library." I slid the device toward Sterling. "I snapped a picture of it before we gave it to the police."

Sterling hesitated, but his curiosity got the better of him. He leaned forward and studied the screen, his blue eyes going misty. "I remember this day. One of the last good memories I have as a kid." He sighed as he pushed my phone back toward me. "Josh was a good guy. He didn't deserve what Jane and I did."

"Why'd you do it?" Poppy tilted her head, her voice soft.

"I was jealous. And stupid." Sterling began to twist his bar towel, his knuckles white. "The moment I laid eyes on Jane senior year, I fell for her. But she only had eyes for Josh. It wasn't long before the two of them started dating. They were our school's golden couple."

"Did Josh know you liked Jane?" I asked.

"I think he suspected, but we never talked about it." He hung his head. "I thought I had everything under control, but then Jane came to see me the weekend after Josh left for college. She brought beers she'd stolen from her dad and had clearly already been drinking. I should have sent her home right away, but she told me she was so lonely. So, we hung out in my room, and one thing led to another…" Sterling's cheeks grew red.

"Little did I know, Josh drove home that weekend to surprise us. He came barging into my room, like he always did, and—well, I'm sure you've heard the rest."

I nodded. It seemed unfair that Sterling had taken all the heat for the affair, when Jane had been the one to arrive at his doorstep, seeking solace. He'd only been eighteen, after all. An adult in the eyes of the law, but really, what eighteen-year-old had it together?

"Did you ever hear from Jane after that night?" Poppy pressed.

"Nope." Sterling, though, sounded hesitant. "Well, actually, that's a lie. She did leave a message on my answering machine several years later. Ten years, in fact."

Poppy and I shared an intrigued look. How did he remember the specific timeframe so readily?

Sterling unknowingly explained away our unvoiced question. "The Sherwins were doing a big memorial at the high school. Dedicating something in the athletic wing to Josh's memory. Jane called and left a message, asking if I would be at the ceremony. *She'd been invited.*" He snorted. "I didn't bother calling her back. She would find out soon enough that I wouldn't be showing my face there."

I did the mental math as I examined my phone, the digitized image of Marjorie's Polaroid staring back at me. Ten years after this was taken…had Jane Zeller reconnected with someone in the photo at Josh Sherwin's memorial? Had that reunion led to Marjorie's birth?

"Hey, boss!" a thick New York accent called from the depths of Roadside Station.

Sterling rapped his knuckles on the bar top. "That's my cue. Sorry, Glenmyre Girls. Chatty time is up." Without another word, he sauntered through a doorway bearing a sign marked "Employees Only."

I nudged Poppy's shoulder. "Anything I missed out on from his aura?"

"No. He was surprisingly honest." My aunt folded her arms across her chest in a discouraged scowl.

I chuckled at her response. Poppy didn't usually get miffed by people telling the truth. "If Jane's diary was right, and Marjorie's dad is someone in this photo, we're not left with a lot of options."

"You're right. Sterling is out, and Josh is most certainly excluded, which leaves Jared—"

"I think we can cross him out, too," I cut her off. "Can you really see Jared sleeping with the woman who broke his brother's heart and indirectly led to his death?"

Poppy pursed her lips. "Grief can make you do whacky things, but I suppose you do have a point."

I studied the telltale Polaroid, a lump growing hard in my throat. "If Marjorie's father really is in this picture, he has to be Grant Finchmore."

Chapter 22

Poppy sucked in an audible breath. "Hexes, Hazel. If that's true, do you know what that means?"

"Where to begin?" My mind spun with the many implications. "Marjorie would've been an heir to the Finchmore empire."

"And Yvonne would have a younger sister." Poppy lowered her voice in dramatic emphasis, even though we were the only people inside the bar. "If Grant is Marjorie's father, he would've had the affair *after* he and Monica were married."

I don't know why I found the matter so shocking. Loads of powerful, wealthy people cheated on their spouses. But Grant and Monica always seemed like such a good team. Ruthless and cold, yes, but very much dedicated to each other.

"Do you think Grant knew about Jane being pregnant?" I asked.

Poppy drummed her fingers on the bar top. "Good question." She pondered for another minute or two. "Constance told us that Jane never spoke about Marjorie's father. Maybe not because she didn't want to, but because she couldn't." Her eyes widened as her theory tumbled from her lips. "People as wealthy as the Finchmores are notorious for using NDAs to keep their indiscretions under wraps.

What if Jane had signed something that kept her from speaking about Grant?"

It felt like we'd landed smack in the middle of an episode of *Dynasty* or *Succession*. More money, more problems, indeed. "Curses. And if Grant found out Marjorie was back in town, asking about her father—"

"He could have taken drastic steps to ensure his shameful secret never got out," Poppy concluded. "It wouldn't be the first time Grant has resorted to terrible deeds to get what he wanted." After all, Grant had been our suspect in the murder of his own son, Kevin, due to some unscrupulous dealings we'd uncovered.

My body hummed with anxiety. "What should we do? Tell Holden what we've learned?"

"Definitely." Poppy already had her phone in her hand and dialed his number.

"Not in here." I tossed twenty-five dollars on the bar to tip Sterling for his candidness before cupping Poppy by the elbow and dragging her toward the exit. "Let's talk out in the car."

Holden's line was still ringing by the time we were situated in my SUV. His voicemail finally clicked on. *"You've reached Chief Holden Whitfield. I'm sorry to have missed your call. If this is an emergency, please hang up and dial 9-1-1."*

Poppy pressed the End button and keyed in another number, switching the output to speakerphone. Before I could ask who she was calling, a familiar voice picked up. "Crucible Police Department, this is Holly speaking."

"Hey, Holly," Poppy greeted the internal affairs officer. "Front desk duty again?"

Holly didn't return Poppy's cheerful tone. "Sorry, Pops, is this important? It's all hands on deck right now." She sounded incredibly stressed.

"What's going on?" Poppy shot me a spooked look.

The sigh Holly emitted crackled against the speaker. "Still waiting to find out. A fire broke out at one of Trae's cabins, so Chief Whitfield and the team are down at Waking Woods assisting the fire department."

"A fire?" I couldn't contain my shock.

"Yeah, hi, Hazel." A loud *bang* sounded from Holly's end. "Look, ladies, sorry to cut things short, but I've got to call the county fire investigator so we can figure out if an arsonist is on the loose." Holly ended the call before we could apologize for bothering her.

"An arsonist? In Crucible?" I felt like I had been shish kabobbed by a broomstick.

Poppy pinched the bridge of her nose. "What's a little arson with your murder, right?"

I tilted my head. "What do you mean?"

"You heard Holly. One of *Trae's* cabins?" Poppy stared dubiously at me, clearly waiting for me to follow her train of thought.

It didn't take me long to catch up. "You're thinking Marjorie's killer set fire to her cabin? Why?"

She shrugged. "Maybe Sterling wasn't the only potential father who visited her there. Maybe Grant came by and wanted to ensure that the police didn't find any trace of him."

"Yeah, but wouldn't he have been too late?" I saw big holes in her theory. "Remember what Trae told us? The police already searched her cabin."

Poppy opened her mouth, but nothing immediately came out. "I guess you're right." She sounded so disappointed. "Perhaps Grant didn't know her cabin had been searched and thought it was worth the risk."

"I'll give you that one." I gripped the steering wheel. "What do we do now? It sounds like Holden has his hands full. Should we tell Declan what we've learned about Marjorie searching for her father?"

Poppy winced. "The logical part of me says yes, but I don't want Holden to get in trouble once Declan finds out what we've been up to..."

I considered her point. "Why don't we invite Holden over for dinner, and we can tell him then? A few hours won't hurt."

My aunt's fingers danced across her phone screen, and soon, an invitation to dinner at my house popped up in our family chat. "What do we do in the meantime? Go talk with Grant?"

"Yeah, no way." I was not about to put myself in a room with a potential killer...again. "We've got to be smart about this, Pops. Grant is an extremely powerful guy. If he gets wind of what we know—"

"Yeah, yeah, it was a bad idea." She grimaced. "I knew it as soon as I said it."

"Why don't we take a breather for a bit?" I suggested. "Let's place a pickup order from Elderberry Inn. One of Bea's chicken pot pies is calling my name." The hearty meal would hopefully make Holden feel better, too, after a rough day.

I couldn't miss Poppy's crestfallen expression. "Fine."

I reached for her hand and squeezed before starting the engine. I understood the agitation she was feeling, but we had to pump the brakes on following this sensational new lead. For our own safety, as well as the integrity of the official police investigation.

I called Elderberry Inn over Bluetooth and ordered family-sized portions of Caesar salad and chicken pot pie.

"Do you mind a little bit of a wait?" Bea Thompson sounded worried. "We're just wrapping a private party, so the kitchen is a little chaotic."

"Not at all," I assured her.

"Great. We'll have it ready in forty!"

Since the drive to downtown Crucible would take us less than twenty minutes, I suggested we swing by Bright Moon and grab a caffeinated pick-me-up.

"Sounds good," Poppy murmured.

We spent the commute in thoughtful silence. Well, my silence was thoughtful. Poppy just looked restless.

As I parked on Rosewood Lane, I noticed the lights were on in Ezra's bookstore. Wasn't he supposed to be hosting Caius?

"Do you mind if I check on Ez real quick?" I nodded in the direction of his storefront.

Poppy slouched in her seat. "No worries. But I'm gonna chill here, okay? Feeling a bit tired all of a sudden."

I studied her muted expression. "Why not grab a coffee?"

"Eh, then I'll have trouble sleeping, and that's been tough enough lately."

I frowned. "Need one of my lavender candles or something?" Poppy rarely had problems sleeping. A perk of eternal optimism.

She waved me away. "Go see your boyfriend, little niece."

Clearly, she wanted a moment alone.

I left her with her thoughts and the keys to my car. "Be back in ten," I said as I closed the driver-side door and headed toward the bookstore.

In the early evening light, I could see Ezra moving around inside, holding what looked to be a long PVC pipe. A few other patrons milled about.

Curious about where Caius was, I crossed the threshold and made my way toward Ezra. "Hey, what happened to your brother?"

He whirled around, his expression momentarily startled before it softened at the sight of me. "Oh, hi, luv. His bus got delayed out of Port Authority. So, I thought I'd open for a few hours while getting some admin work done."

I glanced at the long white tube in his hand. "Does your admin work involve plumbing?"

He laughed. "No. It involves some redecorating. This is a poster tube. And you'll never guess what's inside."

I arched an eyebrow, waiting.

Ezra slipped a rolled-up print out of the tube and unveiled the image. My jaw dropped at the sight of the red and neon yellow graphic splashed across the center.

"It arrived this afternoon," Ezra explained, holding up a poster announcing the release of *Under the Red Barn*. "Marjorie's publisher must really be burning the midnight oil to promote this book."

"Oh my goodness." I assessed the bold print declaring the new, rapidly approaching launch date. "That's…"

"Tacky as all get out?" Ezra finished my sentence with a snort. "Agreed. I really don't want to hang this massive thing up, but I also don't need to get put on the naughty list with my book distributors."

"Would you like some help?" I offered.

As Ezra and I struggled to hang the garish poster in his front window, a trio of familiar figures waved to us outside from the sidewalk.

"Hey, you two. Need help?" Ione Martin asked as she hurried inside, followed by Tula and Tobias Sardolous.

My arms were shaking as I tried to keep the heavy poster material against the glass. "That would be great."

"I'm sorry," Ezra said with bright red cheeks, "my tape dispenser got all tangled."

Ione and Tobias both rushed to my aid, each taking a corner of the poster and holding it in place.

Tula *tsked* as she gently took the tape from Ezra. "Let me get this straightened out."

Behind his mother's back, Tobias rolled his eyes. "That's about as high tech as she can handle."

Ione knocked him with her shoulder. "Be nice to your mom."

"What's he saying about me now?" Tula's stern gaze twinkled in jest.

"Just how resourceful you are, Mother, with technology made before the 1980s," Tobias said while sending Ione a teasing death glare. "Haven't seen a poster this big for a book in…well, never. What gives, Ezra?"

Ezra joined us in holding a corner while Tula worked her magic with the tape dispenser. "Don't ask me. Seems a bit sleazy, considering this poor author died only a few days ago."

Ione lifted her side of the poster so she could read the front lettering. "Hey, wait a second. Isn't this the woman who was killed outside Hazel's place?"

I winced at my name being so closely associated with a murder victim. "The same." My gaze slid to Tula, suddenly remembering she had been one of the people in Marjorie's Polaroid. "Marjorie Zeller. Did any of you guys meet her while she was staying in town?"

Tula fumbled with the tape dispenser before glancing at me. "I did. I actually ran into her last week at your place, Ione."

Ione tilted her head. "Oh, yeah, I remember now. You had lunch with her, right? Odd little scene."

"It was so weird. Only a few days before she died," Tula admitted before slicing off a piece of tape. "Here you are." She handed it to me to press against the poster corner.

"Why did you have lunch with her?" Had Marjorie somehow figured out Tula was one of the people in the photo, even though she hadn't found her in the yearbook?

"Well," Tula said as she handed Ione the next piece of tape, "she heard my last name called when my order was up and wanted to know if I was from Greece." She gave a swath to Tobias. "I guess she had spent a semester there. We got to talking, and when she found out I'd lived in Crucible most of my life, she invited me to join her while we ate our salads. She told me she was doing research for her next book and wanted to know more about the area."

Ezra frowned as he received a piece of tape to secure the last corner of the poster. "She was writing a book about Crucible?"

"She didn't tell me much." Tula handed him the fixed dispenser. "Although from the questions she asked me, it sounded more like a genealogy project than a book."

"What kind of questions did she have?" Ezra, my knight in shining armor, pressed for more details.

"They were about Jane Zeller, a young woman I went to school with." Tula nodded toward the poster. "At the time, I didn't understand why she was interested, but once I learned her last name from the news report about her murder, I realized she must have been somehow related to Jane."

Tobias reached for his mother's arm. "Hey, Mom, we gotta get going. That thing, remember?"

As Tula bobbed her head, I realized our time for getting answers was running short. "What did she ask you about Jane?" My pulse raced with anticipation.

Tula twirled a strand of her long dark hair. "She wanted to know who Jane's friends were in school or if she had a boyfriend."

"That's random." Ione placed her hands on her slender hips.

Tula gave a reluctant chuckle. "That's what Tobias said when I told him about the conversation."

Tobias, however, didn't laugh. "Mom, we're gonna be late."

Ione knocked Tobias's arm. "Hush. Your mom had face time with a *murder* victim. We need more deets." She turned back to Tula, ready for more gossip. Bless her. "Go on, Tul. What else happened?"

"Nothing noteworthy, I'm afraid." Tula's cheeks colored. "I told her Jane Zeller would often hang out with my friend group, but once we all went off to college, I never crossed paths with her again." Her brow furrowed. "Marjorie then asked for a list of people I was friends with, but before I could tell her, she got a call and had to leave in a hurry."

"Did she have you look at old photographs or anything?" I knew I was taking a risk with such an odd question, but I had to know if Tula had identified Grant Finchmore in the Polaroid.

"Mom!" Tobias's clipped reprimand made me jump. "Grant is expecting us."

"Oh my," Tula fretted as she glanced at her watch, "you're right, darling. We can't have Mr. Finchmore waiting on us." But as her son dragged her toward the door, she turned to me. "She didn't show me any photographs, no."

I tried to conceal my disappointment with a smile. "Well, at least you have an intriguing story to share at parties."

"No kidding." Ione snorted.

"Sorry, everyone, but the Finchmores need us," Tobias called over his shoulder as he ushered his mother out of the bookstore.

Ione stared after them. "That boy is too tightly wound when it comes to that family."

Ezra and I chuckled at her assessment. "If only I could find someone as dedicated as Tobias when it comes to hiring a helper for this place." He motioned to the bookshelves surrounding us.

"Good luck with that." Ione patted him on the shoulder. "And don't you try poaching one of my guys."

"Wouldn't dream of it." Ezra cocked his head toward the poster. "Thanks for bringing in all the helping hands, Ione."

"Anytime. Tobias had just guilted me into providing lunch for the Big Melt volunteers, so he owed me a favor."

I grinned. "Seems to be his MO these days," I said and told her about the last-minute candle order he'd made.

"Well, at least we're getting paid good money for it." She bid us goodbye and departed.

Ezra and I studied our handiwork. "What do you make of Marjorie and Tula's encounter?" he asked in lowered tones, mindful there were still patrons milling about the store.

I mulled over Tula's story. "I can't help but wonder if Marjorie targeted her once she heard Tula's name called at Sip. I know her last name is different than what it was in high school, but Tula isn't exactly a common name in this area."

"But we didn't find her picture marked in the yearbook," Ezra pointed out.

"Maybe because she wasn't a potential father candidate."

"But Jane's picture was flagged." Ezra kept poking holes in my theory.

"Tula said they had lunch a few days before Marjorie died. Maybe Marjorie removed the tag because her conversation with Tula didn't pan out."

But then why was Sterling Ildrich still marked in the yearbook? I internally challenged my own reasoning. Did Marjorie suspect he was lying about not being her father?

Before Ezra could respond with his own doubts, his phone rang. "Caius. His bus is probably getting in soon."

I stood on my tiptoes to kiss his cheek. "Then you should close this place and get going. I need to get back to Poppy, anyway."

"Okay. I'll text you later, luv."

As I strolled back to my parked car, I replayed Tula's odd lunch meeting with Marjorie. Amazed by both parties' willingness to share a meal with a complete stranger, I also stewed over Tobias's surly behavior while his mom shared the hot gossip. I understood not wanting to be late for a work thing, but his harsh tone had seemed a bit over-the-top. Did he normally speak to his doting mother like that?

I found Poppy leaning back in the passenger's seat, an old A Wick in Time baseball cap pulled down over her face.

"Pops?"

She pushed back the brim of the hat, and her eyelids fluttered open. "Hey, that was quick. I was just catching a power nap."

"Feeling okay?"

Poppy nodded as she removed the baseball cap. "How was Ezra?"

"Good. His brother's bus was delayed, so he was taking care of some work." I took the hat from her and tossed it onto the backseat, from where she'd probably dug it out. "Had an interesting run-in with Tula while I was there. She and Marjorie had lunch together." I climbed into the car and started the engine.

Poppy straightened in her seat. "Really?"

I drove the short distance up the road to The Elderberry Inn.

"Marjorie approached her while Tula was getting lunch at Sip. Asked her all kinds of questions about Jane Zeller and who her acquaintances were."

"Did Marjorie show Tula the Polaroid?" Poppy clenched the strap of her seatbelt. "Did she figure out that Grant Finchmore was the last man standing?"

I shook my head. "Tula said Marjorie didn't show her any photographs. Their conversation got cut short by a phone call."

Poppy deflated at the news. "Then we still don't know if Marjorie was able to identify Grant from the picture."

"No, we don't." All our burgeoning theories rested on figuring out this key piece of information.

The Elderberry Inn glowed with activity as I pulled into the parking lot. The elegant boutique hotel sat on the north side of the Crucible Commons, the perfect spot for visitors looking to enjoy our town's many amenities. The inn also maintained one of the nicest restaurants in the county, and the luxury cars filling the parking area reflected the high-end clientele the food attracted.

"Want to come say hi to Bea, or do you want to stay here?" I figured I'd offer Poppy the chance to continue her nap. My bestie still looked a bit peaked.

She waved away the idea. "Nah, I'm fine, Hazel. And I'll feel even better once I have some food in me."

We strolled up the pathway that led to the inn's gorgeous porch entryway. From the large windows, I noted the dining room was jam-packed. Thankfully, the hit piece in the *Interpreter* hadn't seemed to affect local businesses.

The aroma of butter, bread, and grilled meats swirled around as Poppy and I entered the grand foyer, my stomach grumbling with appreciation.

"Hello, welcome to—oh, hey, ladies!" Jada Ryan's wide smile greeted us.

"Hey, girl." Poppy gushed, her cheery demeanor returning with a vengeance. "Counting down the days until commencement?" Jada had been a longtime employee that Bea had been training to manage the inn once Jada graduated from the nearby SUNY school.

The young coed practically bounced behind the registration desk.

"Five weeks, two days, and…" She paused to glance at her smartwatch. "Fourteen hours, but who's counting?"

I chuckled at her candid response. "I loved my college experience, but by senior year, I was ready to be done, too."

Jada motioned to the intimate lobby, her black braids sweeping across the tops of her shoulders. "I just can't wait to be here full-time."

"I know Bea is excited, too," Poppy added. Bea was a good friend of hers from high school. "She's so proud of how much you've grown."

Jada's cheeks darkened at the compliment. "Bea's the best. I wouldn't have made it this far without her."

"Yes, you would've," I assured the young woman. "You've worked hard for this and deserve everything coming to you."

"What a hype team." Jada giggled, although her eyes glistened with heartfelt emotion. "What can I help you guys with tonight?"

"We're picking up a dinner order." I glanced toward the open double doors that led into the grand dining area and froze.

Seated at one of the tables, alone, was Monica Finchmore.

Chapter 23

I didn't know what was more shocking. The Finchmore matriarch dining among us mere peasants, or the fact that she was by herself. Usually, Monica was followed by a gaggle of ardent admirers and socialites.

Jada, oblivious to my inner turmoil, reached for the desk phone. "I'll call the kitchen and see if it's ready."

Poppy, however, immediately knew something was up on my end. Her right eye twitched, and she followed my curious gaze.

A heartbeat later, my aunt's white-knuckled fingers wrapped around my wrist. "Hexes," she mumbled under her breath so that only I could hear, "that's one stormy aura."

Before I could pry further, Jada set down the receiver. "Renaldo says your order will be out in ten. Sorry for the delay. How about a drink on the house?" She ushered us into the dining area and toward the long, upscale bar. A complete one-eighty from the décor of Roadside Station.

Nick, the bartender on shift, dipped his chin in greeting. "I'll take care of them, Jada. What can I get you ladies?"

We thanked Jada for her hospitality and gracious hosting, and then Poppy ordered a vodka soda, while I opted for just an unsweetened iced tea.

Nick ambled to the far end of the bar to prepare our drinks, giving me the opportunity to pepper Poppy with questions. "What's up with Monica?" I murmured before casually tossing a glance over my shoulder.

The polished, dark-haired woman dined on a salad and bottle of wine, her attention glued to her phone.

"She is maaaad." Poppy stretched out the syllables to convey the extent of Monica's sour mood.

I gulped. "Any idea why?"

"One way to find out." Poppy hopped down from the barstool she'd claimed and skipped over to Monica's table. "Hi, there, Mon," she exclaimed as if greeting an old friend. "Haven't seen you out on the town in a long time."

I nearly laughed at the shocked expression that eclipsed Monica's face, as if she couldn't believe someone had the audacity to speak to her so informally.

"Hello, Poppy." Her cool response sent a shiver down my spine, but my bestie, bless her, didn't bat an eyelash.

"What brings you here?" Poppy placed a hand on her hip.

Monica's gaze slid from my aunt to me watching their exchange from over at the bar. "Hello to you, too, Hazel."

With a meek smile, I waved and slid off my chair to join this strange tête-à-tête. "Hi, Mrs. Finchmore." I couldn't summon the courage to speak to her like an equal.

Poppy folded her arms, her nose wrinkling. Monica had ignored her question.

"I heard from Tula that you had a lovely time in Turks and Caicos," I added, trying to steer the conversation back to what she was doing here. "Are you excited for the Big Melt?"

"Excited?" Monica's laugh was sharp and pointed. "Hardly. Grant can deal with that Podunk debacle himself." She folded her slender arms, her designer blouse shimmering in the candlelight.

I tried to hide my irritation over her elitist response. I'd never heard any of the Finchmores speak so poorly about Crucible traditions before. Yes, they may have been obscenely wealthy, but they'd always respected the town that had paved the way to their life of privilege. Clearly, something had gotten under Monica's Botoxed skin.

"Debacle?" Poppy tilted her head, her expression neutral.

Monica flicked her wrist. "Good luck convincing people to come to a festival with a murderer on the loose."

Unwittingly, she had given us the perfect opening to ask about Marjorie. "Did you know the woman who was killed?" I asked.

"Heavens, no." Monica looked affronted by the suggestion.

I snuck a peek at Poppy to see what her whim was picking up. Her lips were pressed in a tight line. "Are you sure about that, Monica? Marjorie Zeller doesn't ring a bell?"

"Why would she?" Monica snapped. "I mean, I heard she was a writer or something from *New Jersey*. Like I'd have any connections there."

I almost rolled my eyes at her sneering reaction.

"Well, you used to." Poppy lifted her chin in challenge. I'd never seen her speak so boldly before. "Or have you forgotten about Jane Zeller?"

"Jane? Have you been talking with Tula? What does Jane Zell—" Monica stopped mid-question, her jaw hanging open as her eyes widened.

"Enough of this. I don't have to answer to the Glenmyres." In a fluid motion, she rose from her chair and grabbed her purse. "My husband might respect your little family, but I've always thought you were a bunch of self-important goody-two-shoes."

"Us? Self-important?" I couldn't hold back a scoff. I wanted to say more, but Poppy gripped my elbow. One glance at her face, and I zipped my lips. She looked genuinely frightened.

Monica tossed her hair dangerously close to my cheek. "Ugh, I can't wait to get out of this place once and for all." She stomped past us, knocking Poppy back a step. To our continued surprise, instead of leaving the inn, she stormed upstairs toward the guest suites.

"What in the hexes was that all about?" I turned to my aunt, worried by her quivering lip.

Before she could reply, Nick called out to us from the bar. "Hey, Glenmyres, your food is ready earlier than expected. Would you like these to go?" He pointed to the two drinks waiting for us on the countertop.

"That'd be great, Nick. Thanks," I said with a tight smile.

Poppy directed me toward our abandoned beverages. "Let's talk outside."

Despite the fact that I was nearly bursting with raging curiosity, I obeyed and helped Poppy lug our takeout order to the car. Once we were buckled and on the road, Poppy finally let out a long sigh.

"I think we had it wrong, Hazel. I think Monica was the one who killed Marjorie. Not Grant."

I kept my hands glued to the steering wheel as I did my best to maintain focus on the road. We no longer had the luxury of Grandmaster Jedidiah's protection shield to keep us safe while driving. "What did you see in her aura, Pops?"

Her face dropped into her hands. "It was terrible. Anger. So much rage and hatred. Especially once I mentioned J-Jane."

I realized my aunt was quietly crying and reached out to give her thigh a comforting pat.

"There were also pulsating waves of humiliation." Poppy sounded puzzled. "That, honestly, was the dominating emotion."

"Humiliation?" I repeated. I shouldn't have been surprised. To Monica, reputation and appearance were everything. If the world learned her doting, beloved husband had cheated on her, of course Monica would be mortified. "How do you think she found out about Grant and the affair?"

Poppy shrugged. "I don't know. It must have been pretty recent, though. Her emotional wounds were fresh."

An idea burst into my mind. "She mentioned Tula. Do you think Tula told her and Grant about running into someone asking questions about Jane?"

"It's possible." Poppy tapped her chin. "You think hearing Jane's name after all this time kindled Grant's guilt over cheating on his wife and that's what forced him to come clean?"

I gnawed on my lower lip. "Is Grant capable of feeling such an emotion?"

Poppy smirked at my not-so-subtle dig. "However it came about, Monica is livid."

"You've seen anger and rage in a person's aura before," I began in a soft voice, "and they turned out not to be killers. What makes you think Monica killed Marjorie?"

"I can't quite put my finger on it, but there also was this desperate need to escape." Poppy leaned her forehead against her passenger window. "It just gave me a really bad feeling."

I recalled how Monica had fled upstairs. "She's just learned her husband has been unfaithful. Maybe she wants to escape her marriage. That could very well be the reason she's staying at The Elderberry Inn and skipping out on the Big Melt."

From the corner of my eye, I saw Poppy glare at me. "Why are you trying to undermine my whim reading?"

"I'm not trying to undermine it," I said defensively. "I'm just providing possible theories as to why Monica is feeling the way she is."

"No. *You* don't trust my whim anymore." Poppy's tone was harsh. "You haven't trusted yours since Kevin Finchmore's death, and now, you don't trust mine."

Where the heck was this coming from? I felt my hackles rise at her sudden attack and retorted, "Well, can you blame me? You didn't exactly pick up on our town's last killer until I had a gun pointed at me."

I regretted the unfair words the moment they flew across my lips. "I-I'm sorry. That was uncalled for. I didn't mean to say—"

"Low blow, Hazel."

I winced as I pulled the SUV into my driveway. "I said I was sorry. I didn't mean—"

"Didn't mean to say it's *my* fault murderers are still walking around Crucible? That it's *my* fault people are dying because my whim isn't good enough?"

There wasn't any malice or rage in Poppy's response. Only panic, fear, and sorrow.

"No! No, of course not." I frantically tried to fix my terrible mistake, but by now, Poppy's sobs filled the car.

"B-because I know it's my fault. I'm failing everyone, Hazel."

Parked safely in front of my cottage, I wrapped Poppy in a tight, if awkward, hug. "You're not. You're being too hard on yourself.

You've done so much good with your whim, Pops. You can't blame yourself like this. People who purposely take the lives of others...they likely don't have the conscience to have their regrets reflected in their aura."

Poppy wiped the back of her hand across her red eyes. "I know. I know. You're right."

I studied her, worried. We'd had similar conversations before. What was getting Poppy so worked up about this one in particular? "I'm sorry for what I said, too. I trust your whim. I do. I just want us to consider all our options, or we could send Holden and the police down the wrong path."

Poppy sniffled as she dug a tissue out of her purse. "You're right," she repeated. "I'm sorry for getting so defensive. I honestly don't know what's gotten into me." She blew her nose, and her breathing seemed to steady. "Must be this annoying headache coming on."

"Let's get that nipped in the bud, then." I searched her weary gaze, hoping we could put this uncharacteristic spat behind us. "Are we okay?"

"Yeah, we're okay." Poppy wiped her eyes one final time. "Let's blame it on being hangry. I'm starving, and the smell of the chicken pot pie is driving me nuts."

I let loose a half-hearted giggle. Our takeout meal did smell incredible even from the trunk. I could always count on Poppy to brighten the mood.

"I'll warm up the oven. Can you see where Holden is?" I asked as I climbed out of the car. I grabbed the paper bag containing our food and headed toward the porch.

Poppy trailed after me, her nose in her phone. "He just messaged our group chat. He'll be here in fifteen."

His impending arrival gave me the perfect amount of time to say hi to my fur babies and prep dinner. Still feeling guilty for suggesting Poppy was at fault for me getting cornered by a killer, I insisted she relax on the couch with her drink. She looked like she needed a breather.

As I warmed up the pot pie and tossed the salad, I watched Poppy from my spot in the kitchen. My aunt still seemed out of sorts as she swirled her vodka soda that Nick had poured into the portable alcohol containers Elderberry Inn used for DoorDash and Uber Eats deliveries.

I didn't know what else to do except let her decompress. While I felt bad for snapping at her, I didn't regret questioning her whim. We couldn't just go accuse someone willy-nilly because Poppy saw anger and rage in Monica's aura. Everything Poppy had seen seemed justifiable for a scorned woman in Monica's position. That didn't make the Finchmore matriarch a murderer.

"What I really want to know," I said, speaking to Noli, who perched on her hindlegs, begging for dinner scraps, "is how Monica found out about Jane and Grant. It had to be because Tula mentioned her conversation with Marjorie to the Finchmores, right?"

From what we'd uncovered so far, Marjorie had yet to connect the dots that Grant was, in all likelihood, her father. So, if that were true, and Grant or Monica was our killer, it had to mean that Grant already knew about Marjorie's existence and had come clean to Monica about his affair resulting in a child. After keeping a secret like that for so long, why break his silence now? Could it really be out of guilt? Or was there a more sinister reason for the timely confession?

Chapter 24

I considered Grant's prior corrupt business practices involving his late son, Kevin. He might have been a generous benefactor to Crucible, but he was definitely no saint. I'd thought him capable of murder on numerous occasions. If Grant believed the Finchmore empire was in jeopardy, he wouldn't hesitate to take action. Had he confessed his indiscretions to Monica in an effort to rally the family together to prevent a scandal? And if Monica knew about Marjorie, did that mean Yvonne did too?

"Now, there's an interesting angle," I said to Noli, trying to recall the last time I'd interacted with the young heiress. It took a few more tosses of lettuce leaves to remember. "Yvonne was at the Rose & Raven gig with Blair."

Noli tilted her head, as if to say, *Who, Hazel?*

I chuckled at the pup's reaction before my mind returned to Yvonne. She hadn't seemed on edge or anything at Cold Cauldron. In fact, she'd been rather sociable until Poppy's prying questions had driven her off.

Poppy's prophetic words from that night suddenly rang in my ears. *"The Finchmores arrive back in town earlier than expected, and a woman turns up dead soon after? It's curious timing, that's all."*

Given everything we now knew about Marjorie, it *was* curious timing. Had Grant somehow gotten wind that Marjorie was in the area visiting Constance? Had his illegitimate daughter's presence in Crucible been the catalyst for the Finchmores' sudden return?

"Hey, Pops," I called as I set the salad bowl on the kitchen table. "Remember our run-in with Yvonne and Blair at Cold Cauldron?"

Poppy meandered into the kitchen, leaning against the archway. "Um, I guess so. What about it?"

"Yvonne told us that Grant made them all leave Turks and Caicos early to be more involved in the Big Melt, right? Do you think that's true, or just a cover story?"

Poppy's brow furrowed. "Well, Yvonne was telling what she believed to be the truth, but I still think it's fishy. Grant opens his checkbook every year for the Big Melt, but he's never really been involved in it before." She snorted. "Not like he's been involved this year at all. Poor Tobias is juggling everything on the Finchmore end."

I frowned as I began setting the table. "So, why cut a family vacation early?"

Poppy's eyes widened. "You think Grant found out from his network of minions that Marjorie was here and decided to deal with her himself?"

I nodded when a knock sounded from the front door.

"It's me." Holden's announcement was followed by a cough.

We hurried to greet him, our welcoming smiles vanishing at the sight of our cousin. His face and uniform were covered in soot.

"Holy hexes, Chief." Until now, I'd completely forgotten about the fire at Waking Woods campground. I guessed murder took higher priority than arson. "Did you run into the fire yourself?" I rushed forward to ensure he wasn't hurt.

"I look worse than I feel." He stifled another cough. "Is it all right if I grab a shower real quick before the inquisition begins?"

"Of course." I held my arm out in the direction of the bathroom.

Holden hoisted a small duffle bag off the ground, giving Noli a little scratch as she whimpered to greet him. "Sorry, girl. I'll give you a proper hello in a bit. Don't want to get you all dirty."

With that, Holden hurried to wash up, leaving Poppy and me

speechless—for a minute.

"Jeez, I totally spaced about the fire at Trae's." Poppy ran a hand through her hair.

"Same. I hope everything is okay."

We wandered back into the kitchen. "Do you think it was Marjorie's cabin?" Poppy asked. "Someone trying to get rid of potential evidence?"

I poured three iced teas and went to get the chicken pot pie out of the oven. "We'll find out soon enough." I motioned for her to take a seat and relax. She still seemed on edge to me. "Are you feeling okay, Poppy?"

"Yeah, I'm fine. I mean, as fine as one can be in our situation." She massaged her temples. "And this headache isn't going away."

"Want something for it?" I offered. "Pain reliever? Hot pack?"

She shook her head. "Don't worry about me."

"I can't help but worry."

Holden joined us a few minutes later, freshly showered and in a spare change of clothes. "Something smells good." He sat down in his regular chair, looking like the weight of the world was on his shoulders.

"What happened, cuz?" I scooped a mound of steaming pot pie onto his plate.

Holden scarfed down a bite before answering. "Sorry. Couldn't wait," he said with his mouth full.

I chuckled and dished food out for Poppy and myself.

Poppy launched into her questioning. "Was Marjorie's cabin set on fire? Any idea how it started? Is there anything recoverable from the scene?"

Holden held up a hand. "Pause, Pops. This had nothing to do with Marjorie. It was a cabin being rented by that 'friendly' Canadian couple you guys mentioned."

"What?" I nearly choked on a bite of biscuit and gravy. The welcoming faces of the folks we'd met over the weekend flashed through my mind. "Omigosh, are they okay?"

Holden scoffed. "Oh, they're fine. Besides the fact they're the first people to take up residence in our temporary jail cell."

Poppy dropped her fork. "Jail cell?"

"Turns out," Holden said as he scooped another bite into his mouth, "that our pals from the north have a habit of leaving destruction in their wake. Four motels they've stayed at during their American road trip had suspicious fires on the premises while the Hendersons were in residence." Holden arched an eyebrow. "I assume you can figure out where this is going."

I shook my head in disbelief. "You mean, the sweet ol' Hendersons are a couple of firebugs?"

Holden arched a sardonic eyebrow. "Do I detect a hint of ageism, Hazel?"

"No! I mean—goodness, who'd have thought?" I turned to Poppy, utterly baffled.

Poppy's shoulders curled forward. "I can't believe I didn't see anything suspicious in their auras. Broomsticks, I should have questioned why they were so ridiculously excited by the kindling they'd gathered. But they just seemed like nice, regular people."

Uh-oh. I didn't like where this conversation was taking us. Poppy had already suffered one blow to her ego today regarding her whim.

"Come on, Pops. You're being too hard on yourself again. We were just asking them questions about Marjorie. The Hendersons gave us no reason to think anything else about them beyond that. And we know you were right that they were telling the truth about Marjorie having a gentleman caller."

"You figured out who it was?" It was Holden's turn to put us in the hot seat.

Poppy nodded. "That and much more."

In between mouthfuls of crunchy salad and gooey chicken pot pie, we took turns sharing what we'd uncovered about Marjorie's mysterious reason for sticking around Crucible.

"Her father can only be Grant," I concluded, scraping the last of my dinner off my plate.

"That's quite an interesting theory, cousins. And would explain why the Finchmores lawyered up the moment I reached out to Grant's office about the case." Holden jotted some notes down on a small pad of paper he'd pulled out midway through our conversation. "That is, if Jane Zeller was telling the truth to begin with."

"Huh?" Poppy tilted her head.

"Her daughter just happens to be the love child of a *billionaire*?" Skepticism oozed from Holden's gaze. "Why keep that from Marjorie? You've told me that both Lauren and Constance said Marjorie's mom never spoke about her dad. Why deny Marjorie the right to know her father, especially one as stable and successful as Grant?"

I furrowed my brow. Curses, he'd made a good point.

"You know how people like the Finchmores operate." Poppy rolled her eyes, as if the answer should be obvious. "Grant probably paid Jane to keep quiet. I bet an NDA was involved."

Holden leaned back in his chair and stretched his arms over his head. "You're assuming Grant knew he was the father. Maybe Jane never told him. And if that's the case, he'd have no reason to kill Marjorie."

"Then why lawyer up so quickly?" I countered. "Why not answer your questions about Marjorie?"

Holden chuckled. "I think Poppy said it best."

"People like the Finchmores lawyer up for everything." Poppy propped her elbow on the table as she begrudgingly rested her cheek on her hand. "If I was as important as Grant Finchmore believes he is, I would not want police asking me questions about a murdered woman."

"It wasn't even Grant I spoke with. It was his executive assistant, Mr. Sardolous," Holden admitted. "He immediately referred me to Grant's legal team. And, of course, they weren't very forthcoming, either." Holden folded his arms. "They requested that a copy of the Polaroid be sent to them for further examination."

"Did you?" I asked.

"Heck no." Holden shook his head. "Grant hasn't been charged with anything, so I don't have to share our evidence with his counsel. I told them they could come to the station and review it themselves."

A bemused grin twitched on my lips. "I take it that offer wasn't received well."

"No." Holden rose from his chair and began gathering our dirty dishes. "All I wanted was a quick chat with Grant, and it's turned into a three-ringed circus of bureaucracy."

Poppy's blue eyes twinkled in the overhead light. "If it's a quick chat you want..."

I gnawed on my lower lip, confused by her words. "What are you thinking?"

She leaned forward, eagerness brimming from her. "Tobias might be trained to throw a wall of lawyers at the police, but maybe not at Grant's peers. What if we use our family connections to get a meeting with him?"

"*Family* connections?" I still wasn't following her train of thought. "Why would Grant agree to meet over that?"

"Come on, we're the Glenmyres, and..." Poppy paused as she searched for inspiration. "And it's Holden's first Big Melt as a member of one of Crucible's founding families!" Her excitement grew. "We thought it would be a good idea for the Glenmyres and Finchmores to get together and chat about the town. You know, take stock of things as the town's benefactors and protectors."

Holden tried to stifle a laugh, but it leaked out through his fingers.

"What? It *might* work," Poppy said with an indignant huff. "Grant has always cared about Crucible in his own way. And he respects the traditions of the founders."

"Are you sure?" I recalled our Elderberry Inn visit. "Monica didn't seem too thrilled."

"Well, she's a Finchmore by marriage, not blood." Poppy stared me down. "Grant cares about the reputation of the town and his family. Hexes, he might even be willing to *kill* for it."

I could see in her eyes that she wasn't going to give this up. "It's worth a shot." I glanced at Holden and shrugged. "What have we got to lose?"

Chapter 25

Holden dabbed his lips with a napkin before tossing it on his empty plate. "Fine. If it gets me through the door for a chat, I'm in." He surveyed us both. "I suppose it can't hurt to have Poppy's whim on my side, either."

A hard lump of envy formed in my throat. No one ever wanted assistance from *my* whim.

Poppy clapped her hands in giddy triumph. "And with you at our side, we're at no risk of getting into trouble."

"There's *always* a risk, which is why I'll be armed." Holden's tone left no room for discussion. "And the minute you see something suspicious in Grant's aura, I want us gone."

My aunt deflated at this demand. "But—"

"No buts." Holden stood firm. "We go in, fish around, and see if you can get a read on him. Then, if Grant bites, I'll return through more official investigative channels."

"Fine." Poppy sniffed, clearly not happy.

I studied her intently. Why was she giving Holden a hard time about this? "It's for our safety, Pops. And the integrity of the case," I added. "If Grant's lawyers get wind of something underhanded from

Holden's end, it could spell trouble later down the line."

"I said fine!" Poppy's response was snippy at best.

A frown grew on Holden's face. "Are you okay? You seem a bit out of sorts, cuz."

"I just want Marjorie's killer caught, all right?" She threw her hands defensively in the air. "Is that so bad?"

"No. Of course not. We all want that." Holden spoke in calm, measured tones as if he were negotiating with an agitated suspect, not a family member. "We just need to do this smartly and safely."

"Yeah, yeah, I get it." Poppy batted away his remark. "Should we call Grant now and set something up?"

I balked at the notion. I rarely interacted with Grant Finchmore and certainly didn't have his phone number.

Poppy must have realized the same thing. "I guess I can call Tobias and see if we can get on Grant's schedule."

"You sure he won't refer you to Grant's lawyers?" The corner of Holden's lip twitched.

"No, he won't see anything coming." Poppy snickered. "He'll be a good little minion."

Before I could reprimand her for her degrading comment, Poppy had her phone in her hand, the dial tone ringing through her speaker.

"Hello?" Tobias picked up, sounding out of breath.

"Hi, Tobias. It's Poppy Glenmyre," Poppy said with her signature charm. Her moody attitude from moments ago had completely vanished. "Did I catch you at a bad time?"

Tobias took a few heavy breaths before replying. "Nah, I'm just getting back from a run. Needed to work off all this nervous energy about Saturday."

I guessed the meeting with Grant that he and Tula had needed to get back for had come and gone.

"I'm sure the cooking competition will go off without a hitch." Poppy leaned closer to her phone's mic. "You've put in so much work. We really can't thank you enough for everything you've done."

I marveled at the way she gushed over Tobias's involvement in the upcoming festival. She was really buttering him up.

"All in a day's work," Tobias assured her. "Grant knows how

important the Big Melt is to the community."

"He takes his role as a town founder so seriously," Poppy agreed. "It's wonderful to see. In fact, that's kinda what I was calling about. I'm hoping to set up a little meeting of the minds between the Glenmyres and Finchmores. Our families have always looked out for Crucible, and it might be nice to discuss plans for Crucible's future." Poppy gazed hopefully at Holden and me, waiting to see if her smooth words had done the trick.

"Well..." Tobias's hesitancy radiated through the airwaves.

"We also haven't had a proper sit down to introduce Grant to the newest member of our family," Poppy added. "I'd think that Grant would want to establish a...*connection* with Crucible's new chief of police."

Holden lightly kicked Poppy in the shin, his expression stormy. I could guess why. Poppy was making it seem like Holden would be open to being in Grant's pocket.

But her sneaky subterfuge worked.

"Hmm, yes. Yes, a meeting would be good." Hurried movement on Tobias's end crackled through the phone. "With all the recent upheaval, it would be worthwhile to make sure everyone is on the same page." Tobias now sounded more enthused. "Given the shuffle within the Tarling clan, why don't I arrange a little gathering for all the founding families? A luncheon up here at Finchaven?"

While the offer wasn't quite what we'd had in mind, it still gave us prime access to speak with Grant. Surrounded by guests, he might even let his guard down.

I gave Poppy a thumbs up, and Holden nodded his agreement.

"That sounds great, Tobias," Poppy replied. "A generous offer."

"Let me see, let me see..." Tobias's voice drifted off, and we heard some tapping. "How does Thursday sound for the summit? I'm sure I can get some catering delivered, even though it's a bit last minute."

"Perfect!" Poppy beamed. "Just in time for the Big Melt." The festival kicked off Friday afternoon, with most of the events happening on Saturday.

"Exactly. Okay, sounds good, Poppy. I'll run this by Grant, but you should receive an invite soon." They exchanged pleasantries, and Tobias signed off the call.

My bestie pumped her fists triumphantly in the air once the call ended. "A Crucible *summit.* How glamorous."

I giggled. "It's honestly a good idea. Things have been…trying for the town this past year. The founding families banding together will be an encouraging sign of solidarity."

"I'm still getting used to this whole 'founding families' concept to begin with," Holden admitted. "It will be helpful to see everyone in action."

"I doubt Grant will end up inviting *everyone.*" Poppy tucked a strand of her auburn hair behind her ear. "I mean, the Sherwin clan alone is like sixty people."

I winced at the possibility. The Glenmyres may have been small in numbers, but the same couldn't be said about the Ildriches and Sherwins. "Do you think Philippa Tarling will show her face?"

"She better." Poppy grimaced. "Or people will only talk behind her back even more."

Holden's features tightened. "This is beginning to sound like a circus. How are we supposed to have a private aside with Grant to question him about Marjorie?"

Poppy clenched her fist with determination. "We'll figure something out."

~∞~

Poppy and Holden had left for the night by the time I received an email inviting me to the Finchaven estate on Thursday for a "Founding Families Fête."

"Our little ruse now has a fancy name." I chuckled as I scratched Berg's ears. My aloof gray cat had curled beside me while I typed away at my laptop. I'd been doing some payroll work while watching a new detective show on BritBox.

I RSVP'd and added the luncheon to my calendar. Iggy and Quinn were already on the schedule to cover the sales floor, meaning I just had to make sure this fête didn't derail my candle-making plans. With the Big Melt looming, the shop's inventory would be decimated after the weekend, so I needed to make sure I had candles to sell come next Wednesday.

My phone dinged with a text.

Hey, luv. Caius is settled and has already taken over my apartment. As expected. Any chance your free tomorrow for dinner?

I smiled at Ezra's message. **Of course. Want my help cooking? Should I bring anything?**

He responded immediately. **Let's go out on the town. Caius is waaay too judgy of my cooking skills. He can critique someone else. Was thinking Cold Cauldron or Briar Patch? Which is more "Crucible"?**

Cold Cauldron all the way, I sent back. I loved Briar Patch and its amazing cuisine, but Cold Cauldron was a Crucible staple, and Fitz's paranormal décor was guaranteed to entertain and amuse.

And that's why I consulted an expert. Let's meet at 6:30?

Sounds good. What about the shop? Are you working tomorrow?

Yeah, Caius actually volunteered to come help out. Altho, I imagine he'll end up monopolizing the reading nook.

I giggled at the mental picture.

We texted back and forth about our afternoons before Ezra was summoned away by his hosting duties. I hadn't even gotten the chance to bring him up to speed on our run-in with Monica. We just chatted about our families and their quirks. Ezra admitted that Caius had eviscerated his interior decorating skills the moment his brother walked into the apartment. I, in turn, shared that Poppy and I had gotten into a bit of a tiff—not over *what*, mind you—but had resolved our differences. It felt so nice to connect with Ezra about the mundane.

Our light-hearted conversation also diverted my attention from Marjorie's case for a time. But now, sitting on my couch with Noli at my feet and Berg nestled against my lap, I was back to puzzling out the confusing web Marjorie had woven during her short stay in Crucible.

Had we gotten tunnel vision about Marjorie's search for her father being the motive for her death? This was a woman who'd stolen an entire book from a close friend and published it as her own. Was there someone else out there, beyond Constance, that Marjorie had wronged?

I wondered about Lauren Johnson and whether we'd been wise to write her off with just Poppy's whim reading to go on. I hated questioning the integrity of my aunt's ability, but the words I'd spoken earlier had been from the heart. Someone ruthless enough to commit murder might very well be heartless enough not to be troubled by it.

Was Lauren still staying at Waking Woods, or had she decided to end her vacation early, what with Marjorie's death and our Canadian firebugs causing chaos? She might be someone worth following up on.

I debated texting Poppy this idea but opted not to. She'd know right away I was questioning her whim, and after her emotional response this evening, I didn't want to set her off. Perhaps if things with Grant didn't pan out, I'd broach the topic with Holden.

"Since when have I ever been afraid to go to Poppy about anything?" I cupped Berg's whiskered chin in my palm.

I feared I knew the reason but didn't address it out loud. Instead, I extricated myself from the comfy confines of the couch and got ready for bed, hoping tomorrow would bring more answers than questions.

Chapter 26

My eyes adjusted to the dim overhead lights twinkling from Mason jars as I stepped over the threshold into Cold Cauldron. I'd spent the day holed up at the shop, working on candles. Since the store wasn't open on Tuesdays, it had been blissfully quiet with no interruptions, and I now had several batches of Vanilla Toffee, Dewdrop Bouquet, Lavender, and Berry Blossom candles curing. My crafting sessions had also given me a lot of time to think about everything that had happened over the past week, and the more I mulled over Poppy's and my exploits, the more a troubling realization simmered to the surface of my concerns. But before I got too worked up, I decided to get a second opinion from an informed source.

I had purposely arrived ten minutes early for my meet-up with Ezra and Caius, as I was on a covert mission. I scanned the brewery for my quarry. The evening crowd had yet to descend upon the place, so I had my choice of tables. But instead of grabbing a high top, I headed for the bar.

Fitz was in discussion with one of his staff members, so I perched on a stool and waited for him to spot me.

"Hey, Hazel." Fitz beamed as he sauntered over to greet me. "How's it going?"

"Can't complain." I glanced nervously at my intertwined fingers, wondering if I was really going to do this. I felt a little grimy, going behind my aunt's back. "You all set for the Melt Off?" I asked conversationally.

"As prepped as I can be, I think." Fitz folded his arms across his broad chest. "Gonna be a nail biter, what with all the fancy judges Finchmore is flying in."

I bobbed my head a few more times than his remark warranted, trying to figure out how to approach the delicate subject I'd come to discuss.

Fortunately, Fitz beat me to the punch. "Hey, have you checked in with Poppy today? She canceled our dinner plans for tonight. Says she has a bad headache."

I frowned at this development. *Another headache?* "No, she didn't mention anything to me when I texted her earlier." I'd told her I was gearing up for dinner with Ezra's brother, and she wished me luck with this next big step in our relationship.

Fitz stroked his sandy beard. "She's been getting them a bunch lately, I feel like. I told her she should get her eyes checked." He pointed at my purple-and-gold spectacles from behind the counter. "Since needing glasses runs in the family."

I'd subconsciously leaned away from Fitz's outstretched hand, worried he would knock my frames askew and cause a lifeclock debacle. "Ha ha, yeah." My laughter came out half-heartedly.

This conversation confirmed what I'd feared. The more I reflected on our investigation, the more I recalled Poppy mentioning being bothered by a headache. Their appearances usually aligned with snippy, uncharacteristic behavior from her. If Fitz was also noticing their frequency…an apprehensive pit grew in my stomach. Mood swings. Headaches. Was something wrong with my beloved auntie?

"I'm gonna sneak out of here and bring her some dinner before it gets busy." Fitz pointed over his shoulder toward the kitchen. "Can I get you anything before I leave?"

I shook my head. "Nah, I'll order once Ezra and his brother arrive. Tell Pops I said feel better."

Fitz bid me goodnight and handed control of his brewery to his night manager, Willa. I sat at the bar in contemplative silence, mulling over Poppy. I felt terrible. I'd been so focused on this case and my relationship with Ezra that I hadn't noticed her suffering, beyond her occasional short fuse. Had she seen a doctor for these frequent headaches? Would she go if I asked her?

"Earth to Hazel."

A hand waved in front of my face, startling me so much that I slipped off my seat.

"Whoa, there." Ezra's fingers encircled my right arm, steadying me.

His gentle, familiar grip restrained my hand from immediately reaching my glasses as they slipped down my nose at my sudden jolting. I tried to close my eyes, but it was too late. I'd seen the awful, glowing lifeclock. Not Ezra's, mind you, but the one belonging to the young blond man standing on my left-hand side.

Caius.

"Didn't expect you to faint at the mere sight of me." Ezra's brother gave me an impish grin as he assessed my reaction.

Curses. Curses. Curses! I couldn't get that terrible, neon-sign-bright countdown out of my mind. How in the hexes was I supposed to act like everything was hunky dory when I'd just seen that Caius Walters only had thirteen years, six months, two weeks, one day, and eighteen hours left on this earth? How could I act normal knowing that my boyfriend's little brother was fated to die before he turned forty?

I swallowed, very much aware I had an audience to this inner turmoil. "I just can't believe you're here in the flesh," I finally managed to squeak out, a hard lump still lodged in my throat.

Caius cocked his head, his hunter-green eyes—identical to Ezra's—pinched with slight confusion. "You okay? You look a bit pale."

I shook my head, trying to slow my rapid heartbeat and churning stomach all at once. "I'm fine. Just hungry." I forced a smile.

"You sure?" Ezra's worried gaze examined me head-to-toe.

"Yeah, I'm fine," I repeated. "Sorry for the weird welcome, but that's Crucible for you." I opened my arms to Caius and wrapped him in a tight hug. Traitorous tears leaked from my eyes. *Get it together, Hazel.* But how could I? A million questions swirled in my mind. Caius, at twenty-six, was in great shape. His creamy skin was unlined, and with his blond hair, tall, lanky stature, and square jawline, he looked like a model. How could this kid die so young?

"Eh-hem."

Caius's cough brought me back to the moment, making me realize I was still clinging to him for dear life.

"Oops, sorry." I released him and stepped back, trying to swipe away any evidence of my tears. "You know what? I think there's something in my eye. Let me run to the restroom real quick. Ez, you wanna grab us a table?" I didn't even glance at my probably confused boyfriend. I just dashed toward the washroom.

As soon as the door closed behind me, tears rolled freely down my cheeks. I couldn't even see clearly to check if I was alone in the room. Instead, I bolted into a stall and pressed a hand over my mouth to muffle my sobs.

Oh God, oh God, oh God.

I hadn't had a reaction to a whim reading like this in a long time. But the harsh reality of what I'd seen ate away at me. Caius was fated to die by the time he turned forty years old. Ezra would lose his beloved little brother way too early in life. The unfairness of it all burned as if my heart was on fire. Then a darker, more chilling thought ran through me like a bolt of lightning. What if Ezra and Caius shared the same countdown? Was it possible I had little more than a decade left with the love of my life? Bile rose in my throat.

Stop, Hazel. You can't think like that. You only know what Caius's *fate holds, not Ezra's.*

This situation was exactly what I'd been dreading. Seeing a terrible lifeclock for someone I cared about. I may not have known Caius well, but he was Ezra's brother. Ezra was my future, and I hoped one day, Caius and I would be family. Why did I have to know he would die so young? And more pressingly, how was I going to pull myself together and make it through this dinner?

I closed my eyes, trying to control my tears. *I wish Poppy were here.* My auntie would know what to do, what to say. I could always rely on her to help me navigate a whim-related trauma.

"Um, excuse me? Sorry, I couldn't help but overhear...are you okay?" a familiar voice murmured from outside the stall.

Yvonne? What was she doing here?

In a move that surprised even me, I threw open the door and launched myself into the energy heiress's arms.

"What the—Hazel?" Yvonne, obviously startled, hesitated a moment before relaxing into my sobbing embrace. "Hey, hey. It's okay," she cooed as she patted me awkwardly on the back.

"I'm so sorry." I quickly extracted myself from our clumsy hug. "I-I just—I really needed that." I hiccupped as I wiped my eyes, overcome with embarrassment. My nerves were so frazzled that I'd practically assaulted the woman.

Yvonne studied me a moment, her blue eyes unreadable. "Clearly," she said, not unkindly. She brushed away the teardrops I'd left on her jacket shoulder. At least, I prayed they were teardrops and not gunk from my nose. "Do you need me to call someone for you?" Her continuing concern nearly had me in tears all over again.

I shook my head. "I'm okay. Or I will be." I turned to look at myself in the mirror. "Oof." Red eyes, flushed cheeks...there'd be no way I could downplay this to Ezra and Caius.

Yvonne glanced at my reflection and winced. "Here, I might have something to help." She reached into her designer handbag and dug around before pulling out a small tube. "Reduces the swelling." She motioned around her face, indicating how to apply the cream.

"Thanks." I accepted her offering, trying to decode the name on the fancy label.

"It's a miracle serum from some South Korean doctor." Yvonne shrugged as she watched me apply the cream. "I used it a lot after Kevin died."

My heart went out to her over the loss of her twin brother. *Her brother*...had Yvonne unwittingly also lost a sister? The old Polaroid floated through my mind.

"What brings you by Cold Cauldron?" I asked conversationally, still trying to bury my embarrassment over my emotional outburst.

Yvonne tossed her shiny blonde hair over her shoulder. "Blair is taking some promotional pics of the place for one of the bands she's managing. They don't see the 'value' in road-tripping upstate for a gig." She tossed in some air quotes to show sarcasm.

I chuckled at her evident disdain. "Agenting isn't as glamorous as Blair hoped?"

"Oh, it's not that." Yvonne flicked her wrist. "She's so busy working her butt off that I hardly get to see her." Her lower lip stuck out in a pout.

"Aww." I couldn't help but gush at the sweetness behind Yvonne's moping comment.

She glowered at me. "Don't you dare tell anyone that Blair has made me go soft."

Even though there was some intensity to her words, I detected the slightest amount of teasing. I mimed zipping my lips and handed her back her tube of miracle serum. Indeed, the cream had muted the redness around my eyes tenfold. I *almost* looked like I hadn't been crying, but maybe now Ezra and Caius would believe I'd simply gotten something lodged in my eye.

Yvonne studied me up and down. "Those were some pretty serious tears. Are you sure you're okay?"

"I am, thanks." I wasn't entirely recovered from my lifeclock reading, but Yvonne's presence had coaxed me off a dangerous ledge of despair. "I appreciate your help. How are things with you and your parents?" Given what Holden, Poppy, and I had discussed last night, now that I had her alone, I figured I had to at least try and see if Yvonne would spill any information useful to our investigation.

She did a double take at my topic-swapping. "Um, we're good, thanks."

"I ran into your mom yesterday. She was having dinner at The Elderberry Inn."

Yvonne arched a perfectly threaded eyebrow. "And?"

"Well…" I flailed for a response. "I hope everything is all right. She seemed a bit upset."

Yvonne snorted, her pert nose wrinkling. "Oh, that's putting it mildly. She's furious that Daddy took Tobias's side about wanting us all to attend the Big Melt as a *family* this year. I mean, I'm not too thrilled by it either. Way too much trans fat for my liking. Not sure what's up Daddy's craw. Usually, he's content to sign the checks. But Tobias has him convinced a family appearance will be bankable goodwill for FPT."

"Oh." There was the entitled Yvonne I knew and loved. But was she really telling the truth about the source of her mom's anger? Could Poppy's intense whim reading be chalked up to Monica being aggravated at her husband for choosing someone else's opinion over hers and having to go to a small-town festival? It sounded a bit outlandish, but Monica Finchmore *was* someone who was used to getting her way. "I didn't realize Tobias held that much sway with your dad."

"He doesn't." Yvonne reached into her bag and pulled out a lipstick. "Or, at least, he didn't use to. Things kind of changed after Kevin died. Tobias has been even more glued to Daddy's side, much to my mother's chagrin." She dabbed at her lips with a lovely maroon hue. "I honestly think he likes having someone he can play pretend son with." Sadness coated her admission.

I also noted the slight hint of bitterness lacing her words. Yvonne had long sought her father's approval, giving herself entirely to Finchmore Power Technologies. Yet, she'd always come in second to her twin brother. And it seemed that after Kevin's death, she was still dealing with rivalries for Grant's respect and affection.

I reached for Yvonne's forearm and squeezed, offering my sympathies for her situation.

She glanced at my hand momentarily before shrugging it off. "I'm sure Mother will come around once she gets the new Birkin Daddy bought her." Yvonne dropped her lipstick into her bag. "He had me pick it out after she told him she'd be spending the night at the Elderberry." A wistful look flickered across her features. "Daddy hates it when Mother is mad at him."

Because he loves her so much? Or because he worries what she might do in such a state? I kept these thoughts to myself. Instead, I replied, "That's a generous apology gift."

"The woman knows how to play her cards right, huh?" Yvonne gave herself a once-over in the mirror before stepping back from the vanity. "Well, I best get back to Blair. Bye, Hazel." She turned on a heel and sauntered out the door, her air of superiority and indifference returning with each graceful stride.

I shook my head as I tried to process the weird scene that had just played out. Never in a million years would I have thought Yvonne would offer me—or anyone—comfort. Blair's presence in her life had certainly mellowed her for the better.

But, more importantly, her comments about her mom and Tobias holding sway over Grant caught my attention. I recalled the results of Poppy's aura reading at The Elderberry Inn. Monica had been angry, full of rage and humiliation. While we initially suspected those emotions had been associated with Jane Zeller, Yvonne's explanation put everything in a new light. As a powerful and wealthy woman, Monica was used to getting what she wanted, especially from her husband. If Grant had vetoed her opinion in favor of his employee, I could imagine a wounded Monica summoning those very same feelings, even if the reasoning seemed childish to me.

Then there was this insider intel about Tobias. If Grant had grown even closer to his personal assistant in the wake of Kevin's death, could Tobias have become a trusted confidant? Had Grant confided in him about Marjorie? Maybe we could chat with Tobias at the fête and see what he knew.

Chapter 27

I pushed my building questions for the Finchmore family aside and focused on the matter at hand. I had a family dinner of my own to attend. At least my interaction with Yvonne had helped qualm the terrible fallout from my unintentional whim usage.

Checking myself in the mirror one more time, I smoothed my hair and adjusted my cardigan. *This is as good as it's gonna get.*

I took a deep breath and returned to the main floor of the brewery, spotting the Walters siblings right away. Ezra and Caius had grabbed a corner spot, and Ezra already had my favorite hard cider waiting for me when I reached the table.

"Hey! Is your eye okay?" My boyfriend leaped from his seat to pull my chair out.

I thanked him for the gentlemanly courtesy. "Yeah, just a little sore. Sorry for the rotten timing." I plastered a wide smile on my face as I turned to acknowledge Caius. "It's really nice to finally meet you in person."

"To be honest," Caius said with a chuckle, "for a while, I thought you were some AI-generated image that Ezra had rigged up for our video calls. Nice to know my older brother isn't totally hopeless in the romance department."

Ezra scowled at his younger sibling. "Why would I ever make up a girlfriend?"

Caius shrugged. "I figured you had snapped and got tired of Mom complaining about how she would never have grandkids if you didn't lock down a relationship."

"Oh, shut it." Ezra brooded over his beer.

"You see, Hazel, our parents never ask *me* when I'll settle down and have children." Caius held a hand to his chest. "You know, because I'm *gay*." He spoke in an exaggerated whisper.

Even though his tone was joking, I couldn't bring myself to laugh. I knew how much Caius had struggled after coming out to his parents, and it was clear some of that hurt was still there.

Instead, I chewed on my lower lip, trying to find the right response. We'd entered dangerous territory. Ezra and I had never even had the "kids" talk. Did he want children? Did I?

"I contemplated bringing up adoption before Deleon shattered my heart into a million pieces," Caius continued. He seemed at ease leading the conversation.

"Seriously, bro?" Ezra's mouth dropped. "You were together for like, what, four months? Maybe you should learn to take it slow."

"What? Like you did?" Caius rolled his eyes. "Excuse me, but I don't have the desire to wait around for three years until the person I'm into is nearly killed by a deranged murderer before confessing my love."

My cheeks heated. I guess Ezra and I did have a pretty unique meet cute.

I cleared my throat. "How are you liking Crucible so far, Caius? Did you guys have a good time at The Poignant Page?"

"Oh, it was wild." Caius's sarcasm was evident. "I spent most of the day spicing up Ezzie's website."

"Really?" I pulled up the bookstore's page on my phone. "Holy hexes, this looks amazing! Look at those cute little book graphics." I held the screen in front of Ezra's face.

Caius scrunched his nose. "Cute wasn't exactly the vibe I was going for."

I winced at my misstep. Artists—I'd clearly offended him with my word choice. "I'd love to have this kind of revamp done on my web page. Would you be up for another commission?"

"Commission? You think Big Bro paid me for this?" Caius pointed to the display on my phone. "Nah, that's just me freestyling. The websites I've designed for work are much better than that."

"Wow. You're really talented," I gushed with sincerity.

Our conversation was interrupted by a waiter coming to collect our food order. Once we'd rattled off our selections, Caius turned to me with a critical stare. "So, word on the street is that *another* murder took place in this sleepy town. Got any details?"

I glanced at Ezra, wondering what he'd shared with his brother. My boyfriend mimed zipping his lips in response.

Caius pointed at him. "Ah-ha! So you do know more than what you let on."

Ezra must have seen the confusion on my face. "Caius overheard a few patrons talking about Marjorie's murder and wouldn't stop bothering me with questions."

"I need to know if the place I'm staying at is safe!" Caius huffed with feigned indignation. "Besides, you're dating the hometown hero who's helped solve three murders in the past year. I thought you'd have the deets."

I giggled at the flattering moniker he'd given me. I often felt more like a hometown busybody. "Well, we don't really know much more than can be found online." I hedged around the truth.

Caius held out his palms. "I'm a blank canvas. I don't know anything. Who died?"

"An out-of-town woman named Marjorie Zeller. She was visiting a friend in Crucible."

Caius tapped his chin. "Marjorie Zeller? Why does that name sound familiar?"

"She's the author of a new book that's blowing up all over the Internet." I picked up my cider and took a greedy sip. "*Under the Red Barn.*"

"Oh!" Caius's expression brightened. "What a small world."

Ezra's brow furrowed. "What do you mean?"

"I forgot to mention this earlier when I saw the poster in your store window. The digital design company I work for also does book covers," Caius explained. "One of our artists was commissioned to create the artwork for *Under the Red Barn*. I remember giving feedback on his mockups."

I recalled the red cover on the garish promotion poster and shook my head in disbelief. "Small world, indeed."

"My buddy went through the wringer with that one." Caius leaned back in his chair, his expression pensive. "I guess the author hated everything he originally sent. He had to do five different mockups before the publisher finally took control and approved the cover."

"I thought the publisher always had final say in the cover design?" At least, that was what Iggy had told me, and he was with the same publisher as Marjorie.

"Somehow, the author got ahold of Reggie's email and started flooding his inbox with requests for the design. Totally unprofessional." Caius scoffed. "When Reggie ran it up the flagpole and her publisher found out, I guess she got into some real hot water."

Trouble with Griffinsmith? Lauren hadn't mentioned that when Poppy and I had chatted with her about Marjorie's book deal.

Caius's eyes gleamed as he dished the juicy details. "Reggie told me the publisher threatened to terminate her contract over it, but I guess the woman's agent talked them down."

"Interesting." And now, Griffinsmith was charging forward with the launch of *Under the Red Barn* like it was their golden goose.

"Doesn't seem like Marjorie made very many friends in the industry," Ezra observed as he finished his last swig of beer.

I shook my head. "No, it does not..." Had Poppy and I made a mistake writing off Marjorie's writing world so early on in our investigation? If she was causing trouble for someone at Griffinsmith, that could be a motive to want her gone, as thin as it might be.

"So, Hazel, are you looking into her murder?" Caius propped his elbows on the table.

I tugged awkwardly at my braid. "Um, you could say that." Even though Caius didn't know anyone in Crucible to blab this admission to, I worried about someone overhearing us. My focus was pulled across the room to where Yvonne stood, waiting for Blair to take pictures of the stage space. I certainly didn't want her to know that her dad was now my top suspect in Marjorie's death. "But I've kinda hit a brick wall," I added, hoping to nip this topic in the bud.

Caius frowned, and the arrival of our food prevented him from asking more.

The conversation turned to more engaging topics, with Caius sharing many embarrassing stories about Ezra from their childhood. Well, Ezra said they were embarrassing. I thought they were adorable.

It was nice to see their sibling bond, despite the copious amounts of teasing they made each other endure. Ezra, who was often quiet and composed around our friends, was much more animated and at ease with his brother. It was fun seeing this side of him.

"How long are you planning to stay?" I asked Caius as we congregated out on the sidewalk after the meal. I'd offered to drive them back to Ezra's but they'd declined.

Caius shuffled his feet. "TBD. I'm in no rush to return to the city. Too many memories."

Ezra rolled his eyes. "Again, it was four months!"

Caius ignored him. "Since I can do my design work from anywhere, I'm playing things by ear. So, if you'd like me to take a look at your website, Hazel, I'd be happy to."

"That would be awesome." I beamed. A Wick in Time could definitely benefit from an online makeover.

Caius then scooped me into a hug. "I'll give you two lovebirds a moment." He teased his brother as he sauntered away to check his phone.

Ezra let out a long sigh as he watched Caius walk off. "Jeez. Sorry about him. He can be...such a little brother sometimes."

I laughed. "Nothing to apologize for. I had a great time."

"Yeah? Your eye doing better?" Ezra studied me intently.

My gaze dropped to the ground. I hated lying to him. "Totally fine."

"It's just, you seemed a bit down tonight." Ezra stuck his hands into his pockets. "Is there something going on with the case?"

Keep it together, Hazel. I willed myself not to think about Caius's lifeclock or Poppy's concerning headaches. "Oh, nothing like that.

I'm fine, I promise. Maybe just a bit tired."

"All right, then. Go home and get some sleep." Ezra reached out and pulled me in for a one-armed hug.

I wanted to melt into his chest as I felt his lips press against my hair. He made me feel so safe and warm. "Have fun with your house guest."

I waved as the two brothers strolled down the sidewalk, doing my best to keep the memory of Caius's lifeclock from invading my mind. As I headed toward my car, a nasty thought nagged at me. *If you can't even handle knowing Caius's time, how are you ever going to deal with Ezra's?*

The fear built up within me, and once I was buckled safely in my SUV, a frustrated cry escaped my lips. "Ahh! I hate this!" I hit the steering wheel with my fists, ignoring the immediate pain that sprang up my arms.

"This is so unfair," I muttered, leaning back against the headrest. "What am I going to do?"

As I stared out the window, I wondered if Poppy would have any advice. I reached for my phone to call her, but quickly dropped my hand, knowing she had a headache. I didn't want to burden her with my problems if she was dealing with something of her own.

The warm fuzzies of the evening gone, I drove home in serious need of cuddles with Noli and Berg.

Chapter 28

Wednesday flew by in the blink of an eye, what with tourists beginning to arrive in town for the Big Melt. A Wick in Time fielded a steady stream of patrons, so much so that I worried whether Iggy and Quinn would be okay without a third set of helping hands on Thursday.

"We'll be fine, Hazel," Iggy assured me Thursday morning as I prepared to head over to Finchaven. "It won't be the end of the world if people have to wait in line for your candles."

"Yeah, if anything, it will make it seem like this is the place to be," Quinn called over her shoulder as she stocked a top shelf with Mint Meringue, a new mint and sugary scent I was trying out.

I smiled at my team. "Thanks, guys. I hope this 'summit' won't be too long." Now that the Founding Families Fête was upon us, I felt reluctant to go. Poppy was the face of the Glenmyre clan, not me. But my desire to question Grant overrode my introverted tendencies, and at eleven thirty, I bid Iggy and Quinn farewell.

Poppy and Holden had texted that they'd meet me at the Finchmore estate, so I made the drive to the massive, eco-friendly compound on the northern border of Crucible. Finchaven really was a sight to behold. The manor had been featured in nearly every architectural magazine out there, hailed for its ingenuity when it came to green living. As much as Grant's and Monica's attitudes rubbed me the wrong way, I couldn't deny they were truly friends of the planet.

I slid my Equinox behind another SUV parked in the circular driveway, noting the "Coffee is Life" bumper sticker. I smiled. This had to be Jolie Potter's vehicle. Jolie's mom, Nadine, was one of the ranking members of the Ildrich clan, so her attendance didn't surprise me.

Several other cars were parked in the driveway, and I wondered—a little jokingly—why Grant didn't have a valet out here. I spotted Poppy's Subaru near the front. Of course she would have been one of the first guests to arrive.

I checked my phone to see if she had texted. Nothing. Poppy wouldn't have gone and questioned Grant, alone, would she?

I hurried toward the sleek, modern entrance, eager to track down my aunt. I didn't see Holden's SUV in the driveway, so it appeared he hadn't yet arrived.

"Please don't have done anything reckless, Pops," I prayed before ringing the doorbell.

A smiling Tula greeted me a moment later. "Hello, Hazel. Welcome." She ushered me inside, nearly bowing at the waist.

I gave the estate manager a friendly wave. "Hi, Tula. Nice to see you."

"Do you need me to take anything for you?" She glanced at my satchel and the light linen jacket I wore.

I shrugged off my coat and handed it to her. I'd brought a candle as a thank-you gift for Grant to help break the ice during our questioning, so I opted to keep my bag with me. "Thanks so much." My gaze drifted to the familiar periwinkle scarf around her neck. The one I'd seen her wearing in my shop.

She noticed me staring at the accessory. "Did you ever stop by The Corner Store to pick one up?" She stroked the silky material.

"I did." I blushed, knowing that she'd caught me ogling her. "I went with an amethyst scarf. I didn't realize the artist made each in a one-of-a-kind color."

"Kooky, right? I can't imagine all the work that went into making every single one unique." Tula tilted her head. "Although, I really couldn't tell the difference between 'periwinkle' and 'cornflower' when deciding which ones to get."

"Those are pretty similar," I agreed. "I often get those dyes mixed up when I'm mixing my candles."

"Oh, by the way, your gardenia candle was a big hit with Mrs. Finchmore." She motioned me to follow her through the expansive foyer.

"Wonderful." An idea flickered. "Maybe she can give me some notes on it during the luncheon."

Tula's shoulders stiffened at the mention of her employer. "Mrs. Finchmore won't be joining you today, I'm afraid. Business in the city."

Interesting. It sounded like Monica and Grant were still at odds. Had the Birkin bag not smoothed their rough waters? Or had Yvonne been mistaken about Monica's true reason for being angry with her husband?

We turned down a brightly lit hallway that looked like it was carved totally from marble.

Tula must have seen me admiring the interior, for she said, "This material is made entirely out of recycled plastic. Can you believe it?"

"Really?" My eyes widened in shock. "That's amazing."

"Mr. Finchmore funded the research for the product himself." Tula beamed with pride. "He really is the most incredible man. We're so lucky to have him fighting the good fight."

I nodded, knowing it was best to agree. When it came to the Finchmore family, no one loved and admired them quite like Tula did.

Muted chatter and faint instrumental music drifted up the hallway as we neared a set of glass doors.

"The event is through here." Tula stopped and opened one of the doors. "Lunch will be served in about forty minutes, but we do have some yummy appetizers from The Elderberry Inn floating around."

I thanked her and slipped inside the airy room. It looked like it had specifically been designed as an event space.

I surveyed the crowd, counting the familiar faces I saw. Jolie and her mom were speaking with Philippa Tarling. Maggie Sherwin and one of her uncles chatted with a few of Jolie's other Ildrich relatives. Yvonne mingled with another group of Sherwins and a few Tarling cousins.

I stood on my tiptoes, my stomach flipping with anxiety. Where was Poppy?

I then spotted her auburn hair shimmering over by the window, where she stood with Tobias and Holden.

"Hey, guys," I said once I was only a few feet from them. "I didn't see your SUV outside, Chief."

He pointed to my bestie. "I came with Pops. We were doing a little...*research* before coming here."

I bobbed my head in understanding. As part of his induction into our family, Holden had been reading the Glenmyre Opus, a large, somewhat mystical tome that Poppy kept in a bullet-proof display case at her house. The opus chronicled the many wondrous abilities the Glenmyres were capable of in the days of old, back when Grandmaster Jedidiah and his kin could truly attune with nature and thus channel its awesome power.

"I can't believe you threw this party together on such short notice," I said to Tobias, congratulating him on such a lovely event.

He chuckled. "Well, we'll see how things go. No offense, but the founding families tend to be very *opinionated* about how things are done in Crucible."

"That's a nice way of putting it." Poppy snorted. "I plan on keeping my mouth shut."

"Maggie Sherwin will still come for you." Tobias nudged Poppy's arm in jest.

She winced at the thought. "Ugh, you're probably right." She shot a quick look at Holden and me with a secret wink. "Before things kick off, do you mind if we have a private word with Grant? You know, to properly acquaint him with Holden?"

Tobias glanced at his watch. "Oh, yes, that's right. Grant is very keen to meet our new chief of police. Follow me. He's just finishing a conference call, and we have a bit of time before lunch is plated."

As Tobias and Poppy led the way, Holden growled in my ear, "I still don't like this cover story. I don't want Grant thinking he can buy me off."

"Then tell him that." I threaded my arm through his and tugged him along. "But try not to make him too mad. We need him to open up about Marjorie."

Tobias led us down the same hall I'd just come from with Tula, only at the foyer, we turned left, moving deeper into the sprawling mansion.

We arrived a short time later in front of another set of glass doors, although these were frosted for privacy.

Tobias pressed a tablet mounted on the wall. "Excuse me, Grant. The Glenmyres would like a quick moment with you."

"Come on in." Grant's smooth baritone filtered through the tablet's speakers.

Tobias held the door open for us, and we entered a study that looked like a cross between Harry Potter and *The Jetsons*. High-tech had been fused with steampunk, creating a modern yet warm vibe in the massive office.

"Glenmyres!" Grant rose from his desk, a wide, charismatic smile plastered on his face. "Welcome to Finchaven." With a few powerful strides, he crossed the room, extending his hand for a firm shake.

Poppy and I accepted first, then gestured to Holden. "This is our cousin, Holden Whitfield," Poppy said with pride. "He's Ruthie's grandson."

Grant gripped Holden's hand. "I've heard a lot about you, Chief. Glad we finally get to have a little sit-down." He motioned us over to two couches by a free-standing fireplace.

Behind us, a throat cleared, and I realized Tula was standing in the doorway with Tobias nowhere in sight. "Would you like me to bring you some refreshments, Mr. Finchmore?"

"That would be lovely, Tula." Grant smiled at her, although his expression dimmed once she left. "I've long since given up telling her to call me Grant." He seemed almost bashful at the admission.

"Tula adores you," Poppy reassured him. "She's obviously very proud of everything you've accomplished."

"That she is. Sometimes I think she's more protective of my family than she is of her own son." Grant immediately winced at this blunt remark. "Sorry, that was rude of me to say. Tula is a wonderful mother to Tobias. He's a good kid, too. Would do anything for me. Like a son to me, really. Not sure what I've done in life to deserve such devoted employees."

He clasped his hands together, his expression focused. "So, what can I do for you? How can the Finchmores assist our dear friends the Glenmyres?"

Dear friends? Really? I gulped. How were we going to play this? We couldn't very well come out and ask about Marjorie's parentage without Grant going on the immediate defensive.

"Well, we're obviously concerned about the direction Crucible is heading." Poppy took the first step, her tone measured. "Four murders in less than a year. It's troubling, Grant. Yes, Mayor Mooney acted quickly to ramp up a town police department, but we're worried things aren't moving quickly enough on that front."

Grant's brow furrowed. "I understand the concern, believe me. With crime on the rise, FPT employees are already squeamish about their security."

The Finchmore Power Technologies campus wasn't located far from the Finchaven compound. But it seemed strange to prioritize his employees' feelings over the fact that his son had been one of the four people murdered.

Grant's gaze slid to Holden. "What do you propose to move things along?"

Holden shifted, clearly uncomfortable with the direction Poppy had taken this in.

"Well, unfortunately, it's all red tape at this point. We just feel so helpless about our inability to contribute," my aunt interjected. "It's unbelievable that it's come to this. I mean, the woman who was killed recently, she wasn't even from here."

I took a steeling breath before jumping into the conversation. "Exactly. How could a person with no ties to Crucible end up murdered?"

"No ties?" Grant's eyebrows rose. "So, I take it the official investigation hasn't established any solid leads?" Again, he stared expectantly at Holden.

With his gaze diverted, Poppy and I shared a baffled look. Did Grant somehow not know Tobias had referred Holden to Grant's legal team about the matter?

My aunt cleared her throat. "Well, Hazel and I actually did a bit of digging, since the victim's last name sounded so familiar," she lied with amazing ease. "I realized my sister had mentioned the name Zeller to me before."

"Zeller?" At that, Grant sat back in his seat.

"Are you familiar with the name?" I asked as innocently as I could. It was evident from his reaction that the answer was yes.

"I-I am," Grant murmured. "That's a name I haven't heard in a very long time."

I resisted making an Obi-Wan Kenobi joke and pressed onward. "The woman who died, her name was Marjorie Zeller."

"And it turns out," Poppy said, "that her *mother* was someone named Jane Zeller. She lived in Crucible for a time."

"What?" The color from Grant's face drained. "The dead woman was Jane's daughter?" He began stroking his chin, his gaze somewhat haunted. "Jane Zeller had a daughter? I-I had no idea. Tobias only told me during a briefing that the victim was a thirty-something-year-old author."

Poppy, Holden, and I shared questioning glances. Briefing? Grant's world was so very different than ours. I guessed people in his powerful position relied on others to deliver their local news. It also explained why Tobias had tapped Grant's legal team to deal with Holden; he likely didn't want to involve his boss in such matters until it proved warranted.

Holden must have realized Grant was relatively in the dark about his investigation, too, for he leaned forward, his dark gaze full of authority. "Were you well-acquainted with Jane Zeller?"

Grant ran a hand through his styled, silvery hair. "I suppose you could say that. Jane and I...I made a mistake a long time ago." He didn't elaborate further.

A mistake, huh? I knew what that was code for.

Poppy's right eye twitched. "Grant, did you know Marjorie was your daughter?"

The energy tycoon jolted out of his seat, his blue eyes wide. "What? What in God's name—is this some kind of joke, Glenmyres?" His shock turned to rage in an instant.

"No." I hurriedly came to Poppy's aid. "Marjorie was under the impression that her father was someone in this photo." I dug out my phone and showed Grant the digital image I'd snapped of the telltale Polaroid.

Next to me, Holden looked murderous. *Oops.* We hadn't told him we'd made a copy for our own investigation.

Grant studied the old photo that contained his high school friends. "Why?" he growled.

"Jane wrote in a diary that this was the only photo she had of Marjorie's father," I explained.

Poppy added, "Jared never had a relationship with Jane, Sterling hadn't seen her since high school, and Joshua Sherwin certainly couldn't be the father of a thirty-four-year-old woman."

"I-I didn't know." Grant swallowed, his face now pale. "It was one night. After the ten-year anniversary memorial for Josh. FPT had made a donation, and I'd been invited. Monica was home recovering from a tough pregnancy with the twins." He sank back into his chair. "I was lonely. Jane and I got to talking. One thing led to another…"

I struggled to keep the disgust off my face. His wife had been dealing with severe post-partum issues, and *he* was *lonely.*

"God, I was utterly repulsed by myself the next morning." Grant shuddered. "Thank goodness Tula's father, my dad's right hand, was there to help me sneak Jane off the estate without Monica realizing it. How could I do something so terrible to my wife?

"But at the time, I blamed Jane. I was convinced she'd tricked me into bed, and I told her if she ever contacted me again, I had the power to make her life miserable. She made good on her promise. But I never thought…" He suddenly rose again, his features a storm of emotions. "So, you're saying the dead woman is my *daughter*?"

"That's what we believe." I couldn't quite meet his troubled gaze.

Grant staggered to the side and reached for the back of the couch to steady himself. "I…this is—please excuse me." Without another word, the distraught man stumbled out of the room.

"Should we go after him?" I turned a panicked look to Holden. Had we inadvertently set a diabolical killer loose on a party full of people?

Before Holden could respond, Poppy cleared her throat. "I don't believe he's our guy. He didn't know Marjorie was his daughter."

I gasped. "What did you see?"

"Confusion. Revulsion. Shock." Poppy's eyes glistened with unshed tears. "Understanding. Then, finally, regret and despair."

"Understanding?" Holden pressed. "I don't get that one."

"That he had to be the father." Poppy's lips quivered. "Everything he said about his night with Jane was the truth. He knows it must be him."

Silence settled over us as we processed Poppy's reading. The Grant we knew now was repulsed by his actions as a young man, which softened my attitude toward him a little. He clearly regretted intimidating Jane into silence. With a scary threat like that lingering over her head, it was no wonder why Jane had been so secretive about the truth behind Marjorie's paternity. People in Grant's position got away with terrible crimes all the time just because they had the right people on their payroll. No wonder she never said a word.

The part that gutted me the most was the despair Poppy had seen with her whim. Grant had just been told he'd fathered another child, only to find out she, too, had been murdered. No wonder he'd fled. Despite his many faults, I felt sorry for him.

"If Grant didn't know Marjorie was his daughter," Holden muttered, "that completely obliterates any motive to kill her."

"You're right." I wrung my hands, feeling untethered. "What do we do now? What does this mean?"

"I don't know. My head is spinning." Poppy hopped up from the couch and placed her hands on her hips. "Why would Jane not tell Grant about his daughter? It makes no sense."

"Didn't you hear the way he threatened her? She had to be terrified about how he would react," I pointed out. "He could have done more than just financially ruin her. How many *Dateline* episodes have we seen where a married man snaps and kills his pregnant mistress? It must have been self-preservation."

Poppy tapped her chin. "It could also explain why Marjorie felt that she was owed financial compensation, as her mom never got it." She began to pace around the room. "But if Grant didn't kill Marjorie, who did?"

Holden and I joined her as she wandered over to Grant's sleek, modern desk.

"It would not bode well for us if we got caught snooping, Pops," Holden grumbled, reaching for her elbow to pull her back.

"What about Monica?" I had written off the Finchmore matriarch after speaking with Yvonne at Cold Cauldron, but what if I'd been fooled or purposely misled? Poppy hadn't been with me to do a reading, after all. Yvonne could have simply made up the story about her mother being mad over the Big Melt in an effort to protect the family's reputation. "Maybe she somehow found out about the affair while Marjorie was asking around. Tula could've mentioned her weird encounter to Monica, and it triggered her suspicions?"

"It's worth looking into." Poppy rubbed her hands together. "Makes sense to me."

My stomach cramped with anxiety. "And what if, instead of attending to business in the city, she's fleeing the country?"

Holden held his hands up. "I think you two are grasping at straws. How would Monica make the leap to Grant having a lovechild, anyway?"

Poppy and I opened our mouths to respond when a buzzing sound rattled from my and Poppy's bags.

"Hold that thought," Poppy instructed as we dashed to grab our phones.

My heart skipped a beat as I read the notification. "It's a text from Constance."

Poppy's response came a second later. "Oh, wow, Holden. Take a look at this."

While Poppy showed our cousin her phone, I stared at our group chat with growing bewilderment.

Guys, I found my scarf!

Chapter 29

A picture of Constance's coral bowtie scarf filled the screen. The same scarf I'd seen fluttering inside Marjorie's car at the crime scene. Or at least, I thought I had. How could this be?

"Wait. *This* is Constance's?" Holden took Poppy's phone and studied the image closely. "The stitching is similar, but that's not the same color as the one we found in Marjorie's BMW."

Another message from Constance popped up below the photo. **It was somehow lodged under the passenger seat of my car. All this time! It must have fallen off when I last wore it. Ugh, now I feel so scummy accusing Margie of stealing it.**

"Wait—so Constance's scarf *wasn't* the murder weapon?" I stared at my family in shock.

More messages came from Constance. **But in my anger toward her, it made sense. Even in the crime scene photo Shroud showed me during our first meeting, the scarf totally looked like mine.**

I quickly texted back, **That's what I thought, too!**

But when I called Shroud to let him know about finding the scarf, Constance replied, **he brought over a different pic to my house, one taken at the lab in better lighting. Turns out, the scarf**

found near Margie was rose-colored, not coral. It just looked like mine in the dim light at the crime scene. Shroud and my lawyer just left. I'm off the hook!

Holy hexes. We'd been under the assumption that Marjorie had stolen the one-of-a-kind accessory from Constance and then been killed with it. But if that wasn't the case...who did the rose-colored scarf belong to?

There was a soft knock at the door.

"Uh, yes?" Poppy's voice warbled with hesitancy.

One of the frosted glass doors opened, and Tula appeared with a tray. "Where is Mr. Finchmore?" She tilted her head in confusion.

"He, um, ran to the bathroom," I blurted out the first excuse that came to mind.

Tula carried the silver tray topped with four glasses and a pitcher with ease as she shuffled into the room. "Well, let me pour you some of my special sweet tea to enjoy."

"Thanks, Tula." Poppy smiled.

The estate manager placed the tray on a nearby table and turned her back to us as she poured. "Mr. Finchmore says this is his favorite drink to have after a hard day of work."

As she turned to hand us each a glass, we nodded our heads appreciatively.

"Tula, did you tell anyone here at the Finchmore estate about your conversation with Marjorie Zeller?" I figured Poppy could at least get a reading on Tula, since she hadn't been with me when we'd chatted about her brief encounter with Marjorie earlier.

"Goodness, no." Tula chuckled. "Why would I bother the Finchmores with something so trivial?"

I shrugged. "I don't know. Maybe because you were all friends with Jane Zeller."

Tula's brow furrowed. "Friends is a strong word, Hazel. I only knew her because of her association with Josh Sherwin."

"Oh." My face warmed at her reprimand.

"Truth be told, I didn't care for her at all." Tula folded her arms and glared at us. "I thought she was a troublemaker. And I ended up being right, didn't I? To ruin poor Josh's life the way she did."

Poppy was just about to take a sip of her drink when Tula's words made her pause. "You know, you're the first person we've spoken to who hasn't entirely blamed Sterling for Josh's death."

Tula scoffed. "Poor guy. He was hoodwinked by that woman like Josh was. Ugh, I was so mad when she showed up at our little graduation party. I tried to mask it, but you could totally see my unhappiness in that old Polaroid."

I'd brought the glass to my lips when I did a double take. "Tula, you told me that Marjorie never showed you any photos."

Tula's mouth opened, then closed. "Well," she stuttered after a long moment, "I must have misremembered. Or you misheard me."

"If you saw the photo, you must have been able to identify the other people in it." My pulse began to race. "Why didn't you tell Marjorie the names of the other people?"

The color in Tula's tan cheeks began to drain.

"You must have recognized them." Holden's voice simmered with authority.

"Why not tell her?" Poppy added.

I thought back to our short conversation with Grant and how he thought Tula would do anything to protect his family. "Because you didn't want Marjorie to figure out who her father really was. You wanted to protect Grant from whatever fallout there might be."

"That's absurd." Tula flipped her wrist.

I set my drink down and stepped toward her. Holden and Poppy did the same, flanking her on either side.

"And when it became clear that Marjorie wasn't going to stop her search," Poppy narrowed her gaze, "you decided to silence her for good."

I snapped my fingers as more pieces tumbled into place. "Sofía said she hoped you were enjoying your purchases when I chatted with her about the scarfs, yet you told me Tobias bought one for you as a gift." I pointed to the periwinkle accessory hanging around her neck. "Sofía also said *purchases*, plural. Earlier today, you said you had a hard time discerning periwinkle from cornflower 'when deciding which *ones* to get.' You also bought a rose-colored scarf that day, didn't you?"

Tula reached for her neck, her lips white with rage.

The condemning *Ithaca Interpreter* article about Crucible's skyrocketing crime rate flashed through my mind. *"...left for dead by the side of the road in her broken-down car."*

"When Tobias canceled your dinner date on Friday—if there was even a date to begin with," I concluded, folding my arms in deductive triumph, "you left Lakeside Mulligan's, found Marjorie stranded by her broken-down car, and decided to strangle her."

Holden edged closer to the silent estate manager. "The place where Marjorie was found would've been way out of your way if you'd been driving back to Finchaven, Mrs. Sardolous." His tone was chilling, rooting even me in my spot. "But not if you *always* intended to drive home along the route Marjorie would have taken back to Waking Woods."

Poppy gasped. "You think she purposely did something to cause Marjorie's car to break down?"

"Our techs found a small slash mark on the BMW's back tire," Holden revealed before continuing to press Tula. "Did you stop by the library before dinner and discover Marjorie was there? Did you then sabotage her vehicle so that poor woman would be helpless at the side of the road? A sitting duck for you to come kill her?"

"Ridiculous!" Tula cried. "How on earth would I have known she was even at the library?"

"Because you were already there," I murmured, a memory from my candle shop bubbling to the surface. "When Tobias came in this past weekend, he was on the phone with you. He told you to have fun with your knitting circle." The library event's page from the day Marjorie was killed flooded my mind. "You're a member of the Crucible Crocheters, aren't you? You were at a club meeting when Marjorie and Constance got into their fight!"

Ezra and I had assumed no one in the community rooms would have heard the argument, but this was Crucible we were talking about. Juicy gossip traveled at the speed of light, and no doubt, even the folks in the community rooms would have learned of the scandalous scene taking place right outside their door. "I bet if we ask around, we'll learn that you left their meeting early on Friday to put your vile plan in motion."

Tula, her eyes wild, lunged forward with surprising speed. Before Holden could withdraw his gun and react, Tula had Poppy in a chokehold, a pair of scissors pointed at her throat.

"I swear, you Glenmyres are such an annoying family," she spat out. "Nothing like the Finchmores."

"Omigosh, let her go!" I shrieked, and Tula pressed the scissors harder against my aunt's skin.

"Zip it," she hissed. "You, drop your gun," Tula instructed Holden, "or she gets it."

Holden's jawbone was nearly bursting from his skin, but he reluctantly placed his gun on the floor and kicked it away from where we all stood.

"Does Tobias know you did this?" Poppy whimpered as she struggled against Tula's hold. "Was he meant to be your alibi at Lakeside Mulligan's?"

"Leave my son out of this," Tula barked. "He doesn't know anything. I just told people I was meeting him for dinner to shore up an alibi, so when he 'conveniently' canceled on me, I could say I went straight home."

I sagged against Holden, terror quickly overtaking my body. What was going to happen now?

As if reading my mind, Tula sneered. "You're going to let Poppy and I walk out of here like nothing is wrong." Tula's gaze darted frantically between Holden, me, and the door. Her grip seemed to tighten against Poppy's neck, for my auntie started clawing at her arm.

"Please, Tula, just let her go," I begged. "You don't have to do this."

"Oh, but I do." She suddenly looked regretful. "Can you imagine the scandal this will bring to the Finchmores? I can't let that happen."

"You're not going to get away with this." Poppy gasped, her teeth gritted in pain. "You can't take us all down."

"Are you sure about that?" Tula challenged. "Hazel, Chief Whitfield, you seem parched. Why don't you take a sip of sweet tea?"

Holden and I turned our attention to our abandoned glasses. "No thanks." Holden scoffed.

Tula pressed the scissors harder against Poppy's throat, and to my horror, a thin line of blood slithered down her neck. "Do it."

I swallowed. "You poisoned our drinks, didn't you?"

Tula's smile would haunt my dreams. "I listened to some of your conversation with Mr. Finchmore over the intercom. I knew as soon as you mentioned Marjorie and Jane that you suspected him of killing that illegitimate brat. I had to protect him."

"Just like you had to *protect* him from his own daughter?" Poppy's cheeks were turning paler by the second.

Tula jerked Poppy's body around like a ragdoll. Her years of service had honed her muscles in a terrifying manner. "That's right. But I also had to protect my son and what he rightfully deserves."

"Tobias?" I frowned. "What does he have to do with this?"

"Marjorie only wanted one thing from her father. Money." Tula sneered. "And I wasn't about to let her usurp the fortune that *my* son has worked so hard for."

"What do you mean?" I figured we had to keep Tula talking. Maybe then Grant would come back and interrupt this terrible scene. "Why would Tobias be entitled to anything from the Finchmore estate?"

"You heard Mr. Finchmore say it himself!" Tula cried. "Tobias is like a son to him. And Mr. Finchmore has always told me that my son would be taken care of. That he cherished our dedication."

"H-Hazel." Poppy's arms sagged, her strength draining from the continued pressure against her neck.

Curses. I shot Holden a panicked look. *What should we do?* We couldn't rush Tula without risking Poppy's safety.

"Just drink my sweet tea, and all this unpleasantness will be over." Tula tutted, nodding toward the glasses.

If I pretended to drink the laced tea, maybe Tula would let her guard down a bit. I clutched my fists and moved closer to the coffee table where we'd left our untouched beverages. As I neared, I noted that my bag had tipped over on the couch, the contents dangerously close to spilling out. It was then I saw the twelve-ounce candle I had tucked into my bag to serve as a thank-you gift for today's luncheon.

Sorry, Grant. I'll send you a replacement. I bent down to reach for my glass. Out of the corner of my eye, I saw Tula relax ever so slightly, and I made my move.

Instead of reaching for the drink, my hand darted out and grabbed the candle jar. I whirled around and threw it in Tula's direction, forcing her to push Poppy away and duck. Of course, with my terrible athleticism, I missed her and Poppy by several feet, but the distraction was enough to trigger Holden into action.

He dove for Tula, knocking the scissors from her hand as he grabbed her arms and pulled them behind her back. With Tula subdued, my frightened gaze trailed to Poppy, who lay crumpled on the floor.

"Pops, are you okay?" Tears ran freely down my face as I knelt beside her.

She rubbed her reddened neck. "I think so." She then reached toward the back of her skull. "Ouch. I think I hit my head when I landed." When she pulled her hand away, her fingers were stained with blood.

"Holy hexes," I whimpered, and to my horror, I saw blood on the edge of the bookshelf right behind her. "Holden, we need an ambulance."

Holden nodded his understanding as he cuffed Tula to a nearby chair. He had his phone in hand an instant later, calling in reinforcements.

Tula sat with her head hung in shame. "What is Mr. Finchmore going to think?"

Before I could explode with anger, the man himself barged into the room. "What on earth was that noise?" He stopped short upon taking stock of the chaotic scene: his estate manager in handcuffs, Poppy bleeding, and a candle smashed to smithereens on the floor. "Wha—what's going on here?"

"Just doing what we do best." Poppy winced as she tried to sit up. I placed a comforting hand on her arm to keep her from moving. "Protecting Crucible."

Chapter 30

𝒟espite Poppy's reassurances it was just a little bump on the head, I finally got my bestie to let the paramedics take her to the county hospital. Leaving Holden to deal with the pandemonium at Finchaven, I rode in the ambulance with Poppy. I'd had enough of death and greed for one day. I wanted to be by my aunt's side.

Three hours later, she stuck her tongue out as a nurse left her private recovery room, having checked her vitals. "See? I told you I was fine, Hazel. Just a bump."

I sat in the uncomfortable chair next to her bed. "You don't get a CAT scan and an MRI for just a bump." I wrung my hands as I continued waiting for her test results to come back. The doctors had said it would be an hour or two, and we were already nearing the end of that window.

Poppy rested against a big pillow. "I didn't even need stitches. You worry too much."

Before I could comment further, I heard pounding footsteps, and Fitz burst into the room.

"Oh my gosh, babe. Are you all right?" He dashed to her bedside. "Holden called and told me you were here. I came as soon as I could.

What happened?"

She patted him on the cheek. "I'm totally fine. Calm down. You're gonna give yourself a heart attack."

"*You're* gonna give me a heart attack." Fitz frowned deeply and turned to me. "Give it to me straight, Hazel."

I swallowed. It wasn't really my place to tell Poppy's boyfriend about her medical issues. "She's good, Fitz. We're just waiting for some tests."

He paled. "What kind of tests?"

"Routine scans for a head injury. That's all." Poppy glowered at me, and I shrank back in my seat.

Her words seemed to appease Fitz slightly, and he claimed the well-worn armchair on the opposite side of her hospital bed. "What the heck happened?"

We took turns telling Fitz about Tula's deranged, misguided actions, which, of course, left him stunned.

"She was going to poison you? *Tula*?" Fitz's disbelief that the kindly estate manager had become a ruthless killer was evident.

I nodded. "Holden texted us a few minutes ago. The crime scene guys did some initial tests and found strychnine in our drinks."

"Strychnine?" Fitz asked.

"Rat poison." Poppy shuddered. "She must have sprinkled it in when she had her back turned to us. I noticed something suspicious in her—" She stopped mid-sentence.

Fitz leaned in. "What? What? Is something wrong?"

"Sorry." Poppy smiled weakly as she touched her temple. "Just had a little pain in my head."

I wasn't sure if she was telling the truth or if she was lying to cover her near misstep. She'd told me after we'd received Holden's message that she'd noticed some deception in Tula's aura as she was pouring our drinks but couldn't quite figure out the meaning at the time.

"Jeez, Glenmyres. You dodged a bullet." Fitz gripped Poppy's hand tightly.

"We sure did. But now we can enjoy the Big Melt without fear of a murderer walking free." Poppy smiled and kissed Fitz's fingers. "You're gonna knock the Melt Off outta the park."

Amazed she could be so positive after what we'd just experienced, I decided to let Fitz and Poppy have a moment to themselves. "I'm gonna go get a coffee. Want anything?"

The lovebirds declined, and I took off in search of the hospital café while checking my phone for messages.

Have Pops's results come back?

I actually had the question three times from Holden, Ezra, and Constance.

Still waiting. I texted to them all. **Will let you know when we hear back,** I told Holden, whereas to Ezra, I typed, **Poppy seems to be in good spirits, so I hope we get to leave soon.**

Ezra replied once I was in line to place my coffee order. **If there's anything you need, just say it. I'll be there. Caius sends a hug, too.**

I smiled at the Walters brothers' thoughtfulness. **If you wouldn't mind, Noli could use a walk.**

On it! I'll give Berg some chin scratches, too. I know where you keep the key. Ezra also sent a winky face emoji.

Relieved my fur babies would be in the best of hands, I ordered a latte and responded more to Constance's inquiry. **Just glad Marjorie's killer has been caught and you're off the hook.**

Yes. Very grateful to have you crimefighters in my corner, Constance wrote back. **When you have a moment, I could use your advice, tho.**

Go for it. I had nothing but time while I waited for the busy hospital café to make my drink.

My phone lit up with Constance's contact info. "Hey, what's up?" I asked as I answered.

"This isn't a bad time?" Constance sounded nervous.

"Nope," I reassured her. "I'm giving Fitz and Poppy a moment alone, so I could use the company."

"That's sweet of you. Okay, so here's the deal." I heard Constance take a huge breath. "Lauren Johnson called me about an hour ago. She was going through some of Margie's belongings that were left in her rental cabin and found her outline of *Under the Red Barn*. Well, *my* outline."

I gasped.

"She told me she was initially confused by the outline because she didn't recognize the handwriting as Marjorie's at all. She dug around some more and discovered the first two chapters, as well."

"Omigosh." This was huge. "How did Lauren know to call you?"

"Because I had written 'By Constance Crane' under the chapter one header."

Yet, instead of sounding triumphant, she just sounded sad.

"Well, that's great, isn't it?" I saw one of the café baristas place my order on the pickup shelf. "You can now prove Marjorie stole the book from you." I grabbed my latte and took an invigorating sip.

"I can...but I don't think I'm going to."

"What?" I nearly choked on my beverage. "Why?"

Constance sighed. "I talked over my options with Lauren. I can either stake a claim in the IP and have Marjorie posthumously dragged through the mud. Or Lauren can tell Griffinsmith about everything and simply ask for the book to be scrapped altogether." Her voice sounded heavy with emotion. "I know what Marjorie did was wrong, but she wrote thirty-five really amazing chapters all by herself." She chuckled. "Yeah, I caved and read the copy she left me. It's such a well-crafted story, Hazel. I can't in good conscience destroy such a legacy. Not after what happened to her."

"But she *stole* the plotline from you. You'd be totally within your rights—"

"I know," she interjected. "And I know cheaters shouldn't prosper, but I think the world deserves to read *Under the Red Barn*. Besides," Constance admitted, "this whole nightmare has given me killer inspiration for a new novel, totally separate from Misthollow. I'd like to explore that and let the past lie in the past."

"It sounds like you've already made up your mind," I teased. "What advice did you need, exactly?"

She joined my laughter. "I guess I just needed to talk things through. I'll call Lauren back and tell her I'm going to let this go. Thank you, Hazel. For everything. It's wonderful to know you and your aunt are in my corner. Send Poppy my good wishes, please."

"Will do. I'll be in touch." We bid each other goodbye.

I pocketed my phone and sipped thoughtfully on my latte as I strolled back to Poppy's room. While I didn't necessarily agree with Constance's decision, it was hers to make, and I respected her commitment to her friend, even though Marjorie hadn't shown her the same courtesy.

I arrived at Poppy's door and knocked softly before entering. I immediately froze at the sight of a solemn-looking doctor standing at the foot of my aunt's bed.

"I'm sorry—" she began, but Poppy cut her off.

"She's family. Hazel can hear what you have to say."

I then noticed Fitz wasn't around. "What's going on?"

The doctor cleared her throat. "I'm Dr. Chen, one of the neurologists here at Sacred Heart." She motioned to the folder in her hand. "I wanted to discuss Poppy's test results."

Her tone scared the ever-living daylights out of me. Curses, this couldn't be good. My knees felt like they had disintegrated, and I scrambled to collapse into a chair. "Oh no."

Dr. Chen gave me a small smile before turning to Poppy. "Now, we didn't find any detrimental trauma to your skull or brain from today's incident, so that's a great sign." She took a deep breath. "However, we noted something on the scan and did some further investigation."

"Something on the scan?" Poppy, my always optimistic, bubbly Poppy, trembled.

"Yes. During intake, you mentioned frequent headaches and being more irritable of late, and I believe we know why. Poppy, your scan revealed a mass on your hypothalamus." Dr. Chen's earth-shattering words were gentle. "Now, I know that sounds incredibly scary, but our hope is that it's a hypothalamic hamartoma tumor, which is non-cancerous and benign. However, the pressure it puts on your brain can cause the symptoms you've been experiencing of late."

Tears flowed freely from my eyes. Dr. Chen's medical mumbo jumbo did little to alleviate my burning fears. "Poppy."

My forever bestie looked at me, and to my amazement, all I saw was strength and determination. "What can be done, Dr. Chen?"

The neurologist opened the folder and began flipping through the paperwork. "Well, we can conduct surgery to remove the tumor, or you can begin radioactive treatment to reduce the size."

"What do you recommend?" Poppy kept her head held high.

Dr. Chen pulled out some loose papers and handed them to Poppy. "Well, radiation is a lengthy process, but non-invasive. If you opt for surgery, we could schedule you this weekend and get this thing out of your head. Surgery has risks of its own, but where you're a young, healthy woman, you're not as at-risk as some of our older patients."

"Then let's get the removal scheduled."

"Pops," I interjected, my throat closing. "Don't you want to think about this?"

"What's there to think about?" she shrugged. "I'm not about to have poison injected into my system for weeks on end when there's a much faster solution."

I bit back my concerns. After all, this was her choice, even though I thought the situation warranted a little more consideration.

"I want this thing out of my head, Hazel," my bestie's reply was soft. "I've been so frustrated lately. I hate not feeling like myself."

I swallowed the lump in my throat. "Well, okay, then. I'll be right here waiting."

"You will not." Poppy lifted her nose. "You have to go to the Melt Off and cheer on Fitz."

"As if I'll be able to do that while you're in surgery!" I went to throw my arms up in exasperation, only to realize I was still holding my latte.

Dr. Chen placed a comforting palm on the end of Poppy's bed. "I'll get things prepared on our end. Given your normal bloodwork results, our oncologist is hopeful that this isn't cancerous, but we'll be able to conduct a biopsy as soon as the mass is removed." She collected her papers and headed for the door. "I'll be back shortly with a member of our surgical team to walk you through what to expect."

I felt like I was going to throw up.

"Her aura was optimistic, Hazel," Poppy whispered once we were alone. "She wasn't sugarcoating a bad situation. Please, have faith, okay?"

"Oh, Pops." I threw myself into her awaiting arms, my crippling fear washing over me like a tsunami. As I cried, I thought about how strong Poppy was being, and that made me sob even harder. "I'm so sorry this is happening," I eventually managed through wailing hiccups.

Poppy had tears in her eyes, and I willed myself to be stronger for her sake. "You don't have anything to apologize for, little niece. I'm just glad you're here with me."

"I'll always be here for you." I wiped my face clean and straightened my shoulders. "Of that, you can be certain."

Chapter 31

The next several hours passed in a daze of doctors and paperwork. Poppy and I met the members of her surgical team, and I felt much more optimistic by the end of visiting hours. With space for only one cot in her room, I conceded my claim to Fitz, allowing him to spend the night with Poppy.

"I'm fine, really. Much better than I was," I reassured Ezra as I arrived in the hospital lobby. "I'm getting ready to head home now."

"Want me to come pick you up? You must be exhausted." Ezra's worry oozed from my phone speaker.

I smiled at his thoughtfulness. "No, I'll just grab a taxi or—" I cut myself short as I noticed a familiar figure rocking back and forth in a chair in the nearby waiting room.

"Or what?" my boyfriend pressed.

"Don't worry, Ez. I'll let you know when I make it home, okay? Bye." Without waiting for his answer, I ended the call and hurried toward Grant Finchmore.

"Ms. Wickbury!" Grant rose as soon as he spotted me. "Hazel, I'm glad I caught you."

"What are you doing here, Mr. Finchmore?" I clutched my bag, a bit unnerved by his presence.

"Please, call me Grant." His shoulders sagged. "I figured you might be tired and need a ride home, since your vehicle is still at Finchaven." His pinched gaze surveyed the lobby. "I also wanted to speak with you privately. I realize that I have a lot to apologize to your family for."

Understatement of the year. But I held back my harsh words at his withdrawn and sorrowful appearance.

"May I?" Grant motioned toward the exit.

My curiosity getting the better of me at this unexpected act of kindness, I nodded and followed Grant out to the parking lot. I was too emotionally exhausted to drive, even if he had taken me back to get my car.

We didn't speak until we were buckled into his electric Range Rover.

"Words can't begin to describe how sorry I am for what transpired today." Tears glistened in Grant's eyes. "Tula...goodness, I'm still at a loss for words."

"Have you spoken with her?" I asked.

Grant dipped his chin. "I had to hear it, straight from her. I had to know why she killed my daughter." I didn't need a whim like Poppy's to see the cold, lethal anger radiating from him as he kept his laser focus on the road ahead.

Tula had shared her selfish reasons with us. Had she told Grant the same?

"Apparently," Grant seethed through gritted teeth, "her father had told her about my dalliance with Jane back in the day, making her swear to protect the Finchmore family should my transgressions come back to haunt us." He flexed his fingers on the steering wheel. "Dimitri Dukakis kept tabs on Jane for the rest of his life. He *knew* I'd fathered a child. Eventually, Tula did as well, once her father passed the torch to her."

I released a low whistle. "So, when Marjorie approached Tula at Sip, Tula already knew she was your daughter?"

"Indeed. Tula said she did her best to convince Marjorie to give up such a hopeless search, but Marjorie couldn't be swayed. Not even after Tula told her she couldn't remember the people in the photo."

In the glow from the SUV's headlights, I could see silent tears streaming down Grant's stoic face. "But she worried Marjorie would eventually learn the truth from either Jared or Sterling..."

"And so she decided to silence Marjorie for good?" My quiet remark broke Grant's dam of emotions.

Through his sobs, he managed to pull the Rover to the side of the road and park. "All because she thought I needed protecting. That I was some little child who needed to be saved."

I patted him gently on the back, debating whether I should share the truth with him. "When she thought she had Holden and me backed into a corner with her poison scheme, Tula shared with us that she did it to save Tobias from losing out on a possible inheritance."

"*What*?" Grant snapped, his eyes wild in the budding moonlight.

I nodded. "She didn't want Marjorie usurping any of the Finchmore money you'd promised to Tobias if you found out she was your daughter." I hoped that sharing this would alleviate some of the guilt Grant was feeling over his role in Marjorie's death. The powerful businessman had made terrible mistakes in life, but even he deserved the truth. "Tula's main reason for killing Marjorie was pure greed."

"Oh God." Grant's jaw went slack. "D-did Tobias know about this awful plot?"

I thought back to everything Poppy had seen in Tula's aura. "No. And you didn't hear this from me, but Chief Whitfield and his team have yet to find any evidence suggesting otherwise." Holden had texted earlier that Tobias had been devastated when he'd learned the news about his mother's misdeeds.

Grant pulled a handkerchief from his breast pocket and dabbed at his eyes. "How am I going to make it through this?"

"My advice?" I offered. "Lean on your family. Yvonne would do anything for you, you know. She loves you deeply, despite all your flaws." I was pleased my light-hearted comment tugged a small smile on his quivering lips. "Have you spoken with Mrs. Finchmore about this yet?"

"Vaguely. She's on her way back from the city right now." Grant rubbed at his temples. "This is going to take more than a Birkin bag to fix," he muttered just loudly enough for me to hear. "But I think you're right, Hazel. I'll need my family—what's left of it anyway—to survive this."

I noted the despair layering his sardonic comment. The man had lost two children over the course of a year.

"And this has been a clear wake-up call that I need to begin taking more accountability for my actions," he admitted as he collected himself and pulled back onto the road to resume the drive. "I can't allow people to manage aspects of my life while keeping me in the dark. I had no idea Chief Whitfield wanted to speak with me about Marjorie's case. But I can't find Tobias at fault because that's how I've trained my employees to react. Not to mention all this stuff with Dimitri Dukakis. Goodness, if I'd had any sense, I would have checked up on Jane myself. Maybe then, I would've learned I had another daughter before she was dead."

His painful words echoed in the car.

"What does this newfound resolve mean for Tobias's role at FPT?" As much as I detested his mother's actions, Tobias was an innocent victim in all of this. I hated to see him lose his position after all he'd done for the Finchmores.

Grant sighed. "I'll have to give it some thought."

By now, we'd arrived at my driveway.

"He submitted his resignation once he learned the news about Tula, but..." Grant's gaze dropped to his lap. "I'm hesitant to accept it. Tobias has been wonderful, and I meant what I said about him being like another son. I'd like to think we can move beyond this terrible ordeal and have a stronger bond." However, he didn't sound convinced.

"You won't ever have a second chance with Marjorie or Kevin." I delivered the hard blow as softly as I could. "But maybe by giving Tobias one, you're honoring them both."

Grant was silent for a long moment before his head bobbed up and down in the darkness. "I think you're right, Hazel. I think you're right."

~∞~

Two days later, Fitz, Holden, and I sat together in the hospital waiting room, our gazes locked on the sterile door before us.

"She should be out by now, right?" I glanced at my watch. Saturday had ticked by at a miserably slow speed. "Dr. Chen said it was a six-hour procedure."

Holden squeezed my hand. "I'm sure we'll be getting an update any minute."

"Yeah." Fitz's leg bounced nervously up and down. "I can't wait to tell Pops that Cold Cauldron took first place in the Melt Off. With the Poppyseed Smash, no less."

I admired his high spirits. Due to his girlfriend's weekend surgery, Fitz had sent one of his line cooks in his place to compete in the Melt Off with instructions to win it for Poppy. We'd gotten the uplifting news about Cold Cauldron taking home the gold about four hours into the operation.

"I can't wait to give her an update about the case," Holden admitted with a tired sigh. "It will be nice to put all this nastiness behind us."

Justice for Marjorie had been swift. Given all the evidence and witness statements against her, Tula had formally confessed to her dastardly plan as part of a plea agreement to avoid a life-without-parole sentencing.

I wrinkled my nose. "While I don't think Pops will be entirely thrilled that Tula will be eligible for parole in thirty years, it's good to know the woman will be punished for her crimes."

"Do you really think Tobias will be able to keep working for Grant after everything that's gone down?" Fitz cocked an eyebrow, his gossipy nature resurfacing.

"I hope so." When I'd finally been able to collect my car from Finchaven, I'd chatted briefly with Tobias. He was still dazed and shattered by the whole affair, but his resolve to support Grant and the Finchmores, however he could, seemed firm.

"Ms. Wickbury?" The lead surgeon on Poppy's medical team, Dr. Ali, finally appeared from behind the set of double doors.

I practically flew to her side. "That's me. Is my aunt okay?"

"Ms. Glenmyre made it through with flying colors." Dr. Ali beamed in reassurance. "She's resting in her room now, but she gave us permission before the operation to let you peek in on her once she was out of surgery."

Fitz sagged against me. "Oh, thank goodness."

The walk from the waiting area to Poppy's private room felt like the longest five minutes of my life, but soon, I walked in and saw my bestie's brilliant smile as she gave a weary wave from her bed.

"Oh, good, she's awake." Dr. Ali held up the folder that had been tucked under her arm. "Poppy, I thought you'd be relieved to know that we've already received the biopsy results. The mass *isn't* cancerous. Barring any post-op issues, you should be fit as a fiddle within two weeks' time."

I squealed with happiness, turning my focus back to Poppy, whose smile was significantly less bright. In fact, she had a look of bewilderment plastered across her tired, puffy face.

"Isn't that wonderful?" I gushed as I raced toward her side.

"Y-yeah. So great." Poppy's wide gaze bounced back and forth between everyone in the room.

The surgeon clasped her hands in front of her. "I'll give you all a moment alone."

"Thank you!" I called out to our miracle worker before returning my attention to Poppy.

Her right eye twitched rapidly.

"How you feeling, babe?" Fitz approached her, his voice low and soothing. "You must be wiped, huh?"

"Uh, yeah. A bit." Her focus darted to Holden and me, and I couldn't miss the undercurrent of alarm in her searching stare.

Her strange reaction unnerved me. Was she not feeling well? She seemed a bit disoriented. "Pops, what is it? Are your bandages too tight or something?" I glanced worriedly at her wrapped head. "Maybe we should call the doc back in here."

"No! I'm fine. But Fitz?" She reached for his hand. "I'm really craving a chocolate bar for some reason. Can you run and get me one? I *need* one."

Fitz's lips curled downward at her pleading request. "Are you allowed to eat solid foods?"

"Are you going to tell on me?" she teased lightly.

Reluctantly, Fitz went to the door. "Okay, I'll be right back."

Before he left, he whispered to Holden and me, "Don't mention the Melt Off until I get back, please."

We nodded our reassurances, although I was distracted by Poppy's bizarre behavior. I was surprised asking about the Melt Off results hadn't been one of the first things out of her mouth.

Once the door latched shut behind him, Poppy reached for my hand. Her grip was like ice.

"What's going on, Pops? You look like you've seen a ghost or something," I mumbled nervously as Holden and I perched on either side of her bed.

"Guys," she gulped back a sudden onslaught of tears. "I can't see your auras anymore."

"*What?*" Holden hissed.

I stared at her, speechless.

"Well, isn't it normal for a whim not to work on family members?" Holden asked. "Maybe your surgery interfered somehow with your ability to see our auras."

"No," Poppy cried through gritted teeth. "I can't see *anyone's* aura. Not yours, not Fitz's, not the doctor's."

She turned to me, fear and panic etched into her face. "Hazel, my whim is gone!"

Is Poppy's whim gone for good?

Join the Glenmyre Girls in their next mystery,

Get a Candle on Crime

Connect with Sarah at www.saraheburr.com to learn more about upcoming Glenmyre Whim Mysteries.

Other books by Sarah E. Burr

Glenmyre Whim Mysteries

You Can't Candle the Truth
Too Much to Candle
Flying Off the Candle

Book Blogger Mysteries

Over My Dead Blog
Dearly Deleted

Trending Topic Mysteries

#FollowMe for Murder
#TagMe for Murder
DM Me for Murder

Court of Mystery

The Ducal Detective
A Feast Most Foul
A Voyage of Vengeance
A Summit in Shadow
Throne of Threats
Paradise Plagued
Burdened Bloodline
Sovereign Sieged
Crown of Chaos
Harrowed Heir
Ravaged Reign
Innocence Imprisoned
Ardent Ascension
Eternal Empire

www.saraheburr.com

A Note from Sarah

I hope you've had fun returning to Crucible for Hazel and Poppy's third mystery outing. This was the Glenmyre Girls' most complex case yet, and I hope it's left you satisfied.

If this is your first visit to Crucible, welcome! I hope you enjoyed getting to know Hazel, Poppy, and their weird, wacky whims. Seeing when someone is going to die is a weighty burden, but Hazel will continue to use her power to right the injustices of the world…or, at least, the injustices happening within Crucible. With this stunning development surrounding Poppy's whim and the sad realization about Caius Walters's limited time left on earth, there's more mystery and intrigue for Hazel and Poppy to uncover.

If you liked this cozy sprinkled with paranormal sparkle, please consider leaving a review on your favorite bookish platform. Much like a Glenmyre whim, a review has extraordinary power: it encourages an author to keep writing.

About the Author

Sarah E. Burr lives near New York City. Hailing from the small town of Appleton, Maine, she has been dreaming of being Nancy Drew since she was a little girl. After not finding any mysteries in corporate America, Sarah began writing her own. She writes the Trending Topic Mysteries, the Book Blogger Mysteries, and the Court of Mystery series. Sarah is also the author of the award-winning Glenmyre Whim Mysteries. *You Can't Candle the Truth*, first in the series, was a 2022 NGIBA Best Mystery Finalist and a 2022 Silver Falchion Award Finalist. *Too Much to Candle*, book two in the series, was a 2023 NGIBA Best Paranormal Finalist.

Sarah is a member of Sisters in Crime, currently serving as the social media manager for the NY-TriState Chapter. She is also the creative mind behind BookstaBundles, a content creation service for authors. Sarah is the producer and co-host of *The Bookish Hour*, a live-streamed web series featuring author interviews, and writes as a member of the Writers Who Kill blog team.

When she's not spinning up stories, Sarah sings Broadway show tunes, plays video games, and enjoys walks with her dog, Eevee.